A Dozen Truths

A Dozen Truths

12 Works of Fiction

Edited by

Lou Aronica

and

Aaron Brown

An AuthorsFirst Anthology

The Story Plant
Studio Digital CT, LLC
P.O. Box 4331
Stamford, CT 06907

Story Plant Paperback ISBN-13 978-1-61188-251-3
Fiction Studio Books E-book ISBN-13 978-1-945839-08-5

Visit our website at www.TheStoryPlant.com

First Story Plant Paperback Printing: March 2017
Printed in The United States of America
0 9 8 7 6 5 4 3 2 1

Contents

Join

Eric Andersson

≥≤

Eric Andersson is a young, aspiring writer from Camrose, Alberta, Canada, currently in the fourth year of a BA in English. His interests in terms of reading and writing range widely, from suspense thrillers to fantasy, sci-fi, horror, philosophy, and much more. Really, the only constant is his passion for a good, gripping story.

From the author:

"The idea for 'Join' started with the character of Kyle and his ruminations on the universality of mortality. I remember one image standing out in particular: the image of Skipper, Kyle's childhood dog, lying dead in its grave, young Kyle shedding tears while his parents stand over the grave, father delivering a "respectful, yet passionless" eulogy. I felt like Kyle – and many others in the real world – would easily be able to connect that memory to a fear of the future, a future in which we've died (as we inevitably will) and the mourners who show up to mourn are equally respectful yet passionless toward us post-mortem. From there, it blossomed into a grim character portrait of a tortured psyche, an extrapolation of the realization we all have at some point in our lives: that we are mortal, and our lives will eventually end."

≥≤

He knew he'd have to join them eventually.

He heard their voices whisper in the night: *Soon you'll be with us. Soon you'll be one of us.* Sometimes they kept him up, but other times he found the voices comforting, reassuring, found they actually made sleep easier.

It was the first guarantee of life, and really, to Kyle Dagoni, it was the only one. Sure, taxes were fairly ubiquitous with life, but it was always possible—however unlikely—that a new regime could take over, one that believed in laissez-faire enterprise and in taxing their citizens at the rock-bottom rate of zero percent. So, yes, Kyle joined the lines of taxpayers every year, but that wasn't quite a guarantee.

Kyle wasn't sure when he started hearing the whispers, but he knew it was after this epiphany. There is a time in every person's life, Kyle knew, when the fact of one's mortality comes crashing down, jarring the very foundations of understanding: for Kyle, this was when his dog, Skipper, died.

The memory of Skipper's stiff corpse lying in the ground, legs sticking out at odd angles, eyes wide and unseeing, still made Kyle queasy. Standing above his dog's grave, his father giving a passionless yet respectful eulogy, Kyle let his tears flow, let his sorrow be known. Not only had his dog died—this death had changed everything in Kyle, had allowed him to see the one, true, terrible fact.

He was just like Skipper. He was a creature of meat, his life depended on a series of chemical reactions, and one day all that organic machinery would grind to a halt. There was an end. One day, he'd be just like Skipper, with someone else crying over his grave while another—a minister, probably—gave an equally passionless yet equally respectful eulogy for Kyle Dagoni, a man who'd once walked the Earth, had made his mark on it, and yet now, for most of the world, might as well have never existed.

Sometime after Skipper died, Kyle started hearing whispers. He was never sure whether the whispers were in his own head or whether they were actual dead people trying to talk to him, but they kept him grounded in the fact of his own mortality. Some days, they frightened him. Other days, they consoled him. It really depended on Kyle's mood.

Tonight, he could stand a little whispering.

Soon, you'll be with us.

Soon? How soon? 10 years? 50 years? Would Kyle be the first man to live to 500? Or would he be flattened by a bus tomorrow?

There's no way to know.

Kyle's uncertainty about the origin of the whispers came in part from their tendency to answer him.

Soon. That's all you need to know. We can't wait for you to come. It's fun. You'll have a lot of fun. There's no avoiding it. This is one party you can't miss.

Ha. Parties. One thing Kyle knew nothing about.

Soon. Very soon.

Kyle sighed. But how soon?

Soon.

≥≤

Denny keyed in Kyle's phone number, then hesitated.

Did he really want to drag Kyle into this? Couldn't he invite Ben, or Zeke, or Yale? Did it have to be Kyle?

Yes, Denny thought. He'd told Kyle he'd bring him along.

But Kyle was so...*different*.

Denny and Kyle had been friends since the fourth grade. During junior high, though, Kyle began to change. He brooded, asked to be alone, and progressively went out less and less until lately he barely ever left the house except to go to school, and even his school attendance was slipping. When Denny asked whether anything was wrong, Kyle always said no, that he was fine, but Denny didn't buy it. So, finally, Denny decided he'd take Kyle out, try and get his mind off whatever was bothering him.

It had been Tianne, Denny's girlfriend, who'd suggested a double date. Denny agreed. It would do Kyle some good to finally get out and socialize. He'd spent so many years getting progressively more and more antisocial that now, as the gang edged closer to twenty years of age, Kyle could barely even be considered part of the gang. He never did anything with the rest of them. He never did anything with anyone.

So, Tianne had asked around until she found a friend who'd be willing to go on the double date. Denny set it up with Kyle—there'd been surprisingly little resistance on his part—and they were on their way.

It was scheduled for tonight. Denny hoped Kyle would show up.

"He'd better," Tianne said when Denny brought it up. "Or we'll know there's something certifiably wrong with him. Didn't he used to be all cool and social and everything?"

"Well, he was never cool," Denny said, "but he used to talk to people. He used to go to birthday parties and things. He was never the life of the party, but he was always there. Now he's more like the Phantom of Gugushka."

Gugushka was their town. It was a cesspool of mediocrity. The only reason Denny was still here was he had a steady job. The minute Denny found something better, he was out of there.

Still, Denny worried about Kyle. He hoped going out with someone—and having one of his best friends there—would snap him out of his funk. Denny sighed, looked down at his cell phone again, and pressed the call button.

The phone rang three times. Then:

"Hello?"

"Hey, Kyle," Denny said, "Just calling to remind you about that double date we've got scheduled."

"Yeah," Kyle said.

"We'll come pick you up around 5:30, OK?" Denny said. "Just, please, be ready."

"I will," Kyle said. "Don't worry."

Denny nodded. "I'm worried about you, Kyle. You barely talk to anyone anymore."

Kyle stayed silent.

"Well," Denny said, "I guess I'll see you at 5:30."

"Yeah."

"Bye."

Kyle's end went dead. Denny stared at his phone for a moment, then ended the call, hoping tonight would spark *something* in Kyle.

≥≤

Kyle set down his phone, annoyed.

Stupid Denny, Kyle thought. *Always assuming the worst. Like* he's *immune.*

Denny had to join, too. Everyone did. Kyle wondered whether Denny knew yet, or if he'd just found a way to put it out of his mind. Surely he knew. How could anybody on planet Earth make it to nineteen years of age without discovering that inevitability? No, he must've found a way to keep himself distracted.

Sex, maybe?

Could be. It could be any number of things: sex, sports, movies, books. Who knew? What always confounded Kyle was how anyone could be distracted by these things at all. None of them cancelled the inevitability. None of them made the voices go away.

Soon.

Yes, yes, he'd be joining them soon. So would Denny and his girlfriend, Tianne. And so would the girl Kyle was being set up with, whatever her name was. They would all join the voices soon enough.

That's right. Soon, you'll be with us.

But how soon?

Soon.

Before 5:30?

No answer.

Well, if he wasn't going to be joining the voices before 5:30, Kyle thought he might as well make himself look presentable. With an almighty sigh, Kyle heaved himself off his bed, and trudged off to the shower. Just because oblivion awaited didn't mean he should let down his friends. After all, a girl he'd never met was coming out just to eat dinner with him. He might as well give her a somewhat pleasant evening.

The clock is ticking.

"Louder than ever these days, it seems," Kyle muttered as he went off to get himself clean.

≥≤

Denny's day passed without much incident. He spent a surprising amount of it thinking about Kyle: whether he'd show up, whether he'd actually make decent conversation, or whether he'd finally snap and go insane. Who knew? Maybe this would be just what he needed. After all, a date would pick anybody's spirits up, especially someone as reclusive as Kyle.

Tianne arrived at Denny's around 4:30. Denny let her in, and immediately she started rambling.

"Hey, Denny," Tianne breathed, "glad to see you're ready. Kyle had better be there."

"He will be," Denny said. "Don't worry about it."

Tianne took a deep breath, then nodded.

"Where's your friend?" Denny asked, looking around, peering through the door windows.

"Oh," Tianne said, just remembering, "Annie wasn't quite ready yet. We're going to go pick her up before we get Kyle."

"What? But..."

"But what?"

"Doesn't she live over in Pantin?"

"Yeah. So?"

"Great," Denny said, smacking his forehead, "Just great! That means we need to get going now!"

"Why's that a bad thing? I thought you were ready," Tianne said, leering at her boyfriend.

"I...well, I'm almost ready," Denny said, "Just give me a few more minutes."

"Come on, Denny!" Tianne shouted. "We're going to be late!"

"Yeah, yeah," Denny grumbled, rushing back to his room to spruce himself up a little more. Tianne was a lovely girl, make no mistake, but sometimes her insistence on rabid punctuality—even for the most casual occasions—got on Denny's nerves. So did her propensity to bring up crucial details at the last minute.

Denny quickly swiped on deodorant, brushed his hair, and washed his face, all the time thinking, *Kyle, you'd better be ready. You'd better not chicken out of this. You'd better be ready.*

≥≤

Denny needn't have worried. Kyle was ready by the time the clock hit noon.

Kyle had put on his best (and only) suit, complete with cuff links and lapel. He wasn't wearing the jacket at the moment; after all, it was hot, and he didn't have to wear it that instant.

Soon.

The voices were starting to get on his nerves now.

No need to get so annoyed, dear Kyle, they answered. *We're just telling it like it is. Have a good time tonight, though. You do need to get out more. Just look at yourself.*

Kyle had, but just the same he got up out of his chair and went to the bathroom. The mirror showed the same grisly picture he'd seen when he showered: his pallor had really deteriorated, fading to an almost paper-white, and dark circles hung underneath his bloodshot eyes.

No portrait of fine health, the voices observed, *fit to join us, I'd say.*

Kyle ignored the voices and strode back out to his chair. At the moment, he was checking his Facebook; he didn't really expect anything to happen while on the site, but hey, you never knew. Life has a way of throwing the unexpected our way.

And, as it happened, in just a few seconds a notification popped up on Kyle's page.

Kyle blinked. Notifications weren't absolutely unheard of on his profile, but they were a rare occurrence: he probably only got one per week at most, and the majority of those were game invites. That's probably what this was: just some stupid game invite.

Even if it was a post on his wall, or something he'd been tagged in, what good was it? How would that help prevent him from ending up like Skipper?

It wouldn't. But Kyle clicked it anyway. Apparently, Denny's girlfriend had tagged Denny and him in a status. *Can't wait for the double date tonight!* she said, *long as Kyle Dagoni shows up. #anxious.*

Anxious? Why would she be anxious? Was she worried about him? Kyle almost sent a message to Tianne right then and there, to tell her not to worry, that the only thing wrong with him was he'd realized the inevitable, when he stopped himself. She wouldn't understand. His parents hadn't understood. They'd long ago stopped trying to cheer him up. Why would Tianne be any different?

Still, Kyle knew her intentions were good and appreciated the sentiment. What interested him more was the name tagged alongside him, Tianne and Denny: Annie Cromwell. Kyle was originally going to treat this like a blind date, but his curiosity got the better of him as he clicked the link to her profile, wondering what she looked like, what she was all about.

The Internet lagged a second, then Annie Cromwell's profile blossomed before him. Kyle's jaw dropped. She was *gorgeous*!

She's joining us too, the voices piped up, after having been silent for a full two minutes. *You'll all join us in time.*

Kyle ignored the voices and quickly left Annie's profile, already feeling creepy. But, he thought, maybe tonight won't be that bad. As he logged out of Facebook and rose from his chair, intending to blow a few hours on a meaningless videogame, he found for the first time in a long time that he had something to look forward to.

≥≤

Denny's rush to finish preparing ended up lasting ten minutes. By the time he was finally completely prepared and headed out the door, his girlfriend was fuming.

"We're going to be *late* now," Tianne seethed, "and it's all *your* fault!"

"Yeah, yeah," Denny breathed.

"Don't blow me off!" Tianne said, "Don't you dare blow me off! What do you think Kyle's going to think when he looks out the window at 5:30 and sees we haven't gotten there yet? What do you think?"

Denny finished pulling on his coat as he reached the door of his car. "He'll probably think that we're running a little late," Denny said. "If you're really that worried about him, I can give you his phone number. You can text him, or something."

"Do that," Tianne said. "Give me your phone."

Denny knew there was no point in fighting her. He dug around in his pocket and brought his phone out, handing it to his girlfriend. Tianne took the phone in one brisk motion, then began quickly pounding off a text message. Denny, meanwhile, climbed into the car and started the engine.

Tianne strode around the car and climbed into the passenger's seat. Denny waited until her door was shut, then pulled out of the drive and onto the road. Pantin wasn't *that* far away from Gugushka, but if he was going to get there and back again by 5:30, Denny would have to really floor it.

"Thanks," Tianne said briefly, putting Denny's phone down beside him.

Denny grunted as the car gained speed. "You'd better be there, Kyle," Denny breathed, bobbing his head, making it a mantra. "You'd better be there. You'd better be there."

≥≤

Kyle was back on Annie Cromwell's profile.

He'd resisted as long as he could—several hours, actually—aided by the fact he'd be seeing her in person by dinnertime. However, as the afternoon stretched on, Kyle found it harder and harder to resist at least taking another look at her beautiful face. In the end, around 4:30, he gave in, logged back onto Facebook, and immediately tracked Annie's profile down again.

His second look confirmed his first impression: She was *breathtaking*. Her eyes were an electric shade of blue. Every feature on her face seemed to be perfectly chiseled out of gold by God himself. Her hair was a shining wavy blonde; it was the hair he imagined angels might have.

What good is beauty? It was the voices again. *Even if you two were to end up together—which is highly unlikely at this point, remember—that face will get old, and in the end you'll both join us. See what beauty does then.*

Shut up, Kyle thought. *Just shut up.*

He didn't expect it to work. The voices rarely listened to him; at least, not when he wanted them to.

Why? the voices came again. *You can't escape. You can run, you can hide, but you can't escape your doom.* The voices then started repeating that last line, creating a complex choral arrangement, singing it to the tune of the old Enrique Iglesias song. Sadly, that wasn't the first time that had happened.

Kyle ignored the voices again, looking back to Annie's profile picture. Her sly half-smile, her striking blue eyes, her impeccable skin tone—it was too much. He couldn't resist. Before he knew what he was doing, he found his hand moving the cursor toward the link that would take him to her entire pictures library. Kyle tried to stop himself, but failed. A second later, he beheld Annie's entire pictures library.

Perhaps makeup and Instagram filters deserved the credit for Annie's luminescent profile picture, but here he saw that

Annie's general beauty was completely natural. Here were pictures of her hanging out with friends: one showed her with two other girls Kyle didn't know, standing on a dock in life jackets, a canoe next to them; another showed Annie and three friends in pajamas, beaming and sitting on somebody's bed; yet another showed Annie and another girl—Tianne, Kyle thought—standing in the bathroom, doing duck faces, their phone in front of them.

Good old selfies, Kyle thought. It seems no one is exempt.

Indeed, the voices jumped in again. *No one is exempt.*

Acting as if the voices hadn't spoken, Kyle quickly skimmed Annie's pictures, then clicked on "About". He already knew she lived in Pantin—Denny had mentioned that—but other than that, he didn't know anything about this girl other than the fact she was the most beautiful girl he'd ever seen. She was single and interested in men, which were both good things (at least for him). She also seemed to like a lot of party music: he saw Katy Perry, Kesha, The Black Eyed Peas, even LMFAO in her music likes.

Oh, well, Kyle thought. No one's perfect.

Once Kyle had been through Annie's info, he logged out of Facebook and headed back for his room. He felt exceedingly creepy now. He vowed to himself right then that he wouldn't look up anything about Annie until he met the woman herself. Instead, he lay down on his bed, put his arms behind his back, and waited for Denny and Tianne to arrive.

≥≤

Denny and Tianne arrived in Pantin over 15 minutes late. Just as they passed the town's welcome sign, Tianne's phone began vibrating.

"It's probably Annie," Tianne said. "Worrying." Her eyes shot daggers at Denny. Denny tried to ignore her, keeping his eyes directly on the road. Tianne picked up the phone and answered the call. "Hello?"

Denny's jaw clenched as Tianne listened. Her expression darkened as Denny flicked his turn signal and swerved into town, heading for Annie's house. Tianne had given him instructions, and now Denny was doing his best to remember them: if he was right, the address was 1462 Dorrence Lane. He hoped he was right, anyway. Tianne would throttle him if he was wrong.

"Don't worry, we're coming," Tianne told her friend, holding the phone right up against her ear. "Yes, we're in Pantin now. We'll be there in a minute or two. All right. Bye." Tianne put her phone away and shot a glare at Denny. "If you'd have started getting ready just ten minutes earlier—"

"Yeah, yeah, I know," Denny said. "The place is 1462 Dorrence Lane, right?"

"No!" Tianne exclaimed, slapping her forehead, "It's 1550 Torrence Drive! Can't you get *anything* right?"

"All right! All right!" Denny said. "Don't be so hard on me."

"Well, maybe if you'd just get it right the first time, I wouldn't have to—"

There was more to the rant than that, but Denny tuned her out, focusing on finding 1550 Torrence Drive. It didn't take long: he found Torrence Drive in less than a minute. He turned onto the street, then scanned the houses. He was at 1530. He kept going along the street until he reached 1550, then pulled over in front of the house and stopped with an almighty sigh.

For a moment, Denny and Tianne sat in silence. Then the front door of 1550 Torrence Drive opened, and Annie Cromwell rushed out. She wore an elegant red dress, which she had to hold up as she ran to the waiting vehicle, her purse slung over her shoulder. As soon as she opened the back door and climbed into the vehicle, Tianne turned around to face her friend.

"Sorry we're late," Tianne said. "Denny decided he'd put off getting ready."

Denny shot Tianne a look but knew better than to say anything. When Tianne was worked up like she was, there was no arguing with her.

"Oh, that's all right," Annie said. "Not a problem."

Tianne didn't seem to be convinced. "You sure?" she asked. "I really am sorry; we would've been on time—"

"It's *fine,* Tianne," Annie said. "Really."

Tianne huffed and turned around. Denny continued to clench his jaw, staring straight ahead, keeping the vehicle parked.

"Why aren't we moving?" Tianne demanded, "We're late as it is! Get moving, Den!"

Denny took in a deep breath, then moved the vehicle into drive and pulled out. This was going to be a long night. *Kyle,* Denny thought, *if you don't show up, I'm going to throttle you.*

≥≤

Kyle Dagoni waited at the front door, eager for Denny to arrive.

The clock crept closer to 5:30, and as it did, Kyle got antsy; he found he couldn't sit or lie still for more than a minute before the excitement of the occasion became too much. By the time the clock hit quarter-to, Kyle was pacing. He felt something, deep down, something he hadn't felt in too long.

Genuine excitement.

Yes, the knowledge of his mortality still plagued Kyle's psyche, but at the moment he found he was able to ignore it. Even the voices hadn't bothered him for nearly a half hour now, not since that last modified Enrique Iglesias tune.

So he waited. Every minute or so, he peeked out the door to see whether they'd come yet.

They hadn't. Not yet.

So, Kyle stood, fidgeted, paced. As he waited, he worked on what he'd say to Annie when they were introduced. Perhaps a simple *Hey, I'm Kyle*. Nah, she'd probably already know that. What about asking something about herself? That was never a bad idea. It might get her to do most of the talking, which would give Kyle the double advantage of not having to talk much and giving the impression he was a good listener. But what should he ask? *Where are you from*? Nah, he already knew that. *What was it like growing up*? Nah, that was too broad. *Do you hear voices in your head, voices that you're pretty sure are either the calls of the deceased or a sure sign of mental insanity*?

Something told him he shouldn't bring that up. She might not cotton to the knowledge he heard voices no one else could hear. Or maybe she'd dismiss him; he could imagine it now: *What, and I'm guessing you see dead people, too? You're gonna have to try a little harder than* that, *Kyle.*

Kyle took another peek out the door. The street was still empty. He turned, took in a deep breath, and let it out slowly. Despite himself, he was starting to get nervous.

A soft soprano sang faintly in the distance. Kyle paid no attention. It was probably the neighbours cranking their music. The strange thing about their neighbours: While most neighbours who played loud music played something rowdy, like rock or rap, and blared it so loudly the stereotypically middle-aged-to-old occupants of the house had no choice but to bring in the law, these neighbours often played classical opera. Thus, hearing a trembling soprano suddenly emerge out of the blue was not a strange occurrence.

The soprano grew louder. Soon, it was joined by several other sopranos, then altos, tenors, and basses, filling out a complex choral arrangement. The notes they sang were beautiful, but somehow menacing.

When the choir began to sing words, instead of just notes, Kyle froze. This wasn't the neighbours.

Come be with us, the voices sang. *Come to the still dark water and meet with us. Come touch the frigid waters and freeze with us.*

Kyle rubbed his temple. Not this. Not now.

Submerge yourself beneath the waves and breathe with us, the voices sang. *COME UNDERNEATH THE WATER AND JUST SING WITH US.*

Kyle ran to the bathroom. He barged inside, and threw open the medicine cabinet.

SUBMIT YOURSELF TO DESTINY AND SING WITH ME, a voice sang, female, high and lovely, then rejoined by the whole choir, in a booming finale, a phrase that shook Kyle's very bones: *JOIN US IN THE CHOIR OF ETERNITY*!

After several tense moments of rummaging, Kyle found what he was looking for. Those pills. Those *stupid* pills. The pills the psychiatrist had given him. "Take these," that idiot had said, "and those voices should disappear." The worst thing of all was that little smile he'd worn as he sat in his posh leather chair, glasses halfway down his nose, eyes giving off a condescending twinkle as if to say, *You and I both know you're just crazy.*

Of course, the pills did nothing. But right now he was willing to try anything; he wanted a nice evening with Annie, Denny, and Tianne; not an evening of shivering in the corner of the table, listening to voices.

Kyle staggered out of the bathroom, the choir still booming in his ears. He stopped, put his hand on the wall to steady himself, then went forth again. Somehow, he was able to find his way to the kitchen; disorientation was beginning to set in.

Breathing heavily, Kyle pawed at the cupboards for a moment before he finally got one open. It was the cupboard with cups in it; Kyle grabbed one and took it to the tap. Kyle flipped the water on, threw a pill in his mouth, and filled his cup with water. Then, as the choir drowned out all surrounding sound, Kyle chugged the glass, throwing the pill down his throat.

There's something missing, isn't there, Kyle?

The voices again. He knew the pill wouldn't work; even if it did, it would take a few minutes.

Don't you hear it?

Kyle staggered to one of the dining room chairs and plopped himself down, head in hands.

We need another tenor, Kyle.

The choir still sang, but the song was softer now, the notes more delicate. Kyle heaved in breath after breath.

You'll do fine.

Amidst the chaos, the doorbell rang.

≥≤

Denny waited on the front stoop, arms crossed, eyes narrowed.

Would Kyle come out? Surely he'd hear the doorbell; Denny had told Kyle several times to expect them at 5:30, and they were late. There was no way Kyle wouldn't be waiting.

Denny rang the doorbell again and waited. He tapped his foot and listened closely for signs of life: he could hear nothing from inside the house. Quickly growing impatient, Denny pressed the doorbell a third time, lips spreading into a grimace. This was it, wasn't it? All of Kyle's assurances—Oh, I'll be there, he said, I'll show up—led to this: in the end, once again, a no-show.

Then Denny heard a thump and a muffled shout come from inside. Denny paused. What was going on in there?

"Kyle?" Denny called, knocking on the door. "Kyle? It's me. Denny. We're here."

Another thump, then silence. A shiver went down Denny's spine. Something about this made Denny uneasy. He couldn't put his finger on it, but something about what was going on pointed to more than just reclusiveness on Kyle's part.

"Kyle?" Denny called again. "Come on. We're waiting."

Denny waited anxiously for a reply. He hoped Kyle hadn't hurt himself. It certainly wouldn't do for he and the girls to show up just to find out Kyle had gone and done himself an injury. He'd much rather spend the evening at a restaurant than at a hospital.

Still, there was silence. Denny reached for the doorknob, intending to test it; if it was locked, Denny swore, he would pound it off its hinges.

Fortunately, that was proven unnecessary. Just as Denny's hand was about to touch the knob, the door swung open. Denny took a step back, startled, as Kyle emerged from the house, dressed in a suit, hair combed back, a half-grin on his face. Denny was stunned. He hadn't seen Kyle this full of life in years.

"Kyle!" Denny stammered. "You're...hey!"

"You thought I wasn't coming, didn't you?" Kyle said, looking from Denny to the vehicle. "No, I was waiting here. You guys are late."

"I know," Denny said. "Don't mention it in front of Tianne. She's kind of sore about it."

Kyle nodded and walked toward the car. Denny followed, still stunned at how *composed* Kyle was. He was happy for him, but just the same, there was something in the way Kyle strode to the car, something in the gleam in his eyes...something that suggested a purpose, but not a benevolent one. Perhaps Kyle was unaware of it, perhaps that gleam didn't indicate anything but a physical reflection of some inner excitement, but all the same, Denny didn't like the looks of it. People didn't just shed melancholy.

No, something was off. As Denny walked back to the car, twirling the keys in his hand, he resolved to keep a close eye on Kyle. Just to be safe.

≥≤

As Kyle strode to Denny's car, he thought of only two things: the voices and Annie Cromwell.

He wasn't sure exactly why—whether it was the doorbell ringing or the pill he took actually working this time—but just as soon as Denny came, the voices stopped. The choir disappeared. In the moments that followed, the voices made not a peep. It was a relief, but Kyle was under no delusions: They'd be back. He hoped they'd hold off until the night was over, though. Why?

Annie Cromwell, of course. He couldn't afford to be distracted when *she* was in front of him. Yes, tonight, he was all Annie's. The voices could screw themselves for all he was concerned.

Naturally, Kyle was still shaken up by the whole choir ordeal: the reveal of the voices' true intentions had awakened a maelstrom of emotions, one which threatened to blow down his newfound composure and leave him weeping in the passenger's seat. They wanted him to sing with them. They wanted him to join them. Sure, he'd already known this, but the choir had really hammered the point in, especially the part about when. How soon? He'd always asked that, and the voices' reply had always been, "Soon." No more, no less.

Now he knew just how soon.

Not tonight, though. As Kyle opened the passenger door and crawled into the car, he resolved to push the voices out of his mind. They could sing to him all they wanted tomorrow: Tonight, Annie's voice would be the only one in his head.

And, speaking of Annie, there she was.

Kyle saw her the moment he sat down in the car. She sat behind the driver's seat, watched him get in with a smile on her face. She was even more beautiful in person than she was in her pictures: Her eyes sparkled in the low light, and the sunbeams, which cut through the cramped interior of the car, lit her hair like a midsummer bonfire. As Kyle sat down, she looked at Tianne, then back at Kyle.

"Hi. I'm Annie."

It took Kyle a moment to fully comprehend the magnitude of the situation. Annie Cromwell—that same stunning ideal of femininity he'd seen on his computer just hours earlier—was speaking to him. *Him!* The Phantom of Gugushka himself!

"Nice to meet you, Annie," Kyle said, every word out of his mouth sounding, to him, like the dumbest syllables ever spoken. "I'm Kyle...but I'm sure you know that already..."

Annie watched Kyle as Denny climbed into the driver's seat. "All right," Denny said. "We ready to go?"

"I was ready an hour ago," Tianne grumbled from the back.

"I'll take that as a yes," Denny said, and he pulled the car out of the drive, finally heading for the restaurant. Beside him, Kyle fidgeted. Who knew? This night could be big. In fact, he had a feeling this night would be a turning point; tonight, after years of misery and melancholy, things would finally take a turn for the better.

≥≤

The restaurant they were going to was called Eleanor's, a locally-owned restaurant that had stood in Gugushka for over fifty years. The founder, Bill Yarbeck, had built it as a fast-food chain, but when that didn't get off the ground the restaurant remodeled itself as a more upscale joint, and surprisingly, business picked up then. In fact, business got so good that several big restaurant chains came calling trying to buy them out, but both Bill and his son Ben, who took over when Bill died, refused to sell.

Though the citizens of Gugushka liked to refer to Eleanor's as "upscale," it really wasn't that fancy of a place: In a town like Gugushka, "upscale" mostly referred to the amount of time it took for your meal to arrive. If you waited at the counter and got handed your food five minutes after you ordered, you were a fast-food joint. If you had to sit down and wait half an hour, you were upscale. That's exactly the place Eleanor's was.

As they pulled into the parking lot, Kyle grew nervous. Was he really ready for this? Was he really ready to dive straight into a social situation like this again, after keeping mostly to himself for so long? What would this accomplish, really? Wasn't he just running away, trying to flee the inevitable?

No. He had to keep his eye on the moment. His fate was the same as everybody else's, and yet he was pretty sure nobody else obsessed over death like he did.

Denny looked for a parking spot. There were only two: one stood between two badly-parked pickup trucks, obviously driven by two tools who didn't give a second thought to proper driving etiquette. The other was on the opposite end of the lot, but it rested between a properly-parked car and a properly-parked minivan.

"Sure is busy tonight," Denny remarked. "Good thing we have reservations."

"You *did* make the reservations, right?" Tianne asked, her voice acid.

Denny sighed. "Yes. I did. Look, I'm sorry we're a little bit late. I think they hold your reservation for, like, a half hour after the time. We'll be alright."

They'd ended up ten minutes late. Denny had sped almost all the way from Kyle's to the restaurant, at the urging of an incensed Tianne.

"They'd better," Tianne growled. "Or I'm going to—"

"Look, can't we just have a nice night?" Denny snapped. "Forget that we're a little late. We're here. Can you just shut up about it already?"

Tianne looked like she'd been slapped. "Excuse me?"

"Can you just—"

"Guys!" It was Kyle this time, surprised at himself for jumping in. "Come on! Tonight's supposed to be fun. Let's just go in there...and have a good time."

Denny grimaced and drove silently toward the open spot. Tianne crossed her arms and glowered first at Annie, then out the window. Annie and Kyle simply sat, not sure what to do in the presence of their clearly-agitated friends. Soon, Denny swung into the spot, and Kyle unbuckled his seat belt, eager to get out of the car.

The evening was warm; a cool breeze drifted through the air, tussling Kyle's hair as he stood up and took a deep breath of fresh air. The voices were still silent.

Denny and Tianne each slammed their door and stomped silently off toward the restaurant. Kyle followed, anxious; he and Annie walked abreast, both silent, until they'd crossed the parking lot and approached the doors.

"So," Annie asked, breaking the silence. "You go to school or anything?"

"Yeah," Kyle said. "Well...yes and no."

"What's that mean?"

"I'll explain inside," Kyle said; he ran forward and opened the door for the other three. Denny and Tianne stormed inside without a word, and Annie walked in slowly, flashing Kyle a smile of gratitude on her way in.

Something deep inside gave a shudder of pleasure. Kyle grinned. She was so *beautiful*.

Inside, Eleanor's was a heavily stylized piece of history: the place was set up in the style of the 1950s as an homage to the restaurant in which founder Bill met his wife, the restaurant's namesake. The theme was so dedicated that the interior looked like a period piece: framed photos of Elvis, Frank Sinatra, and many other musicians from the '50s that Kyle didn't recognize were hung around the restaurant, and the place was painted in mostly unassuming colours, giving it a relaxed feel.

Soon, a waitress was there to take them to a table. The four followed as the waitress led them to a booth, ideal for four. She left as the four climbed into their seats, no one speaking a word.

Some old jazz band played on the stereo. Kyle twiddled his thumbs, wondering what he should say first and whether anyone would speak at all. Maybe everyone would just sit around and glare at each other all night. Who knows? Denny and Tianne were still in a foul mood, and, after his initial burst of enthusiasm, Kyle felt the old reclusiveness setting in quick.

Fortunately, Kyle didn't have to start the conversation.

"So," Annie spoke, and Kyle found his eyes irresistibly drawn to her. "This is a...nice place."

"Yeah," Kyle said. "Used to come here all the time with my family. They've barely changed it since I was a kid."

"I like it...Tianne, why didn't we ever come here before?"

"I dunno," Tianne said. "Some reason."

"Your menus," the waitress was back; she handed out four menus, then asked, "What would you like to drink this evening?"

"Give me something strong," Tianne said. "Whatever you've got."

"Ma'am, I—"

"Surprise me!"

"All right," the waitress jotted down a quick note. "I'll need to see your ID, then, please."

"Me, too," Denny said, handing his driver's license over to the waitress with Tianne's, then, under his breath, added, "Gonna need it to get through tonight."

"What was that?" Tianne snapped.

"Nothing, nothing."

The waitress looked at the licenses for a second, then handed them back. "All right, looks good."

Tianne fell silent, but her accusatory glare never left Denny.

"I'll just have a water, please," Annie said. "Somebody's got to drive."

"I'll have that, too," Kyle said. "Denny, are you sure you're fine with someone else driving your—"

"Yeah, it's fine, don't worry about it," Denny mumbled.

Don't worry about it!

Kyle jumped in his seat, flailing every which way. He looked frantically about: Where had that come from? Who'd said that? Had it been Denny? Had he echoed his own sentiment, loud as he could, right in Kyle's ear?

"Whoa, Kyle, settle down," Denny said. "What's up with you?"

"I..." Kyle looked around the table and saw three concerned faces looking back at him. "I...nothing. Nothing, I guess. Just... just a little nervous." Kyle chuckled and glanced at Annie. Boy, he was toast now. No way she'd have even the slightest interest in him after *that* outburst.

Annie continued to surprise.

"So, Kyle," Annie said. "What was it like growing up here? I've heard a lot about this place...it seems..."

"Meh." Kyle said. "The word you're looking for is *meh.*"

"A cesspool of mediocrity," Denny interjected.

"It can't be *that* bad," Annie said.

"No one said *bad,*" Kyle said. "Just kind of...*meh.*"

"Oh," Annie remarked; she stared off into the distance for a moment before speaking up again. "I grew up a ways south of Pantin, down in Kellesburg. I loved it there...I was disappointed when my parents came and told me we had to move."

MOVE!

"Gah!" Kyle shouted, twisting around to see who'd shouted.

"Seriously," Denny exclaimed. "What's *wrong* with you?"

Kyle breathed heavily. "Just a little...high-strung, I guess...yeah."

"Are you sure you're OK?"

"I'm *fine.*"

But he wasn't. He knew now what the shouts meant.

The voices were back.

Brilliant.

Guess who's back, the voices sang, *back again! Yes, we're back! Tell a friend! Guess who's back, guess who's back, guess who's back...*

Kyle closed his eyes, shook his head. He had to ignore them.

"Here you are," a voice spoke from beside the table. "Who had the waters?"

Kyle's eyes flickered open: the waitress stood beside them, watching Kyle curiously; Annie, Denny and Tianne also had their eyes on him, each expressing a different level of concern.

"Oh," Kyle said, "Yeah. That was me. And Annie, here."

The waitress gave out the drinks, then took out a notepad. "All right. Do you know what you want to eat?"

"I think we'll need another minute," Annie said.

ANOTHER MINUTE!

Kyle struggled to keep his composure.

THE TIME DRAWS NEAR! ANOTHER MINUTE!

"Kyle, are you sure you're all right?"

Annie's hand rested on Kyle's shoulder: she'd gotten out of her seat, apparently, and now crouched next to him, watching him carefully, her sparkling eyes gushing fountains of concern. Denny and Tianne just watched, unsure of what was going on. Kyle came back into his own head, drew away from the voices, and noticed he was shaking: his breathing was laboured, he was barely able to keep still.

"I...I think I need a minute."

The voice was distant, unfamiliar to his own ears; it didn't seem like he had spoken. Before he knew what he was doing, Kyle staggered onto his own two feet. Annie watched next to him, concerned. Kyle turned away from her and stumbled through the crowd of patrons, looking around at the tables, watching each man and woman with a curious kind of pity. How did they do it? How could they keep the knowledge out of their minds?

Of course, they didn't hear voices speaking to them. That probably helped.

Even still, Kyle thought, how did they do it? As Kyle stumbled past the groups of tables, the rows of booths, and moved for the occasional waiter, he watched the people seated. He saw a father and mother, both quite overweight, eating with their three pudgy children, all five of them with smiles on their faces. He saw three girls, probably around Kyle's age, seated at a table with drinks in their hands; they smiled, they laughed, and one of them even cast a glance in Kyle's direction, but he ignored them as he headed for the bathroom, looking only to wonder what they had and he didn't, why he felt like he'd been gnawed through from the inside out and why there was no such indication they'd felt the same.

Soon, Kyle reached the bathrooms. He pushed open one door, then a second, as he found himself in the tight space that passed for the restaurant's bathroom. Of course, Eleanor's didn't need a big bathroom, but this place was barely bigger than a broom closet.

Kyle approached the sink, twisted the silver faucet, and thrust his hands underneath the stream of cold water. He kept his hands underneath for a moment, letting the cold water chill his hands, enjoying the way the stream flowed overtop his skin, then cupped his hands, collected the water into a pool, and splashed it on his face.

The moment the water hit, the singing started again.

AVE MARIA! the choir roared back, *AVE MARIA!*

Something's missing, isn't it, Kyle? a voice called to him, *Something very important. The song must be sung, but there aren't enough people here to sing it. Isn't it tragic, Kyle? Isn't it just so depressing? Just listen to the harmonies: They're so empty! So incomplete! It's a travesty!*

AVE MARIA! the choir continued, *AVE MARIA!* Yes, Kyle could hear it. There was a line missing in the vocal harmony, a line near the top of the choral arrangement: The more Kyle listened, the more it stood out like a sore thumb.

The time has come, the voice continued. *It's time for you to make a decision.*

What kind of decision?

A choice that—

AAAAAUUGH!!

Kyle's eyes had been closed; he hadn't noticed that. How long had his eyes been closed? He was lying on the floor; suddenly, he could feel the hard tile underneath him, digging into his shoulder, his hip, his tailbone.

"SOMEBODY GET AN AMBULANCE!"

Kyle heard shouts: He got up slowly, opened his eyes. He noticed the blood straightaway. It pooled on the floor next to where he stood; his shoes were covered, his pants smeared in the stuff. It took another moment for Kyle to realize the blood was coming from him.

He noticed the mirror next. It had been intact when he'd splashed his face, but now it was shattered, with several large shards completely missing. Kyle looked down again and noticed, among the blood, several large shards of glass. Then he saw his hands. Each hand was red with blood; the blood poured from them, dripped to the floor like some horrible faucet God forgot to turn off.

"What...what's happening..."

The bathroom door burst open. Two men came in; one began tearing paper towel out of the dispenser, fast as he could, while the other put both hands on Kyle's shoulders, and looked straight into his eyes.

"Are you alright?"

"I...I don't know..."

"Come on. There'll be an ambulance here soon. Who were you eating with?"

"I...Annie...Denny..."

The other guy quickly wetted the paper towels and started wrapping them around Kyle's hands. "Hopefully this is good enough until the ambulance gets here," the second guy said, trying to get the paper towels on his hands.

"What the hell happened here?" the first guy asked, looking straight at Kyle again. "What in God's name happened in here?"

"I...I can't remember..."

Both bathroom doors were open now. A crowd had formed: it looked like everyone in the restaurant had shown up. Kyle's eyes searched for Denny, for Annie, for Tianne, but he couldn't see any of them.

He did hear something though; something light, off in the distance: *Join the choir of eternity. Join the choir of eternity.*

"Let us through! Let us through!"

Kyle was being carried now. The two guys had wrapped his hands in an insane amount of paper towels—which were already turning red—as they carried him through the crowd, dazed and confused, hoping the ambulance would get there soon.

The wall adjacent to the bathroom featured a large window, which overlooked the town; outside, life went on as vehicles buzzed to and fro, their drivers completely unaware of what was going on in the little restaurant. Directly outside the window was a small square of grass, which lay adjacent to the edge of the parking lot. Kyle had always found it strange that a small square of grass would be there—it seemed like wasted space—but that's not what he watched now.

Outside the window, eleven blurred figures stood, wrapped in robes.

Join the choir of eternity, the figures sang. *Join the choir of eternity.*

"Where is the ambulance?!"

"They'll be here soon."

"KYLE! KYLE! WHAT HAPPENED?!"

"We've got to stop the bleeding!"

"You're getting blood everywhere!"

Join the choir of eternity.

Kyle watched the choir outside, watched how they swayed to the music, listened to their song. Tears began to flow from his cheeks: the beauty, the absolute perfection of the notes, the amazing cadences of the unearthly tune, ruined by one missing part. One missing harmony.

Join the choir of eternity.

He hardly knew what he was doing: one moment, he was in the arms of the two men. Next, he was moving, on his feet again, the towels peeling off his hands as he ran toward the window. Then, before he knew what was going on, he felt an incredible amount of pain as he flew forward, the entire world sparkling around him, all reality reduced to a series of crashes and screams.

Just a moment later, he came to rest at the feet of the choir.

They were silent now, all eleven of them. As Kyle stared, their blurred, undefined forms came into sharper focus. He could tell now that each of the eleven wore a robe, black as coal, which billowed around their bodies. Each member of the choir also carried a book, which he, or she, or *it* held before itself, to read music off of, supposedly. As the beings came into focus, the only thing Kyle wasn't able to see was their faces; these remained blurred, mysterious.

Sing with us.

Kyle's breathing had reduced to a rasp. Panicked shouts surrounded him, but he paid them no mind—*couldn't* pay them mind.

Lights flashed in the distance: the ambulance.

Ave Maria.

"A...Ave..."

"Get him in! Get him in!"

Kyle had no idea he was being carried; in his mind, he was still with the choir.

"Ave...Maria."

Then, having sung those fateful words, Kyle lost consciousness.

Lost

Steven Manchester

≥≤

Steven Manchester is the author of the #1 bestsellers *Twelve Months, The Rockin' Chair, Pressed Pennies,* and *Gooseberry Island* as well as the novels *Goodnight, Brian* and the national bestseller *The Changing Season*. His work has appeared on NBC's *Today Show*, CBS's *The Early Show*, CNN's *American Morning*, and BET's *Nightly News*. Recently, three of Manchester's short stories were selected "101 Best" for the *Chicken Soup for the Soul* series.

From the author:

"I grew up with two brothers and now, being middle-aged, we're as close as ever. Our conversations, however, are much different from what they used to be. We no longer talk about aspirations or conquests; we usually discuss kids, retirement plans, and even doctor's visits. Given where we came from, I often recognize the dark comedy in this current phase. I recently finished a novel, Ashes, about two estranged, middle-aged brothers who travel cross-country together. It was the perfect vehicle (no pun intended) to highlight the painful challenges and funny realities of getting older. "Lost" is a short story set in the world of my novel, *Ashes*. I hope you enjoy it."

≥≤

The rain smothered the windshield—sheet after pounding sheet—and it didn't look like it was going to ease up any time soon. A country western song played on the radio, just loud enough for Tom to feel his ears threatening to bleed. He looked at Jason, his giant brother hulking behind the SUV's steering wheel, and couldn't decide if there was more scar tissue on the ogre's knuckles or his furrowed brow. Jason had been in Corrections for twenty eight years, time enough to lose any sense of idealism he'd once had and add more than a few extra pounds to his mid-section. *Once an animal,* Tom thought, stifling a yawn, *always an animal. Pop sure trained him well.* The impromptu cross-country trip still felt surreal to Tom. *The sooner we get to Seattle and spread the old man's ashes,* he thought, *the sooner I can return to my life.* But for reasons he preferred to ignore, the truth of it didn't make him feel any better. He looked back at Jason and sighed. Being at this point in his life—where time was much too precious to spend with anyone but someone he cared about—his brother was just more unwanted baggage. *Whether I'm here or there,* he thought, *I can't win either way.*

Although Jason was clearly struggling to read the road signs in the monsoon, it didn't stop him from babbling on and sharing another of his twisted memories. "When I first started staying over at Josie's place," he said, "I didn't know her parrot could talk." He shook his head. "One night, about two in the morning, I got up to take a leak. As I passed the bird's cage, I heard something whisper, 'What are you doin'?'"

In spite of his foul mood, Tom chuckled aloud.

"I must have jumped a friggin' mile," Jason said, grabbing for his chest. "And it took a few seconds before I realized it was the parrot talking." He shook his head. "With my heart pounding out of my chest, I leaned into the cage and screamed, 'What am I doin'? What the hell are you doin'?'"

"Did the bird answer?" Tom asked.

"He didn't make another peep," Jason said, shrugging. "After changing my shorts, I hurried back to bed." Grinning wide, Jason shook his head again. "I'm still having nightmares over that one."

"You're really sick, do you know that?" Tom said above the nauseating country music yodeling in the background.

Jason nodded. "My relationship with Josie didn't last long, anyway."

Although a wise voice in his head begged him not to ask, Tom couldn't help himself. "And why's that?"

Jason's grin erupted into a full blown smile. "Josie had a bad habit of applying the Heimlich maneuver on folks who weren't choking." He nodded. "Trust me, if you want to make someone shit themselves, just sneak up behind them while they have a mouthful of food and start squeezing for no reason." He began making a mock choking sound. "It ain't pretty," he added, laughing at his own sick humor.

Fighting off a pair of heavy eyelids, Tom shook his head before glancing toward the back seat where their father's ashes sat in a plain, walnut box. *You're the reason Jason's so screwed up,* he told his deceased father in his head; he then gave the subject a little more thought and cringed. *You're the reason we're both screwed up.*

Jason and Tom's father, Stuart Prendergast, had been a *bastard* in every sense of the word. And by all accounts, he'd been that way since childhood when his game of choice was playing the neighborhood undertaker. Whether or not he'd intentionally killed any of his clients was always a bit hazy from the stories, but once their hearts stopped pumping he was happy to give them a proper burial in the expanding graveyard he'd established. By the time he'd grown into a man—and the role of father—Stu had submerged himself into a pool of alcohol where he prided himself on being able to swim with the best of them. The only thing heavier than his drinking habit was his hands, which he often used on his terrified sons.

≥≤

In the hypnotizing rain, Tom stared out the side window, watching the world whip by in one massive smudge. It didn't take long before his head grew heavy, wedging itself between the passenger head rest and the window jam. "How long have you been divorced now?"

"Not long enough," Jason quickly replied; he was serious.

"So the process wasn't so bad, then?" he asked, trying to sound as nonchalant as possible.

Jason sighed heavily. "If I'm being honest, it sucked something awful. If it had been just me and the old lady, it would have been as easy as getting a rotten tooth pulled." He looked at Tom and smirked. "One quick yank and a few days of pain, and it's all over." His eyes drifted off for a moment, and his face turned sorrowful—in a way Tom had not witnessed in years. "I'll never forget the morning Miranda confronted me about the break-up. 'Why are you and Mom splitting up?' she asked. 'You guys haven't even been fighting.' She sounded like a six-year-old again, confused by the whole nightmare. I can still remember how she..." Jason stopped, while his Adam's apple bounced from the emotion that had obviously ambushed him. He peered out the driver's side window, lingering in the awkward silence for a few extended moments. "'And that's the point,' I told her. 'Your mother and I haven't fought in years.'" He swallowed hard. "I can still picture the pain in her eyes when I let her know it had been years since her mother and I cared enough to waste our breath."

"Damn," Tom muttered involuntarily.

"I know," Jason muttered, "but Miranda still couldn't understand how the marriage was coming to an end after everything our family had been through." Jason took a deep breath. "That's when I told her it had been a loveless marriage for as long as I could remember."

Tom grunted his disapproval again.

Jason's head whipped sideways, his eyes turning to threatening slits.

Oh shit, Tom thought, his backside puckering like it did when they were kids—just before his brother beat him down.

Instead of striking out, Jason slowly nodded his head. "It definitely wasn't one of my finest moments. To this day, it's still the dumbest thing I've ever told my kid." He paused. "It was the absolute truth, but I still shouldn't have said it," he muttered, now talking to himself.

Tom nodded. *I imagine you've said a lot of dumb things to your kid,* he thought, knowing he'd lose teeth if those words left his lips.

"As much as I wish I could have spared Miranda the pain, I just couldn't stay with her mother. The toxic relationship was killing all of us." He took a deep breath again and exhaled. "I was suffocating, you know?" He nodded. "I think we all were back then."

"Fighting apathy can be exhausting," Tom said, drawing a sideways glance from his brother, prompting him to quickly change the subject. "I wish I'd been a better dad," he blurted, immediately scolding himself for sharing something so intimate with his long-estranged brother. *That was stupid,* he thought. *Why am I even talking to this donkey?*

"And how's that?" Jason asked, leaning in toward the windshield to read the next blurred road sign.

Tom shrugged, careful to take better care with his words. "I don't know," he said. "Even though my kids live under the same roof, I've spent years taking them for granted." He shrugged. "I was always too damn busy chasing down money and success, you know?"

Jason shook his head. "That's what fathers do, right?"

It wasn't the sarcastic reply Tom had expected, and he was taken aback, leaving him suddenly speechless.

"Though I'm not surprised," Jason said. "You've always been completely self-absorbed."

Now there's the asshole I know, Tom thought. "You don't even know me!" he barked.

Jason laughed. "Relax, lollipop. I'm just playing with you."

"Whatever," Tom said, ready to surrender to the sleep that was trying to claim him. *I guess it serves me right for even trying to have a normal conversation with the Neanderthal.*

"I was just playing," Jason repeated. "Success is a good thing."

"Yeah," Tom said, closing his eyes, "as long as it doesn't cast a shadow so wide that our children are left in the darkness."

"Oh, I don't think either one of us has to worry about that."

Tom opened both his eyes and his mouth, but nothing came out, surprising himself.

"I knew you'd agree," Jason said, chuckling again.

He's still as crude as he is honest, Tom thought, nestling his head back into the window jam where his unrelenting mind began to ponder their current stations in life. He and Jason were now middle-aged, taking longer—much longer—to get anything done. *But what I lack in energy and enthusiasm,* he told himself, leaving out his brother, *I make up with experience and wisdom.*

"You know, at this point in life, we should be doing what we want," Jason said, letting Tom know he was contemplating the same thing. "We've raised our kids..."

"...And we're on the back-end of our careers," Tom interjected.

"So we should be able to eat anything we want," Jason added, grinning.

"What?" Tom snickered, peering out from his cozy corner. "That's the last thing you need to be doing, tubby. With your weight, you'll be lucky if you don't join Pop in..."

"A few years ago," Jason interrupted in his booming voice, "people started asking me, 'Are you putting on weight?' I'd tell them, 'No. Actually, I just lost forty pounds.' 'Wow, you look great!' they said."

"You don't take anything serious, do you?" Tom asked.

"Actually, I do," Jason countered. "Just last month, at the prison, I filled a specimen cup with apple juice, labeled it, and placed it into the urinalysis testing fridge. When I finally spotted a few younger officers standing close by, I opened the fridge and started guzzling the juice. 'God, that's twangy,' I told them. 'I definitely need more fluids.'" Jason started laughing.

"Nope, nothing's serious to you," Tom said, struggling not to laugh along with him.

"It's how I've stayed alive *and* sane all these years," Jason answered, any hint of humor erased from his face.

Tom nodded. *The second part's debatable,* he thought, *but I get it. I can't imagine what it's like to be locked in there every day with all those rapists and murderers.*

For a while, besides the rain, only the God-awful country music filled the cab of the SUV until Jason showed some mercy and shut off the radio. As the rain drummed off the SUV, creating a soothing rhythm, Tom stared out the passenger window and noticed that a speeding train was running parallel to them. *I can't remember the last time I rode on a train,* he thought, focused on the long line of passenger cars. "Are you happy with life?" he suddenly asked aloud; it was no more than a thought that had slipped off his tongue, surprising him as much as his brother. *Stupid,* he scolded himself again.

"Happy with life?" Jason repeated in a tone that dripped with cynicism. "Who the hell is happy with life at our age?"

Stop talking, Tom told himself. *Just stop!*

"I suppose when we were kids," Jason said, "there were times when I..."

But Jason's voice had turned muffled and distant, sounding just like their father's—minus the man's threatening tone. Tom felt like he was a young boy again, listening to the deep voice of a man talking in the other room. He tried to nod in response to something Jason had said, but his head wouldn't budge. Two deep breaths later, his mind was removed from reality—set free to roam the unrestricted dream world he preferred to dwell in.

≥≤

After one final bite of dry toast, a black Lincoln Continental waited patiently just outside the marble foyer. Tom donned his coat and hat and darted for the open door. Once inside the car, a wave of heat hit his face, removing all of winter's discomforts.

Shamus Donovan, his friendly driver, looked over the front seat. "Where to?" he asked.

"How about FAO Schwarz, for starters? I'm in the mood to buy some toys."

"As you wish, sir."

While Shamus Donovan parked at the base of a giant teddy bear and exited the car, Tom spent the time admiring the even burn on his Cuban cigar. It was a gift from a colleague, the smoothest tobacco he'd ever tasted.

"We're not open until ten," the store's self-appointed lawman bellowed to Shamus just outside the car, "and I don't care which rich cat is sitting behind that tinted glass."

Tom lowered the fogged window and smiled at the angry little man, who evidently expected a different reaction and was taken aback by the sincere gesture. Just as Shamus threw up his hands, Tom stepped out of the car. "Would it be a problem if I spoke to your manager, sir?" Tom asked, killing him with holiday kindness.

Another seemingly angry soul approached. "I'm the manager. What's the problem here?" His voice was colder than the December wind.

"There's no problem," Tom claimed before glancing down at his Rolex, "I know we've arrived a bit early and that you're not open for another forty minutes, but I was hoping you could help me."

"And how might I do that?" the manager asked, his teeth chattering in the frigid air. Tom was obviously not the first person to ask him for a favor.

Tom grabbed his cell phone, punched in several numbers, and lifted his index finger for the irritated man to be patient. There was a brief pause. Tom grinned kindly at the man before speaking to the person he telephoned, talking loud enough for everyone to hear. "Rick, it's Tom. I need you to get in touch with The Salvation Army and the Marine Corps Recruiting station. Have each of them bring the biggest truck they own and report to the front of FAO Schwarz within the hour. Also, I want Channel Twelve and someone from the *Times* to cover the story. Have them here twenty minutes after the trucks arrive." There was another pause, enough time for Tom's grin to widen. "Yes, Rick, the manager has been kind enough to open early for us. He wants to ensure that every orphaned child in this city believes in Santa Claus this year." After one last pause, Tom concluded, "That's correct. I don't want my name mentioned. Mister..." Tom placed his hand over the phone and looked up at the store manager. "I'm sorry," he said, "what did you say your name was?"

"Fiore," the shivering man replied. "Faust Fiore." His eyes were as big as flying saucers, his mouth half hung in shock.

"Mr. Faust Fiore is the kind soul who deserves all the recognition, Rick," Tom concluded. "Be sure he gets it." He ended the call with a smile.

"I suppose we could make an exception this one time," Mr. Fiore squeaked.

≥≤

It was nearly noon when Tom wrapped up his shopping frenzy. Hundreds of Barbie dolls and an equal amount of superhero action figures made their way toward the register. He purchased every stuffed animal, yoyo, and sled in the store. Pyramids of board games, sporting goods, and baby dolls were stacked inside one of the dozen shopping carriages being pushed in the giddy man's wake. In record time, Tom had personally selected a mountain of toys. Each time he threw something that beeped, whistled, or cried into a carriage, he felt the spirit of giving illuminate his soul. *It's already the best Christmas I can remember*, he thought, feeling his face glow.

Sharing the same truth, Shamus Donovan giggled like a young schoolboy from the first aisle to the last.

Tom threw the gifts onto his platinum card while Shamus shuffled out the door to pull the car around back. As Tom tiptoed out the back, the first rolling camera made its way through the store's front door. Turning back, he couldn't help but smile. Faust Fiore was being swarmed upon by a pack of hungry media. "He can have it," Tom whispered, ducking into the limo—to where Shamus was still giggling.

"Where to?" the Irish chauffer managed through his glee.

"I don't know about you, Shamus, but all that shopping's made me hungry." There was a thoughtful pause. "I think we should get some lunch. How does the Four Oaks sound?"

Shamus pointed the car west, his face confused over the lunch invitation. After a few awkward seconds, he nodded and grumbled something incoherent.

≥≤

The limo pulled into the front of the Four Oaks. Tom had belonged to the private club for years. Though he disliked most of the arrogant and pompous asses that frequented the place, its creative chef grilled the best swordfish he'd ever tasted. *And no one's going to deny me that*, he'd decided long ago.

Tom jumped out of the back and nearly watched Shamus's face go white when he opened the driver's side door. "Why don't we valet the car today?" he suggested.

Shamus couldn't speak. He merely slid out of the seat, threw the keys to the valet attendant, and followed his boss into the dark mysterious den.

In the foyer, a paunch, middle-aged man quickly approached, smoking a cigar half the size of his face. "Tom, we've missed you at the Racquetball Club of late," he snorted, awaiting a reply that never came. "The offer still stands, old boy—double or nothing?"

"I've been busy, Charles. Why don't we just call the wager at even?"

The man strutted away with a smile that engulfed his bloated face.

Tom turned to Shamus. "It was like taking candy from a baby, anyway," he whispered. "Chubby Charles doesn't have an athletic bone in his body, but for as long as I can remember he's been hell-bent to beat me at..."

"Your regular table, Mr. Prendergast?" the maître d' interrupted. His face showed blatant signs of disapproval, each sign directed toward Shamus.

"The regular," Tom countered. "And since it's Christmas, why don't you spoil us by sending over a bottle of Dom."

The man nodded robotically, shot another bad look at Shamus, and scurried off.

≥≤

Tom Prendergast and Shamus Donovan finished their swordfish, the bottle of bubbly, two warm brandies, and a pair of fine cigars. Shamus looked like he'd finally discovered heaven while Tom sat amazed by how little he'd known about his kind chauffer prior to their lunch. *Life really does get in the way of the important things,* Tom thought, vowing to never let it happen again.

"Well, hello, Tom Prendergast. Isn't it fancy meeting you here?" purred a woman so beautiful that even her soft, shapely body couldn't distract from her angelic face. Without being offered, she took a seat. She smelled like gingerbread.

Tom grinned wide. Shamus swallowed hard. "Hello, Tricia," Tom started. "It has been some time, hasn't it, my sweet?" Tom had a way with the ladies, even those who appeared unapproachable. If his looks couldn't reel them in, then his charm blew them ten feet out of the water. This petite goddess was no different. She was nearly drooling. "I hear you're still modeling that beautiful face for the world," he said with a wink.

"It pays the bills for now," she kidded, "at least until you marry me and make me an honest woman." Her smile could have melted the silver butter dish.

Tom stood, grabbed her hand, and kissed it softly. He then glanced over at Shamus and winked. "Ms. Tricia Quintal, I'd like you to meet an old friend." There was a strange pause. "Mr. Shamus Donovan."

Clearly taken aback, Shamus nodded slightly.

Tricia smiled. "Nice to meet you, Mr. Donovan," she crooned, but quickly gave her undivided attention back to Tom. "So, what do you say?" she teased.

Tom smiled. "Tragically enough, I don't think my schedule would permit a wedding right now, but I'll give you a call sometime in the near future, okay?"

She stood, smiled brilliantly, and walked away. Her eyes, however, never left his gaze until the foyer swallowed her whole.

"Women," Tom chuckled. "The greatest test of a man's will..."

Shamus ran the cloth napkin across his mouth and, to Tom's surprise, said, "Then you are a very strong man indeed, Mr. Prendergast." With a chuckle, he...

≥≤

Tom awoke. It took a few strange moments to register any sense of reality. Like a chapped desert, his mouth felt completely dry, letting him know he'd been snoring—maybe even struggling to take in air from his mouth while he slept. He opened and closed his lips a few times to try to generate some moisture—nothing. *Happy with life?* he repeated in his head. *Maybe when I sleep, but that's about it.* Trying to wipe the cobwebs from his mind, he thought about that for a moment. *It's pretty sad when I can only find happiness in my dreams,* he decided, *where my true aspirations can be fulfilled.* Having recently turned fifty, most of the sand in his hour glass had already sifted through his fingers, and he was struggling to reconcile it.

"Welcome back to the real world," Jason said. "And you really need to go see a doctor about your snoring. Do you use one of those CPAP machines at home?"

Tom tried to shake his head, but his neck was all knotted up from being wedged in the window. Instead, he moaned, still trying to locate a few drops of saliva somewhere in his mouth.

"Carmen must really enjoy that at night."

Who gives a shit! Tom thought. *Whatever Carmen enjoys, it sure as hell isn't with me.* He yawned wide before looking over his shoulder at his father's wooden box. *My life's more than half over and this is where I'm at?* he thought. *Unreal...*

Returning completely to the present, Tom realized the rain had finally stopped, leaving behind a sky so blue it looked like he could fish in it. He also discovered that Jason was eager to pick up the conversation where they'd left off.

"So why all that talk about divorce earlier?" he asked.

Tom half-shrugged. "No reason," he quickly answered, concealing his emotion behind another long yawn.

"Bullshit!"

"Listen," Tom said, wiping the sleep from his eyes, "if I needed to talk about my marriage, you'd be the last person in the world I'd confide in."

Jason smirked. "So, you're not ready to talk, then," he said sarcastically. "I'm here when you're ready."

Old, jagged feelings shot to the surface, increasing Tom's blood pressure. "What I need is for you to make a pit stop somewhere so I can use the bathroom," he said, looking out the window. "Where are we, anyway?"

Jason held his smirk, fighting off his laughter.

"What?" Tom asked, hardly amused. "We're lost, aren't we?"

"Chill out, sleeping beauty. I might have taken a wrong turn a ways back, but no big deal."

"How in the hell..."

"Chill out," Jason repeated, only this time he wasn't asking. "It was raining something vicious," he said before pointing to the GPS stuck to the center of the windshield, "and sometimes Google Maps can be wrong so..."

"If you were using my map," Tom said, unfolding the giant paper square onto the dashboard, "then we wouldn't be lost."

Jason looked at him and shook his head. "As long as we're together," he said sarcastically, "then we can never be lost."

Tom looked at him in disbelief. "You think this is funny?" he asked, feeling his blood throbbing in his ears.

"I do," Jason said, "I really do."

As the bickering ensued, Jason drove onto the shoulder of the road and whipped the SUV into a U-turn. At the lip of the asphalt, the SUV hopped back onto the road. Tom looked back just in time to see his father's box of ashes bounce once and then twice until falling onto the back floor. He leaned over the front seat to ensure the lid was still closed and that none of the contents had spilled out. *The old man's fine,* he decided and, with a single shrug, he turned back around, leaving his father on the back floor.

"Next bathroom I see, we'll stop," Jason promised.

"Gee, thanks," Tom said, the needle on his annoyance meter tacking in the red.

"We need gas, anyway," Jason said, "and I'm out of snacks."

"Of course you are. And lottery tickets too, I'm guessing," Tom said sarcastically.

Jason peered at his brother and grinned. "Listen, you have your retirement plan, and I have mine."

Tom drew in a deep breath and held it for a few counts. *It'll be a miracle if I survive this trip,* he thought. *Between my simpleton brother and a box of ashes that hardly deserves this effort, it'll be a friggin' miracle.*

"Oh, good!" Jason blurted, breaking Tom's train of thought. "A gas station." He steered the SUV into the lot and parked beside the pumps. "It looks like we're not lost anymore, Tommy."

Sure, Tom thought while the rising bile in his throat triggered a slow burn. *We're exactly where we should be.* He felt ready to vomit.

Ollie
Carmen Siegers

≥≤

Carmen Siegers started her working life as a broadcast journalist, first in radio in small town Alberta, and then at a television station in Calgary. Covering news was a way to tell stories on a daily basis, but her first love, the movie industry, still called. So one September, in a version of autumn renewal not unlike heading off to college for the first time, she packed up her things and headed to the west coast to start over with a new vocation: working in the playback department on a short-lived television show called *Broadcast News*. Although that show was cancelled before the end of its first season, she stayed in Vancouver and continued working in production until last year when the call of family and friends led her back to the other side of the Rockies. She is currently at work on several short stories, a book, and an idea for a television pilot.

From the author:

"It was a real life missing pet ad that inspired me to write "Ollie." The family had put up several photos, all very compelling to me because

> I felt they told a story, provided an intimate peek into their life. The one that got me especially was the Christmas photo—the kids in front of the tree surrounded by opened presents, posing with their big, fluffy cat. I didn't know these people, and I don't know if they ever got their pet back. I really hope they did. But that's when the voice of Ruby first came to me as I thought about what it means to be a kid coping with loss and emotions that are way too adult for such a young perspective. When you have no context for what is happening around you because you've only spent a decade so far in this nutty world, you are only just discovering how it can turn upside-down on you."

≥≤

It was when Ollie went missing that everything fell apart. But if I really thought about it, it started before that.

We were packing up the campsite after one week of vacation. It had rained five days out of seven, including a huge downpour last night. My little brother and I slept in the tent, and my brother had rolled against the side, so everything was soggy when we woke up. It smelled nice out, though, kinda like a Christmas tree. But now that the sun was out, so were the bugs, and I was slapping at my legs and scratching where they already got me. Mom and Dad were arguing loudly again. This time it was about the tent and the fact that my mom was trying to stuff the wet, green canvas back into its sack.

"You can't put that in there. It'll rot. What's the matter with you?" my dad said.

Mom told him to drop the tone, that she was just trying to get us packed up so we could get out of there. Dad called her a bad word, and she told him he could go to H-E-double-hockey-sticks, only she didn't say it exactly like that. She said the real word.

I had finished my assigned task of putting our sleeping bags in the trailer and our croquet set, badminton paddles, and box of board games in the back of the truck, so I decided I would take Ollie for one last walk. Ollie was our amazing cat. He walked with us just like a dog. He'd do tricks too. He'd roll over, sit, and we almost got him to play dead. He hated the rain, though, and he'd been hiding out in the camper trailer for most of the trip. I searched in there, under the cushions—his favorite spot—then in the cupboards, and even under the sleeping bags that still felt damp and sure smelled like a wet cat. Maybe Mom already put him in the truck. I looked all over—in the back, in the cab, under the seats, feeling with my hands.

"Ollie," I called softly.

My little brother, Jake, trudged in from two campgrounds down where he'd gone to say good-bye to his new friend who shared his love of skateboarding, hunting for frogs and whacking stuff with sticks.

"Is Ollie with you?"

Jake shook his head. He was scratching a big scab on his elbow, his reminder that wheels and gravel don't mix well.

"Mom, have you seen Ollie?" I tried to say it kinda casual.

"He was in the camper," she said.

My dad was laying out the tent on the ground in an exaggerated fashion. My mom was rolling her eyes.

I told Jake our cat was missing and we needed to find him fast.

We walked quickly, my brother and I, our heads swiveled in all directions as we peeked into other campsites, darted into bushes. The branches scratched our arms and legs, but we kept going.

"Ollie, Ollie, Ollie." I yelled out to the wilderness.

"You sound like you're skateboarding," my brother said, and then laughed at his own joke.

"Shut up," I said. His face crumpled. I stopped. He frowned at the ground. His hands were balled up as fists.

"I'm sorry," I said.

"S'okay," he mumbled as he stared at his sneakers and kicked the dirt. A very tiny sniffle escaped before he angrily shook his head.

"I'm really sorry." He looked up at me.

"I guess I'm really stressed about Ollie," I said.

"Yeah," he said. "Me too."

We started walking again and kept calling his name.

"Who's Ollie?" asked this old woman.

She stood at the edge of a campsite that was filled with a big trailer, a picnic table, and a large tarp strung from the trailer to hang over the table. Red, blue, and yellow patio lanterns were strung across it too. The woman wore a pink plaid shirt, long beige shorts, and a fisherman's hat with gray curly hair poking out from under the hat. Her glasses were on a chain around her neck.

"He's our cat."

My brother piped up: "He's all dark gray, and he has a really fluffy tail."

The woman squinted at him. She put on her glasses.

"He's about this big." I used my hands to show Ollie's size.

The plaid-shirt woman was frowning. She looked from me to my brother and back to me.

"Oh dear. Well, cats are certainly tricky. They don't really come when they're called, do they?"

"He's a really smart cat," I said. "He can even do tricks like beg for food and high five with his paws."

My brother nodded his head. "He walks us too," he said. "Like yesterday we went to the beach, and Ollie walked in front, and every time we stopped, he stopped and waited for us."

"There you are." Mom was red-eyed and out of breath. "Did you take Ollie out?"

"We can't find him."

"Oh no. No. Not now." My mom slapped her forehead. The plaid-shirt woman studied my mother.

My mother explained to her that we were in a hurry, and we had to leave so our Dad could get back to work.

"We can't just leave him, Mom. He's our family. You wouldn't leave me or Jake, would you?" I challenged her, my hands on my hips.

"Oh, Ruby. Not now," Mom said.

"I'll keep an eye out for him. We're here for the month." The plaid-shirt woman indicated her camp spot with the huge RV and the patio lanterns.

"Oh, that would be great," Mom said. "I'm Nancy." Mom held out her hand to the woman.

"Carol," said the woman.

Mom reached into her purse, found a pen and scrap paper, and wrote out our phone number. "We're from Calgary."

Carol said they were too, and wasn't that a good thing. She stuck the piece of paper in her pocket and smiled at us.

"Don't worry."

"He's a really great cat," I said. And I realized a few tears were rolling down my cheeks.

We followed our mom back to the campsite, but I kept looking everywhere for Ollie as we walked. I started to protest again when we saw our Dad, but he just pressed his lips together and glared at my mom. I figured I'd better zip it. As we pulled out of the lot, I stared out the truck window, my face pressed against the glass. I kept telling myself that Carol and her family would find Ollie, and even though we don't ever go to church, I still said a little prayer because I figured it might help.

On the way home, we stopped for lunch at a diner.

"You're so careless. That's where they get it from," my dad was saying to my mom.

I had stopped eating, and I was watching the rest of the diners.

"Finish your sandwich, Ruby." My father pointed at my mostly untouched meal.

"I'm not hungry."

"I didn't spend twelve bucks so you could take a few bites and then waste it. Finish it."

My stomach rolled, but I picked up the sandwich and took a bite. Tried to chew. Tried to suppress a sick feeling.

"Don't yell at her," my mother said.

"Who's yelling?"

A couple of people looked over. My father lowered his voice.

"Would it kill you to back me up, just for once?"

"You're being a bully," my mother said.

My father raised his hand. I stopped chewing. For a second I thought he was going to hit her right there in the restaurant.

Instead he slammed both his hands on the table. My brother and I jumped. My father cursed, pushed himself out of the booth. His fork clattered to the floor. More people looked over. He turned and walked out of the diner, slammed the door so that the bell echoed angrily. I stared at my plate as I swallowed hard, willing the big lump of mashed-up sandwich to go down. Chew and swallow.

"You don't have to finish that." My mother was looking at me. She was avoiding the stares from other people.

"It's OK, Mom."

"Is it?" she asked. She covered her face with her hands. *Chew and swallow,* I reminded myself. Jake had his head down. He was holding on to his tablet, but he wasn't playing his game anymore.

When we walked out of the diner, Dad was sitting in the truck out front, staring straight ahead. Mom opened the side doors, and we piled in. She got in the front seat and fastened her seatbelt with a quick glance at my father as she clicked the buckle into place, but he didn't look at her. Instead, he looked at us in the rearview mirror.

"Ready?"

Without waiting for our answer, he turned the key in the ignition, cranked the radio, and gunned the gas pedal. My mother flinched as he peeled out. My father turned up the radio a little more."I miss Ollie," said my little brother.

≥≤

We were still hopeful Ollie would come back to us. When we first got home, my mom called the shelter near where we were staying every day, but there was no sign of him still—nothing to report. My mom and dad had gone from screaming at each other to not talking to each other at all. I thought maybe everyone was just sad because we had lost one of our family members. And then one night before supper, Mom said, "We have news."

"You found Ollie?"

My mom looked down at her hands.

Dad said, "Your mom and I are getting a divorce."

I felt sick. My brother wanted to know what that meant.

"It means your mom and I aren't going to live together anymore."

My brother said, I know, but what did that mean for us?

The next day, my mom got a call. "Hello? What? Yes, I remember you."

Mom looked at me and gave me a huge smile. She mouthed the word "Ollie."

I ran down the hall to get my brother.

We were back in the kitchen as mom hung up the phone.

"The woman from the campsite. She and her husband...they spotted Ollie yesterday. They'll be here in a couple of hours."

Mom gave us a huge hug. We all held onto each other. My mom was crying again.

We watched from the window, my brother and I. We saw the big RV pull up, and before Carol could even get out of the cab, we were out the door right there to greet her. Carol still had on the same hat, but she was wearing a heavy blue sweater now and holding Ollie, who was squirming and twisting toward us.

"It's pretty lucky," she said. "Another day and we would have been gone too."

I grabbed Ollie and buried my nose in his thick grey fur as I breathed in his musty cat smell. His fur was a little matted up in spots. My brother patted him while I hugged him so tight, and Ollie didn't squirm or try to get away. He purred and nudged my chin.

"He really is a pretty neat cat," Carol said.

"He really is."

And I thought, *at least we had Ollie back*. We hadn't lost him forever.

Losing Will

Marcia Gloster

≥≤

Marcia Gloster knew even as a child that she wanted to be an artist. While attending Rhode Island School of Design, she spent a summer studying painting at Oskar Kokoschka's School of Vision in Salzburg, Austria. Upon graduation, she set aside her brushes to pursue a career as an award-winning book designer and art director in New York and London.

Four decades later, Gloster experienced a powerful vision that unleashed memories of her summer in Salzburg that led to the writing of her first book, *31 Days: A Memoir of Seduction*. With a renewed passion for painting, she has since exhibited her work in New York City, New Jersey and Pennsylvania. Her forthcoming novel, *I Love You Today* (The Story Plant, April 2017) tells the story of a young woman determined to succeed as an art director in the "Mad Men" era of the 1960s.

Gloster has one daughter and lives in New Jersey with her husband, James Ammeen.

From the author:

"As I was writing my new novel, *I Love You Today,* about a young woman determined to succeed in the male-dominated world of advertising in 1960's New York, I recalled summers spent on Fire Island and the unexpected angst that seemed to pop up despite the serenity, peace, and beauty of sky, ocean, and beach. In "Losing Will," an overconfident and arrogant publisher seduces his loyal and adoring secretary and, with little regard for her or the woman he intends to marry, expects to have her at his beck and call."

≥≤

Summer 1968

The moment Kathy set foot on Fire Island, she was entranced. The evening was unusually warm for the Friday before Memorial Day weekend, and the setting sun cast a rosy glow over a wide beach and weather-beaten wooden houses, many not much more than shacks. The place held the aura of peace and solitude; a world away from the cacophonous glass towers of the city. She had been told there were no vehicles on the island and smiled at the only ones in evidence: a couple of decrepit bicycles parked randomly in a rusting bike rack and several battered toy red wagons scattered about.

"Come on, Kathy, snap out of it," Brad said, intruding on her thoughts. He had commandeered one of the red wagons that appeared to be the sole conveyance for luggage, groceries, or whatever else required transport. Throwing their duffle bag into it, he handed her a slip of paper. "Tony wants us to pick up a few things. You go to the grocery store. I'll get the beer."

"Grocery store?"

Brad laughed. "Behind you."

Kathy turned around, realizing she was, in fact, standing in front of the entire town of Fair Harbor: a liquor store, a small general store, and an even smaller, ramshackle cafe. Tony's list was brief: potato chips, Tab, eggs, and milk. Kathy added English muffins, a can of Maxwell House, cream, bacon, and jam.

Following Tony's directions, they walked along narrow intersecting boardwalks to a well-worn house that rested on delicate wooden pilings and faced the beach. Tony was on the porch, sprawled in an Adirondack chair and downing a beer. He jumped up and, after shaking hands with Brad, enveloped Kathy in a bear hug, shouting, "Kathy, I get to meet you at last." With a smile she extracted herself as Susie, Tony's girlfriend came out, introduced herself, and helped her carry the groceries inside.

The summer rental had been Brad's idea. According to him, everyone-who-was-anyone at least at KLP, the advertising agency where he presided as one of the head art directors, had taken shares in group houses on Fire Island that summer, particularly Fair Harbor, the town most popular with artists and writers.

As Brad grabbed a beer and joined Tony on the porch, Susie pointed Kathy in the direction their bedroom. It was small and furnished with a queen-sized bed, a couple of night tables, and a small dresser. As instructed, Kathy had brought her own sheets and towels. After making the bed, she put her and Brad's swimsuits and other beach clothes away and returned to the porch.

A few minutes later a couple arrived, pulling another of the ubiquitous red wagons piled with suitcases. Tony introduced them as Rick, a tall, sandy haired creative director at Doyle Dane, and Pam, a petite blond secretary at a law firm. Tony had mentioned they were living together and planned to get married, as Rick said, "one of these days."

Annie, the only single in the group, was the last to arrive. Kathy had met her several months before when Annie had joined Simon and Schuster as an assistant editor. Within the first weeks, Kathy, a book designer, had thought she seemed a bit lost and invited her to lunch. After a few weeks and several more lunches, Annie, in a moment of trust and candor, had opened up to Kathy, confiding why she had left her previous job Random House.

≥≤

After graduating from college, Annie, a journalism major and aspiring writer, had been unable to find a position as an assistant in a publishing company. It wasn't that her skills were lacking, or so she was told, it was that there never seemed to be a job available. And yet, the young men she graduated with appeared to have no problem finding editorial jobs quickly. In the summer of 1963, skirts still covered the knees, Betty Friedan's *The Feminine Mystique* had just been published, and career-minded girls were relegated to the steno pool, a place Annie adamantly refused to go.

The day she had been offered a job at Random House as the secretary for Will Richards, she had jumped at it, convinced she had at last found her way into publishing. Richards, with his tousled dark hair and seductive stare, was an executive editor fourteen years Annie's senior and known as much for his arrogance as his astute ability to recognize promising writers and propel them with alacrity to the *New York Times* Best Seller list.

After a few months of purely professional interactions, he began quietly asking Annie to go out with him for drinks. Naïve and insecure, she had turned him down the first few times until one day, asking herself why not, she had relented. Since she knew he usually frequented the Four Seasons or P.J. Clarke's, she was a bit taken aback when he took her to a small, shadowy bar far from the office. After the expected small talk, office gossip, and a couple of martinis, he got to the point, admitting he had become attracted to her. Aware of what "attraction" meant, she blushed and responded that while she was flattered, she wasn't "that kind of girl."

Not about to give up, he stroked her hand. "Annie. That's what intrigues me about you. Girls today are all too ready to jump into bed at the least suggestion." He had smiled and kissed her fingers. "I respect you. We'll take it slow."

She wasn't sure what slow meant, but after a few days without any further mention from him, she thought, with just a twinge of disappointment, that was the end of it. That is, until the following week when he called at midnight, sounding half-drunk and saying he desperately needed to talk to her. It was only when he arrived that she realized that talking wasn't what he had in mind. Unable to restrain her thinly veiled desire for him, she had succumbed to his seduction. Over the many late nights that followed he had whispered that he cared for her and promised she wouldn't remain his secretary for long; he would move her into the more rarefied realm of copyeditor and then editor. His one caveat, however, was that since they worked together, their "relationship" had to remain a secret. Although unsure she was doing the right thing, she rationalized that although he was her boss, he wasn't married, and perhaps he would one day come to realize he truly loved and needed her.

Over the ensuing months and years, she managed to maintain her fantasy despite the frequent and all-too-painful calls from various girlfriends whom he invited to accompany him to industry parties and charity events. Meanwhile, she suffered and waited, holding on to her late night dreams. In the all-too-harsh reality of the office, however, she would observe him sitting back in his chair smoking the last of his Cuban cigars, laughing and sharing his twenty-year-old single malt with one of his famous authors while scornfully reminding herself she was nothing but a secret in his life, in truth his mistress, albeit one who answered his phones, read his manuscripts, smiled at overbearing authors, typed his correspondence, and laughed at his often-crude jokes. That is, until the day Melanie Burrows-Hastings walked in with a broad "Hallo" and a gigantic ring on her finger. While waiting for Will to finish a meeting, she dabbed gloss on her lips while casually mentioning that she had just come from being photographed for an upcoming issue of the newly-launched and much-discussed *New York Magazine* in one of her chic little Chanel suits while showing off her large diamond and sapphire ring that, she giggled, Will had proffered when he asked her to marry him a few days before. Annie had choked back a sob, coughed up congratulations and run for the ladies room before anyone could see her tears.

Since Melanie had been calling several times a day, Annie had known that Will was dating her. She was supposedly a distant relative of some obscure pilgrim who either floated over on the *Mayflower,* or more likely, Annie thought unkindly, had swum behind it. She was tall, blond—although possibly not, Annie conjectured in another moment of pique—and attractive, if skinny, horse-faced young women were one's type. She was also a member of the younger, hardcore New York society known as Ladies Who Lunch. That her family was involved in the publishing business Annie was sure was a strong motivation for the ever-ambitious Will.

≥≤

A couple of nights later, when Will tried to embrace an incensed Annie in her tiny West Village apartment, she pulled free and faced him. "When were you going to tell me you were engaged to that stick figure, Melanie?"

"I'm sorry, Annie. I know I should have told you before. It just happened so fast."

"Fast? What? You just happened to pick up that huge ring off the counter in Macy's?"

"Actually, it was Cartier," he whispered.

Annie took a breath, walked to the door, and opened it. "Get out."

He shook his head and reached for her. "Annie. I've never seen you like this. I love this fire I'm seeing in you."

"What fire?" she said, unexpectedly dissolving into tears. Will enfolded her in his arms as she sobbed against his jacket.

He petted her hair. "Annie. You know I love you. But this is an important step in my life, my career. I'm sure you can understand that."

"And what, other than your secretary, does that make me?" she sobbed. She'd tried to spit out "mistress" but couldn't say the word.

He kissed her gently. "You're my special girl. I want us to always be together. It will be difficult, but we'll make it work."

She could feel herself weakening. "I don't know."

"Annie," he whispered. "I have a surprise. There's a copyeditor's job about to open up. It's yours if you want it."

Annie held back mentioning that it wasn't exactly a surprise; she had known about it for days and had been waiting to bring it up to him. She understood why he was offering it now and well aware that she was once again being seduced. Nevertheless, she threw her arms around his neck.

After he left that night she lay back on her pillows thinking it might be time to face an all-too-bleak reality. It was 1968; she had worked for Will for over five years, and any hope that he would finally come to his senses was rapidly waning. She had always been there for him, keeping his secrets, putting up with his eccentricities and lying, although not without the occasional twinge of guilt, to aspiring writers, promising he'd call them back. Their lovemaking spanned the sweet to the intense, so how could he not be as much in love with her as she was with him? And though an "I love you" occasionally slipped through his lips, she knew it was time to come to terms with the inevitable; there was no way she could compete with Miss Burrows-Hastings and her social connections. In a moment of resolve, she promised herself their relationship would end at his marriage, or if she could manage it, even before, whether he wanted it to or not.

≥≤

A week later she finally moved into the copyediting area, away from her minute-by-minute interaction with Will—not to mention the all-too-frequent phone calls from the Minnie-Mouse-voiced Melanie. Now Will had to call her or stop by, whispering that he'd see her later. A couple of times when she told him she was busy—she had at last gone out on several dates—he turned on his heel and hadn't spoken to her for days. Despite her anxiety, she was beginning to feel stronger, finally having come to terms with the fact that what she wished for was never going to happen. She'd had her share of dates before but had always put them off, sure that Will would one day wake up and realize he couldn't live without her.

One afternoon about six months later, after Will dropped a manuscript on her desk with a whispered, "Last night was wonderful," she watched him go over to the office of one of the editors and have another whispered conversation. With a sinking feeling she wondered if she was the only secret in his life, something that had never occurred to her before. Later that day she overheard a couple of editors talking, one mentioning that invitations would be going out any day for Will's wedding in October. Holding back tears, she closed her eyes, recalling their passionate lovemaking the night before when he had said not one word. That same afternoon she went to an unoccupied editor's office and called several employment agencies.

≥≤

Kathy was the last person to be judgmental. She too was in love with an arrogant, ambitious, and charming man who had long resisted any discussion of commitment. Listening to Annie's frustrations about Will, she wondered at the forces that drove such men: their relentless quest for power, success, and notoriety, not to mention love, or, if not precisely love, sex at any cost. It was girls like her—and Annie—who were drawn by the confidence, excitement, and sensuality they evoked, only to end up in the long or even short run, heartbroken.

One day, in an effort to convince Annie to end it with Will, Kathy in turn confided that after three of years of dating the ever-evasive Brad, who refused to talk about any future beyond the next Saturday night, she finally had enough. "If a man continually tells you he doesn't want to discuss the future, much less marriage, at some point you have to believe him."

"So what did you do?

Kathy took a breath. "One night after Brad told me, once again, that he didn't want to talk about it, I calmly nodded and left his apartment. I didn't take his calls for weeks. It was awful. I was always on the verge of tears, and all I wanted was to run back to him. I kept imagining him going to bars and meeting other women. But I kept my resolve, and one afternoon he showed up at my office with flowers and saying we should talk."

"And did you?"

"I told him no. There was nothing to talk about."

"So what happened?"

"He asked me to marry him."

She laughed. "In the office?"

"Yep. And on one knee. With everyone in the art department cheering him on. I still wasn't sure he'd really follow through with it. But here we are two years later."

Annie shook her head. "You are so lucky, Kathy."

"I'm not sure luck has anything to do with it. It's more about coming to terms with what one wants, especially after one is told he can no longer have it. If I were you, I'd stop answering Will's calls. If he really wants you, he'll leave Melanie and come to you. If he doesn't you'll know you've made the right decision."

Annie shook her head. "I don't think that will work. I doubt that he's really in love with Melanie, but she's too good a match to pass up. My problem is that I'm not ready to give up."

"Even Brad says he's just stringing you along. If nothing else, listen to a man's point of view."

That was the day, determined to get Annie out of her dark, lonely apartment, that Kathy invited her to share their summer house on Fire Island. With her dark curls and big blue eyes, Annie was curvy and a good four inches shorter than Kathy's five foot, eight-inch height. At first she said she wasn't sure; she didn't like the way she looked in bathing suits.

"No one likes the way they look in swimsuits," Kathy laughed. "Come on, Annie. You're pretty, and you have a cute figure. It's time to get out there. We'll get you a bikini and maybe even a boyfriend."

≥≤

By the time everyone regrouped on the porch it was getting close to midnight, and after a final drink of the night, they all retreated to their various bedrooms.

The next morning Annie and Kathy were stretched out on the beach catching rays while Susie, determined to be the first with a tan, was sitting up roasting herself with a reflector. Pam and Rick had gone down the beach to visit friends.

A raucous volleyball game had begun a few houses away, and Brad and Tony went to join in. It was a perfect day: blue sky, white puffy clouds, and gentle waves rolling in on the soft sand beach. Annie had started reading *The Electric Kool-Aid Acid Test*, not because she was into drugs but that she considered Tom Wolfe an intriguing writer. Kathy, trying to delve into *Master and Margarita*, thought Annie had seemed somewhat anxious all morning, and after attempting, without much response to have a conversation with her, she had given up on both Annie and her book and closed her eyes.

A short while later she heard Annie exclaim, "Oh. Hi," in apparent surprise. Opening her eyes, Kathy was shocked to see a man in large sunglasses and a baseball cap standing over them.

Annie jumped up, her face scarlet, and without a word began walking back to the house. The man followed her.

A couple of minutes later Brad appeared. "What was that all about?"

Kathy shook her head. "That, I assume, was the ever-ubiquitous Will."

"How'd he get here?"

She shook her head. "I don't know. Maybe he's in a house nearby. I'm not sure Annie knew. You can see she's smitten, though."

He shook his head. "From what I hear, the only person he's smitten with is himself. Should I speak to her?"

"Hearing it from a man might be good for her. But please be gentle."

He sat down next to her, suddenly seductive. The thought of another guy about to have sex was turning him on. "I have an idea. Maybe we should go inside as well," he said, pushing a bikini strap off her shoulder.

"This may not be a good time. I think we should leave them alone."

"Any time with you is a good time, Kathy," he said, leaning in to give her a kiss. He glanced around as if pondering some other possible spot. "Okay, for now. But you'll pay for delaying the inevitable."

"Delaying?" she said, laughing. He nodded, looking more serious than she would have expected.

≥≤

After a little more than an hour, she saw Will leave the house and walk towards low dunes where a narrow path between the towns was barely discernable through high beach grass. He didn't glance back. A few seconds later, Annie emerged, her eyes following him as she buttoned an oversized flowered shirt over a different swimsuit.

When she returned to the beach, Kathy asked, "Did you know Will was going to be here, on Fire Island?"

She sighed. "He told me that Melanie's family had a house in Saltaire. But honestly, I didn't know it would be so close. I can't believe he came here."

"Come on, Annie. It's time to get over him. When he was single it was one thing. But now he's cheating on his fiancée, and soon she will be his wife. You don't want to be part of that."

Kathy saw tears come to her eyes. "What am I going to do? I love him."

"It's time to give yourself a chance. There are lots of single guys in the houses around us."

≥≤

On a Saturday in early July, Tony borrowed a surfboard from one of the houses down the beach. They had all seen the movie, *The Endless Summer*, and with good-sized waves that day the guys were determined to show off. Apparently it wasn't quite as easy as any of them anticipated; as soon as one got up on the board, he just as quickly fell off.

Kathy, Annie, and Susie had put down a couple of towels on the beach and were playing Scrabble while occasionally looking up and laughing at the debacle just off shore. At one point they watched as Brad stood up precariously on the board just to wipe out within seconds.

Still giggling, they turned back to the game as he came up toweling off sand and bits of broken shells. "What's so funny?"

Annie looked up at him. "You. Falling off the surfboard."

"Come on. Your turn," he said, grabbing Annie's hand. She got up, protesting as he pulled her toward the ocean. But ignoring the surfboard, he introduced her to a dark-haired young man he had met playing volleyball. Kathy could see she was a bit flustered, but as Brad dove into the next wave they laughed and started talking. A few minutes later, Annie returned. "Did you know Brad was going to do that?"

"No. I never know what Brad is going to do. Was he nice?"

"Actually, he was." She smiled. "He said he'd see me later at the party."

≥≤

Tony had announced that he was throwing a watermelon party. He had gone up and down the beach inviting everyone from the houses around them. That morning, he bought several watermelons and, after boring holes into them, poured an entire bottle of rum into each and left them on the kitchen counter to marinate. Later, he cut up the booze-soaked melons as Susie passed around her homemade appetizers: cheese puffs, water chestnuts wrapped with bacon, and pigs in blankets.

Within an hour, almost thirty of their neighbors had arrived and, totally plastered, were having seed-spitting contests over the railing. Annie unexpectedly became tearful, and Kathy, who told a suddenly-amorous Brad he'd just have to wait, went to console her in her room. "Annie. Please. You have to come out. There are some really nice guys here. That dark-haired guy, Jerry, is looking for you."

Annie wiped her eyes and took a deep breath. "I was fine till I saw how Brad looked at you. It's like he can't get enough of you. He reminds me of Will. That's what I want."

Kathy shook her head. She was well aware of Brad's glances and what they meant. "Be careful what you wish for, Annie. Brad's got some weird thing this summer about having sex in unlikely places." The sunny days of heat, sand, and sea topped off by beer and booze had created a seductive stew for all of them; particularly the guys who continually eyed the girls walking the beach or running into the waves in the tiniest bikinis they could find.

"Consider yourself lucky. I think every girl would wish for such a thing. Especially with Brad. But he only has eyes for you."

Kathy laughed. "Well, I can't say it's not fun. A little weird, though."

"Okay," Annie said, sounding suddenly determined. "Just give me a minute." She got up, brushed her unruly curls and put on lipstick.

As Kathy went to look for Brad, she saw Jerry walk over to Annie with a slice of watermelon and a smile.

Brad was waiting impatiently on the porch, a beach towel draped over his shoulders. "Come on, Kathy. It's almost sunset. Let's go for a walk."

Stepping carefully over slippery watermelon seeds, Kathy asked, "Are you sure you mean a walk?"

"Well, there are some nice dunes with a few trees down the beach. It's pretty secluded. I think we should go have a look at them." He held out his hand.

With a sigh, she put her sunglasses on. "Sure, why not?" she said, taking his hand.

≥≤

Kathy and Brad returned to see Annie running up the steps to the house. For once she was in a swimsuit without any sort of cover-up.

"Look," she said breathlessly, showing them a pail filled with grey shells. "Jerry convinced me to go clamming with him. It's was fun, but kind of weird feeling around with your toes. He's bringing more. We'll clean them and have them for dinner."

Kathy smiled at her excitement and Brad stepped back with an appraising glance. "I like your swimsuit, Annie. Lose the cover-ups. You have a nice figure. You shouldn't hide it."

She blushed, whispering, "Thank you, Brad," and ran inside.

Kathy reached up and kissed him. "That was sweet. Thank you. She needs all the confidence she can get."

≥≤

In mid-August, while watching what had become an increasingly bloodthirsty volleyball game, Annie asked Kathy to take a walk with her.

"Is everything all right?" Kathy said, getting up.

"I'm not sure how to deal with Will. Everything is changing."

"That's not really surprising, if you think about it. You've met someone, and Will's getting married in a few weeks."

"I've already told him I can't continue to see him, that it's gone far enough. But then he tells me how much he loves me and how can I do this to 'us?' He called last Wednesday around six, saying he'd be right over. He didn't even ask if I had plans, just assumed I'd be waiting for him. I was going to tell him no, but it somehow came out as yes. But he didn't show up until after eleven. He didn't even bother to call. By then I was frantic and when I asked him why he was so late, he brushed me off, saying it wasn't important. I guess something finally snapped, and I told him to get out. That's when he started yelling at me, saying some really nasty things. Somehow I managed to tell him I never wanted to see him again."

Kathy sighed. "Good for you."

"Not so good. I spent the night crying and wishing I could take it back. The next day he called to apologize and asked if he could come over later. I don't know how I did it, but I told him I had a date. He became really furious. Apparently it's all right for him to get married, but I shouldn't see anyone else. It appears that you were right; he's called every day since. It seems the more I say no, the more he insists on seeing me. But it's not easy."

"Keep reminding yourself that you're no longer his other woman. Concentrate on Jerry. Brad says he really likes you."

"Really?"

She nodded. "Yes, Annie."

≥≤

Suddenly it was Labor Day, the last weekend of the summer, which meant three days of booze, sun, and sex. In Brad's words, "perfection." All summer long he'd somehow found dark, secluded corners, assorted dunes, and stands of scruffy pine trees that Kathy had never noticed. The girls in the house had become very aware of his preferences and watched giggling as Kathy returned blushing and more often than not still brushing off sand or pine needles stuck to her back. The guys just guffawed and handed a preening Brad a beer.

That Saturday, Brad convinced Tony and Susie and even Rick and Pam to go dancing one last time at Flynn's in Ocean Beach. Annie asked Jerry, and after drinking and frugging to Creme, The Doors, and Stones till closing, they walked home arm-in-arm along the beach becoming pink with the first rays of dawn. As they approached their house Kathy looked around, "Where's Annie?"

Brad shook his head. "Don't worry, Kathy, she's fine. I think we should have a look at those dunes, don't you?"

Laughing, she pulled him away. "No, Brad. No dunes. I'm going to bed."

"I guess that works," he said with a grin.

≥≤

When they got up it was close to noon. As Brad was concocting his special Bloody Marys, Annie walked in, looking disheveled and still in her clothes from the night before. Without looking at anyone she darted red-faced to her room. Brad nodded his approval while Kathy restrained herself from applauding.

≥≤

"Uh oh."

"What?" Annie looked up, shading her eyes.

"I think your friend is here."

Annie turned, her eyes wide at seeing Will. She got up quickly and walked toward him, at the same time glancing nervously down the beach, no doubt looking for Jerry. Kathy saw Will try to take her hand and Annie pull back. After a brief but heated discussion, he put his arm around her and they walked back toward the house. Kathy watched in disbelief.

A short while later, Annie emerged, followed by an angry-looking Will. He said something, and she shook her head. Tight-lipped, he quickly descended the stairs and retraced his steps back the way he had come.

Annie waited until he disappeared then ran to a worried Kathy.

"Annie. Are you okay?"

She nodded. "Will insisted we had to talk and, since I didn't want Jerry to see us, I told him to come back to the house. He just took it for granted that I'd make love with him. When I refused, he got angry. It was as if he hadn't listened to anything I've said in the last weeks. I told him again that it was over and he was kidding himself by thinking that Melanie hadn't become suspicious by now. He just waved it off, saying I was overreacting and she was oblivious. I'm not so sure. I can't believe that she's so clueless."

"In other words, to use a phrase, he still wants his cake and to eat it too. But you're right about Melanie; by now she has to be wondering about his walks every weekend."

Annie nodded. "I guess I should be flattered. He should have thought about this five years ago. Now it's too late."

≥≤

By Monday afternoon the final volleyball game had been played and the net taken down. All over the beach, groups were either having last picnics or gathering up towels and beach toys to be put away till next summer. A few guys and even a girl or two were challenging the fairly flat waves on surfboards as the sun cast long shadows on the sand.

Brad looked around, drained his beer, and coaxed Kathy up to the roof for one last summer fling. After spreading out towels, they watched a small plane putter by, trailing a tattered banner advertising Coppertone. Kissing Kathy's neck, Brad untied her bikini top and, picking up a bottle of baby oil, he began slowly massaging it into her back. With a sigh, she turned to him in a kiss. Whatever misgivings she had about making love on the roof in a group of houses that all had the same roof heights vanished in a haze of desire as Rob pulled her up to straddle him. Suddenly hearing a thrumping sound, she looked up seeing a helicopter heading straight at them. "Oh my God," she shouted. "There's a helicopter coming."

Brad groaned. "So am I."

Laughing, she rolled off him and reached for a couple of towels. As the helicopter approached, it veered off to the right, and Brad waved with her bikini top. The people inside waved back. They looked at each other and collapsed in laughter, tears running down their cheeks. As they picked up their towels, Kathy glanced down at the beach, seeing Annie walking along the shore with Jerry. "Brad. Come here. Look."

Out of the corner of her eye, Kathy saw movement on the path. It was Will, obviously looking for Annie. Brad saw him as well. "Uh oh. Should I go down and intercept him?"

"No. Let's see what happens. For some reason I think this will be all right."

They watched Jerry put his arms around Annie and kiss her. As they moved apart, he grinned, appeared to say he'd be right back, and ran down the beach. She watched him, her eyes shining.

As Jerry ran off, Will walked quickly towards Annie, his eyes narrowed in fury. Without a word, he grabbed her shoulders and kissed her roughly.

Alarmed, Kathy watched Annie push him away, at the same time becoming aware that a tall, blonde, slightly horse-faced woman had emerged stealthily from the tall grass at the edge of the same path that Will had taken. She stopped abruptly, removed her sunglasses and stared wide-eyed at the scene before her, all the while twisting what appeared to be a large shiny ring on her finger.

Tonic and Spirits

Craig Ham

≥≤

As a boy, Craig Ham often travelled with his parents through the high desert of Nevada and the Mojave Desert of California, exploring ghost towns, collecting old bottles, and researching the Old West. A software developer and writer, he lives with his wife in the Los Angeles area. His story "The Mobius Comet" was the First Place Winner in the 2013 Writer's Digest Eighth Annual Popular Fiction Awards (Science Fiction category).

From the author:

"A disillusioned medicine peddler with a traveling museum struggles with his own humanity after concocting a plan to make some easy money in a town terrorized by ghosts."

≥≤

There is something unsettling about old battlefields— something known to those who wander these sites alone. A desolate, forlorn feeling pervades the land, as if the violent deaths have been absorbed into soil and rock, into the veins of the leaves and the roots of the whispering ash and willow trees.

In such unhallowed land, weeds nourished by soil soaked in the blood of the fallen do not pulse with the serenade of crickets, gnarled trees twisted in mock agony shelter no birds, and in the small hours of the morning, glowing orbs float through the writhing mist.

This palpable echo of past deeds is well-known to the inhabitants of Redemption. The town was founded just east of such a battleground. The people of this isolated settlement do not venture anywhere near the actual site of the slaughter after dark, nor do they tend the mound where the multitude of bodies were laid to rest. The site could be put out of mind and simply shunned, but for one reason. The storms. The sound of thunder against the distant purple mountains is occasion to go indoors, or, time permitting, to seek holy ground. Church bells peel out a solemn warning, "Closed" signs are turned in the windows of the mercantile shops, the blacksmith abandons his anvil, and mothers rush to the schoolhouse, where their children are retrieved with no need of explanation. Even stray dogs tuck their tails between their legs and retire beneath the claptrap walkways. Then, as signs begin to sway and windows rattle, as jagged fingers of blue lightning reach out across darkened sky, silence and the sounds of whispered prayer descend upon the town.

It was on such an evening that Dr. Alexander Pettifog, Esquire, rolled into town. His large, boxed wagon was pulled by a team of mules, with an extra horse tied behind. The side of the wagon was covered with ornate Gothic lettering: "Pettifog's Traveling Museum of Amazing Artifacts". Along the middle of one side, it read: "See the Amazing Spirit Urn of Solomon, Recovered from the Ruins of Ancient Arabia". On the other, "Hear the Spirits Speak!" Words like "Electrifying!" and "World-Famous" were thrown at sudden eye-catching angles here and there inside quotes, and below the museum lettering, it read: "Tonics, Bitters, and Spirits."

"Dr." Pettifog, purveyor of ancient antiquities, reputed former head of the archaeology department of an eastern university and self-described theosophist and psychic extraordinaire, was making as grand an entrance as he could after two weeks on the desert trail. Drowsy from the day's journey, he stirred to the sound of church bells pealing, quickly stashed his small beaker of medicinal whiskey in his pocket, and straightened up with a loud but satisfying cracking sound in his back. It was at this moment that he noticed the citizenry of Redemption busily engaged in the act of deserting the streets.

For a moment or two, Alexander considered the possibility that the hasty retreat had been occasioned by his arrival. He quickly realized, however, that no one was paying him the slightest bit of attention. Not even the tip of his black felt bowler hat to a pair of elderly ladies bustling past the front of his wagon was acknowledged.

The church bells rang out once again as thunder rolled across the sky. Red-fringed clouds roiled quickly overhead, veiling the afternoon sun, lengthening the shadows. The wagon swayed, rocked by a sudden gust of wind. Alexander pulled back gently on the reins.

"Best be gittin' indoors, mister."

Pettifog turned in the direction of the voice. A young couple had paused on the walkway. The young man stood holding one hand on his wide brimmed hat. Wind whipped the girl's dress.

Pettifog had driven his wagon across desert soil frothed in alkali, down gullies sculpted by rain falling on parched soil that could not drink quickly enough. He had worked his wagon through canyons scoured by sand and littered with boulders. His nostrils still carried the bitter smell of alkali blown by hot winds and dust devils. The few trees he had recently encountered were stunted and gnarled, denied the luxury of height or spread. He welcomed the relief promised in the sonorous roll of thunder passing overhead, the promise of freshness in the dark and normally penurious clouds. He scowled at the couple.

The girl was tugging at her beau's arm. "Come on Jasper...Let's go." The lines on her forehead were creased beneath her bonnet.

"Suit yourself," said the young man, "but I'd get out of the street if I was you." They hurried away.

"Oh, you would, would you?" Alexander muttered to himself, nodding his head.

Just then, a small boy appeared at the side of the wagon. He looked to be about eight years old and stood with his fingers looped around a pair of red suspenders. He had nicker shorts, a shirt too large for his frame, and a somewhat dilapidated straw hat that was pushed back on a large mop of dirty blonde hair.

"Are you in a circus?"

Alexander looked down at the boy, and for a brief moment thought he saw someone else. Something pulled on his heart-strings, and a familiar heaviness weighed down on him briefly while the wind moaned. The same weight that pressed on him in the long, open nights in the desert when the sky was heavy. He took a breath and cleared his throat.

"Get outta here, kid."

A gust of wind knocked against the boy. He folded his arms and stood his ground. "Can I see what's in the wagon?"

"You got a nickel?"

"No, sir."

"Then get outta here."

The boy thought for a few seconds, then looked down and spat. He cocked his head sideways at Alexander, stuck his tongue out, and took off down the street.

He watched the lad run away, and a smile stole the corners of his mouth. A distant look glazed his eyes again for a moment, while the wind buffeted his wagon, rocking it with increasing ferocity.

"You'd better get that wagon to the livery stable."

Alexander shifted back around to find two men standing nearby. The one who addressed him was heavyset, bald, with mutton-chop sideburns framing a red face blackened with soot. He stood with his hands on a mule-skin apron.

"Directly ahead, next to my smithy. Better get there directly. Storm's coming through."

"Sir," replied Pettifog, "if I was afraid of a little spring shower, I would have settled in Yuma."

He extended a paper to the men. An advertisement outlining the wonders of his traveling museum show. The smithy waved his thick arms impatiently.

"Don't make me wait, mister. Come on, Caleb."

The other man, older, remained where he was and scratched coarse, gray whiskers. He looked up at Alexander, raising his unruly eyebrows over red-rimmed eyes. His nose was shot through with a network of red spider-veins above a thick, gray moustache.

The old man narrowed his eyes. "You got medicine?"

"Have I got medicine? Not only do I have medicine, I have cures." The old man's eyes brightened in a flash.

"Cures from the Orient, cures from our physicians back east, herbal remedies from the apothecaries of Europe. Dr. Harter's Iron Tonic—guaranteed to put hair on your chest and strength in your arms—Lash's Bitters, Pepto-Magan..."

"Joseph!" A woman's cry echoed into his pitch from down the street. They all turned. "Where's Samuel? I need to get Samuel to the church!"

≥≤

Marcella Aragon had heard church bells and dropped the skein of white lace. A cold gust of wind met her on her way out of Beaton's Mercantile, and thunder clouds had begun to gather at the edge of town. Samuel was not waiting outside as he should have been. She had rushed down, turned the corner onto the main street.

Joseph and Caleb were speaking with a medicine peddler in the street. The smithy answered. "He's not at the Mercantile?"

"No. He's not there." The edge in her voice grew sharper. Joseph shrugged.

Marcella crossed the road, scanning the walkways, searching the street.

She hurried to Joseph and laid her hand on his thick arm, and he patted it in return.

"He'll turn up. We'll fetch him right now, won't we, Caleb. Come on." He grabbed the arm of the old man and started to leave.

The medicine peddler spoke. "Pardon me, ma'am." The stranger stood partway up, bowed slightly, and tipped his bowler hat. His face was weathered and darkened by sun. Crow's feet at the corner of his eyes and laugh lines around his mouth promised a pleasant disposition. He looked taller, more broad-shouldered than he ought to have been, and his left cheek was scarred. The most striking thing about him, though, was his eyes—bright cobalt blue, penetrating. They shone out from the shadow of his derby hat.

"Is he a little tow-headed fellow with suspenders and a chewed-up straw hat?" His accent was southern.

"You've seen him," she said excitedly. "Where is he?"

"Last I saw of him, he was high-tailing it down the street that way," he nodded, "towards the livery stables, I suspect."

"Thank you." Somewhat relieved, she turned and began running toward the stables. "Bring Caleb, Joe," she said. "We have to be going," she turned back, "*now*." An arc of blue lightning webbed the sky as if in response to her entreaty.

The storm clouds were beginning to spread over the town, bringing a cold wind and the smell of rain. It was happening faster than before. She already thought she heard whispering in the wind.

She called out ahead for Samuel, but the wind snatched away her words.

≥≤

Alexander watched her make her way briskly down the street. She moved with a certain natural grace that caused him to pause in carnal admiration for a few moments.

Tipping his hat, he turned and sat back down. "The pleasure was all mine, ma'am." The blacksmith noticed his attention and shot him a daggered look.

"You got any Winslow's Syrup?" The old man was peering around at the side of the wagon.

Alexander winked at Caleb. "Very popular, and highly effective. You're a man that knows his medicine. Mrs. Winslow's Soothing Syrup—direct from Curtis and Perkins—is only one of the wonders I carry in this wagon.

"Do tell."

"By the way, gentlemen, what if I told you that inside this wagon repose the remains of Imhotep, Pharaoh of Egypt, architect of the Great Pyramid of Giza?"

Joseph stepped toward the wagon.

"Mister, this ain't the time. I'm warning you..."

"What?" asked Caleb.

A few other men had paused briefly to watch.

"A mummy," continued Alexander in a slightly elevated and imperious tone. "The wrapped remains of an ancient King of Egypt."

The old man scratched the back of his head. "You got a dead feller in there?"

"Among other things. There's also an urn that contains a djinn."

The man smiled a nearly toothless grin. "Now that, I'd be interested in."

"Not that kind of gin, though I do have something like that as well, no this is a *djinn*—a genie—like the one in Aladdin's lamp, found in an ancient city beneath the sands of Arabia." Thunder pealed again, and the other men moved away quickly.

The old man looked at him blankly, so Alexander handed Caleb a paper. It fluttered in the wind.

"Here. I'll see you at the show I'm having tomorrow evening."

Joseph grabbed Caleb's arm again and pulled him away. "Now, old man."

Caleb took the proffered paper and hobbled off, quickening his pace to keep up with his captor.

"Pass the word!" Alexander called out as they disappeared around a corner.

He hadn't exactly found the artifacts in Arabia. He had acquired them in Chicago, from a Frenchman of somewhat dubious reputation. It had come to Pettifog's attention that this particular gentleman, who called himself "Dupuis," a surveyor with a rather vague association with the Cairo Museum, had some artifacts to sell. Having recently incurred the necessity of a timely change in address and finding himself uncomfortably short of funds to prolong said relocation, Pettifog was interested.

The actual origin of the pieces was, of course, unimportant to Pettifog as long as they looked authentic and could be acquired for a reasonable sum. A midnight visit to a dockyard holding bin revealed a rather handsomely decorated sarcophagus, complete with a well-preserved mummy, a half-dozen congealed rolls of papyri, several crates of pottery, a large bronze urn of intricate and curious workmanship, and a variety of assorted figurines, votaries, and small statues of various therianthropic Egyptian deities.

Dupuis was asking far more than Pettifog could give. After much haggling, accusation, protestation, questions as to the legitimacy of the other's parentage, general negotiation—and due in no small part to a certain urgency on both sides—a price for the lot was agreed upon, and an exchange effected. Alexander considered himself the winner as the lot would easily fetch a good deal more from certain parties with whom he was acquainted. Antiquities were the rage in certain quarters, and the mummy alone was worth the price that Alexander gave Dupuis.

Due, however, to a slight miscalculation as to the degree of interest in retrieving the artifacts in question on the part of certain persistent co-claimants to their title, Alexander was forced to relocate with great haste, with the artifacts in tow. Along the way, he discovered that people were willing to pay to see a mummy and the accompanying tomb artifacts. As long as he remained relatively mobile, it seemed a winning strategy. And, of course, there was always the popular and reliable medicinal trade.

As it turned out, of the tomb artifacts, the unusual urn was one of the more popular draws. Cast in bronze, it was nearly two feet in height with a large circular base and a fluted top sealed with a series of concentric, bronze rings. It was covered in markings: etched curved letters and figures in a language that no one ever recognized, which made it quite easy for Alexander to "interpret."

The strangest thing about the urn, however, was the noise that frequently emanated from it. Whispers, harsh and guttural, hissed from the urn if you sat with it long enough. The whispers were faint, and even Pettifog could never swear for sure that he heard articulate sounds at any particular moment, or whether it was the effect of a strange and persistent hum of the metal. It was, however, an effect noticed by many, and again, they were easy for Pettifog to "translate," depending on the needs of the situation. It came in handy particularly for séances.

≥≤

Marcella was frantic. "Bill, he's not here!"

She had searched the stables, the loft, the smithy. Samuel was nowhere. She had called him until she was hoarse. William had come from the Church along with Felipe the deacon, then told her to settle down.

"God is with us, Mary."

Joseph and Caleb waved at them from across the street. She tried to run to them, but William held her fast. "Felipe and I will take a look. You stay here with these brethren. I can't worry about you too."

The sky continued to darken as they stood looking up at the clouds streaming by. The air was damp.

"But look at it, Bill. There isn't time. It's happening already." She tried to pull away. William looked up into the darkness.

"I don't understand. It shouldn't have come up this fast. Oh, the wages of sin. Felipe, see to my woman here. I'll tend to Samuel. I'm sure he's inside somewhere."

"I'll go with you," said Joseph, walking up holding a lantern.

"God is with me," said William. "He is my shield. You stay here. Felipe, take her inside."

≥≤

The streets were deserted. Overhead, the sky had darkened at an alarming rate.

The clouds, gliding quickly a few minutes before, had stopped, ominously. Alexander noted with consternation a pulsing network of red veins of lightning making its way through the billowing clouds overhead.

It was also quiet. Very quiet. Alexander's mules began to get skittish, and the horse whinnied, pulling back on the rope behind the wagon. Then a sound—distant but persistent. It sounded like canons, or hooves—a rhythmic booming noise, not unlike the sound of a marching army or cavalry caught on the wind. Alexander was all too familiar with the sounds. Shiloh. Fredericksburg. His heart pounded in his chest. The wind shifted, and the sound was muted. Odd thunder or some kind of atmospheric phenomenon.

He could make no sense of the situation. Then he remembered something. He had heard of tornadoes, even sheltered against one as it passed overhead in the Territories in Oklahoma. That might explain things. He shivered slightly at the implications. He released the wooden brake of the wagon and flicked the reins. His wagon creaked, clanged, and groaned through the street. The wind seemed to be coming from all directions, and the wagon staggered like a drunkard on his way home.

He couldn't afford to lose his wagon. He'd heard of whole farms being swept up in prairie whirlwinds, cows dropping from the sky miles away from their pasture. He whipped the reins hard and yelled at the horses.

Dust and straw, hats and water from the troughs whipped by him. His own hat flew off as he strained to keep the horses on their urgent task. He saw the blacksmith, heavy and stout, holding a lantern, waiting along with old Caleb by his side as he approached. The blacksmith was motioning for him to hurry.

He struggled several more yards, then turned the team in towards the livery. The blacksmith took the bits of the lead horses and pulled them quickly into the open stable.

"Obliged!" Alexander said, not sure they could even hear him over the roar of the wind. He stood up on the wagon and looked back out at the sky, nearly dark as night. A fog had begun to flow through, whipped by the wind.

"This is some squall. I've never..." Just then, in a sudden flash of silver light, he saw a small, yellow dog dart out across the road about halfway down the main street, running as if the devil himself were chasing him. A few seconds later, another figure followed. A little boy with short pants and suspenders.

Tossing the reins aside, he leapt off the wagon. "Hey you! Boy!"

He ran out into the swirling mist. "Boy! Samuel!"

The mist was growing thicker. He plunged into it, waving his hands, heading in the direction he saw the boy running.

He heard the blacksmith calling after him.

In the distance a dog was barking, yelping excitedly. He turned toward the sound and moved through the mist. Overhead, the sky began to pulse, and the fog around him glowed red. The dog was close by.

Another crack of thunder overhead, sounding like canon fire. "Samuel."

He found the boy kneeling against a water trough a short distance away. He turned and looked back at Alexander, straining to hold onto the struggling dog, still yelping and clawing.

Alexander ran to the boy, scooping both of them up. "What do you think you're doing out here, boy?"

The mist flashed again, bathing them in a rosy glow. The sound of men yelling pierced the fog.

"Your ma's beside herself."

He carried the boy back—the way he had come, he hoped. He was unable to see more than a few feet as he walked.

"Your dog would have taken care of himself... "

The yelling was closer, the sound of many men. Angry. Then came the crack of gunfire.

"What in the name of..."

He saw something briefly, a face, contorted in anger, eyes bulging and red as embers. The face was skeletal—lit for an instant by a flash of lightning. The mouth was open in a scream, the jaws impossibly elongated.

Alexander froze, still holding the boy and his dog. The mist cleared for a few moments, and his blood turned to ice water.

They stood silhouetted in the mist, their hair jutting out at odd angles, haloed by the dim, red light behind them. They were soldiers, or could have been soldiers. The uniforms hung on their frames, their lips were half gone, giving them a death leer of teeth. Pairs of red eyes began to appear everywhere in the mist.

The boy screamed and buried his head in Alexander's frock coat. The dog growled, deep and throaty, baring his fangs, his eyes wild with fear, scratching to get loose.

Alexander tried to say something, but all he could manage was a croak.

"What in the name of Daniel Webster...?" He tightened his grip on the boy.

Another thunder clap and the fog moved in around them again, obscuring the phantoms, or whatever they were. He heard the sound of metal striking metal, groans, and screams. The mist smelled of sulfur and sweat. The voices sounded increasingly distant. The boy sobbed, hugging Alexander's neck so hard it was a stranglehold.

The glow of a yellow lantern appeared, coming closer and closer. He braced himself, then let his breath out in one large sigh when he made out the stout, bald figure of the smithy.

"Mister! This way. Hurry!"

"Like a bat out of hell!" said Alexander, lunging forward with his charges. "Samuel?!" the smithy turned and called out.

"He's here, Mary! Parson, we found Samuel!"

The woman came running up from behind them in the mist. "Samuel. Oh my god, Samuel. Are you alright?"

"Nothing a good hickory switch wouldn't fix, I'd reckon," replied the smithy, visibly relieved.

The woman nearly collided with Alexander, pulled Samuel and the dog to her bosom, smothering the boy in kisses, repeating his name.

"We'd best get back inside!" the smithy held the lantern out and began herding the woman and boy back toward the stables.

Alexander felt faint. The swirling, sickly fog swirled around him as the others moved off. His knees could barely support his weight. He took a few steps and wiped a wet oily dew off his forehead. As the fog wrapped tightly around him, the glow of the lamp went dim. Then it was gone.

He lost his bearings. Stumbling forward, he tried to call out. Again, he heard voices. Angry, harsh, guttural voices. Then sudden flashes of red and clouds of black smoke. He tried turning around and heard the sound of thunder once again. It died away but seemed to melt into the sound of hooves, louder and louder until he was sure he would be stampeded.

On his right he heard the clash of metal, the whiz of balls, the dull thud of arrows, screams. It was all around him. More flashes, more shadows, whiffs of sulfur and a coppery smell. What was it—that smell...familiar. Blood. His heart pounded in his chest. A face lunged at him through the fog. A skeletal face with a tomahawk buried in his skull. The face dropped down into the mist, and behind it was the face of another abomination, this one with long, black hair, braided, with the same eyes, red as fire, the face splattered in blood. The mouth opened in a war cry.

A sudden gust of air threw him back like the kick of a mule. He lay sprawled on his back as the wind rushed over him with such force that it flung his feet over his head, turning him in a great arc onto his face, as if he were a flapjack on a grease pan. He lay face down, stunned. Slowly, he raised his head out of the wet dirt and turned himself over. He gazed in unbelief at the mephitic vapor, roiling, flashing, and surging in great eddies, carrying voices and shadows, wind and screams, and the acrid smell of war. Then a sudden, brilliant crack of light, and all became blackness and quiet.

≥≤

He was aware once again of muted sounds. Someone was speaking in garbled tones, and he could make out a painfully bright glow. Blurred shapes moved over him while a throbbing rush filled his ears. He could distinguish voices. "...Water...Doc..." He closed his eyes, blocking out the light, returning to blessed darkness. Even his eyelids hurt. His mind found his throat, and he tried to clear it. It felt like coals being raked from a rain gutter. His mouth was as dry as the desert he had just crossed.

"...Mister...Mister...you okay?" He opened his eyes, and the figures resolved slowly into two silhouetted heads, haloed in a misty light. He felt an arm under his neck as one of them raised him up to a seated position. His head pounded and throbbed. He groaned.

"Did you get Doc Wilson?" Several pair of legs moved around him. The elderly man supporting him was talking to someone.

"Let's take him over there."

"He might be hurt." A woman's voice.

"I'm all right," Pettifog rasped.

"Let the doc be the judge of that," another voice, familiar, the smithy.

He found himself being lifted by several sets of arms and carried in jerks and tugs across the street and up a small flight of stairs. Then the wind stopped, and the light dimmed. He was inside a room that smelled of alcohol and ether. A low, resonant voice came from somewhere.

"Okay, gentlemen, just lay him down here on the table...I'll take it from here."

He felt warm fingers on his forehead, winced as his head was being turned. People filed out, the door shut, and a clock was ticking somewhere in the room. The doctor's breath smelled of whiskey.

"That's a nasty one."

A sharp pain shot through his neck as the doctor touched the back side of his head. "Let me clean it up, and you'll be back up slick as a whistle."

Pettifog swallowed painfully, pushing the saliva down the racking dryness of his throat. "Just lay still until I'm through, and don't try to talk right now. You'll need to take it easy for a while."

≥≤

Some time later, Pettifog lay with a bandage on his head, looking around at the small apothecary of equipment which served the doctor—calipers, assorted tortuous instruments used for probing or extraction, a jar with several smashed and otherwise deformed bullets, a variety of bottles of different shapes, colors, and sizes with raised glass lettering, a wash basin, a shelf of thick books on anatomy and surgery, and, of course, the omnipresent smell of alcohol and iodine. The doctor had left the room, most likely to administer himself a dose of "nerve medicine."

The clock ticked on.

Then a distant knock, the sound of a bell, the doctor's low, sonorous greeting, a woman's voice, another man's voice.

Pettifog stirred as she entered the room.

"The doc told us you were awake," she said, crossing to stand at his side. Her petticoat rustled, and the scent of lavender and lilac toilet water filled the room.

"Samuel's mother, I believe." His voice was hoarse, his throat still raw. He strained and tried to sit up.

"No, no, no..." the doctor rushed forward and gently pushed him back onto the pillow.

"You need a little more rest before you get out of that bed."

≥≤

His head was bandaged in linen, and his face darkened with streaks of grime, accentuating the sky blue eyes he flashed up at her. Marcella felt compelled to look into them. In the muted light from the window behind him he looked worn but almost handsome. His face was rugged enough without the scar that cut across his cheek like a crimson lightning bolt just to the lower edge of his left eye. With it, he looked like he could be dangerous. One arm was out over the blankets. It was dark, ribbed in muscle, the kind she'd seen on men that toss feed sacks all summer. His fingers and hands were rough, calloused—not the hands of a gambler or piano player like she expected.

"I just wanted to thank you for saving my boy. Samuel told me what happened." She held her hands together.

William edged her aside and extended a hand. "Reverend Wilkes."

The man tried to move his arm, then grunted in pain. "I wasn't thinking." Wilkes withdrew his hand.

"Your wagon's still sitting at the livery stable, and the mules and horse are being taken care of—free of charge, of course," she said.

William flashed warning eyes at her.

"I'll be over there presently," said Alexander. His voice was low, raw. "I would appreciate someone keeping a good eye on the wagon."

"Felipe will see to the wagon," said William. "I'm sure there's nothing to worry about in this town, but I agree there is undoubtedly much in that wagon to provoke covetousness among some, incite them to sin. I'll give you the benefit of the doubt and assume you are unaware that my town is dry. We have no need of liquor here. The devil already has far too many tools at his disposal."

"Dry?"

I'll have it locked away in the shed...until you're able to retrieve it, of course....Mister...?"

"Dr." croaked Alexander. "Dr. Alexander Pettifog, Esquire. And the distillations in the wagon are medicinal in nature, sir. I do not own a traveling saloon." There was a strained silence.

"Don't worry about a thing, Dr. Pettifog," said Marcella.

Alexander returned her smile, his eyes lingering a moment more than necessary. "I'm afraid you have me at a disadvantage," he said.

William stiffened, then placed his arm around her. "Where are our manners? This is my fiancée, Mary Aragon."

Alexander nodded at her, causing her heart to skip a beat in spite of herself. "Ma'am."

There was another pause. Wilkes continued.

"I feel a need to apologize for Samuel. He had no right being out and endangering the lives of everyone. I assure you, he is being dealt with. I suspect he will find it somewhat difficult to sit down for a while."

Alexander cleared his throat. "About the boy," he said. "Far be it from me to offer unsolicited advice to either of you, but he was trying to save his dog. As reckless as that was, it was also courageous, and I don't think that quality should be beaten out of anybody."

"Well, Mr. Pettifog, I take it you have no children. Foolhardiness is no virtue, and men are accountable for their sins. Spare the rod and spoil the child. That's what the Good Book says."

Marcella thought she saw Alexander's eyes blaze a brief moment in anger. He waited a few moments before speaking.

"The Good Book says a lot of things."

He struggled to sit up and winced at the effort. He turned to her.

"I'm not sure what happened out there, Miss Aragon. Perhaps you can explain it to me." He kept his eyes on her. She felt uncomfortable with his stare, though there was no reason to be so. It was probably their uncanny color.

Wilkes started to say something, but the doctor intervened.

"Yes, yes, Mr. Pettifog, I'm sure you had quite an experience, and you're entitled to an explanation, but I think you should rest right now. There'll be plenty of time to discuss the... events...after you've recuperated."

He glanced over at Wilkes and Marcella and nodded to the door. "Yes, of course," said Wilkes. He tipped his hat.

"Mr. Pettifog."

Wilkes took her arm, but she held back for a moment. She laid her hand on Alexander's arm and squeezed it briefly, feeling his warmth and the hard sinew of his arm. She wondered for a brief second what lay under the blanket and then turned and made her way back out into the street before anyone could notice that she was flushed.

The doctor sat down in the chair next to the bed. He leaned back and pressed his fingers together.

"You were lucky. We've lost five people so far to that..." He motioned to the dark outside. "You familiar with the Indian War in these parts? Back in '58?

"Can't say that I am."

≥≤

Pettifog slept in fits and starts. The apparitions in the fog, given shape and meaning in the doctor's explanation, returned in the fog of his dreams, waking him several times throughout the night with a start. Each time the slow ticking of the clock and the occasional bark of a dog quieted his pulse and let him relax enough to drift back off.

The sun filtered in through wooden slats in the window. He awoke weak and sore to the sounds of wagons and idle conversation outside, but he was in no mood to remain in bed. A plan had hatched in the brooding of his sleep.

The doctor was nowhere to be found, so he rose and found his clothes and boots folded on a nearby table. His derby hat was also there, brushed of dust. His boots were shined and waiting on the floor.

After he dressed he decided to forego his morning toilet and shave and go directly to his wagon, his first order of business being to check its contents. He kept it locked during travel, and the key was still around his neck, but he could take no chances.

The smithy appeared hungover and barely acknowledged his presence aside from a tired wave. He checked on the mules and horse and found them contentedly chewing hay. Making his way to the wagon, he took the key and opened the latch on the back.

Once inside, he opened a small iron box and withdrew a single jeweled ring, breathing a sigh of relief. He had found it secreted in the mummies wrappings, around the neck of the corpse. The ring alone would fetch a large sum from the right collector. It was inscribed with writing, Hebrew from what he could tell, and made of an unusual metal—not gold, nor bronze, nor silver— something else. It contained a large green gem of some kind embedded in the center of a pentagram. He would have it appraised as soon as it was prudent. Meanwhile it would prove even more valuable. It was obviously hung around the neck of the corpse when he was wrapped. The ring was one of the artifacts that had escaped Dupuis's perusal of the lot. So much the better for Pettifog, who already had more than one serious buyer awaiting his return.

He slipped it on the index finger of his right hand and opened the sarcophagus. The mummy was within another coffin within a coffin, like a Russian doll. In the center, the kernel of the sarcophagus, lay the body of the king, shrunken, limbs like old dried tree branches.

Opening the inmost sarcophagus, he carefully pulled out a staff with a ridged portion near the top, which turned into a kind of looped cross—something Dupuis had described as an "ankh," a symbol of eternal life. This one was different in that the arms extended out from where the cross met the loop—and the arms were designed to hold a removable bronze globe about the size of a man's head. The staff could be embedded into a pyramidal base that had been inserted into the coffin, as well. Both the base and the globe were in compartments at the lower corners of the sarcophagus. The reason for such a design was anybody's guess, but the staff had an interesting property, one that was obviously unknown to Dupuis when he sold the lot to Pettifog. With the staff assembled and set into its base overnight, the quartz crystal ball would begin to glow green. Alexander had made the discovery soon after he had begun displaying the artifacts in his traveling museum.

The night he made the discovery, he had donned some of the loose paraphernalia, including the ring that he had discovered wrapped up in the mummies bandages, and was pointing out the various artifacts to an older couple. He had described the globe as jasper quartz. The elderly woman had asked why it was green. When he had reached out to touch it, small bolts of electricity had jumped from the surface of the globe to his fingers. Yelling, he had withdrawn his hand and explained it as the presence of spirits.

After arranging a quick séance for the two startled observers, he had closed the museum and experimented with the globe. He discovered he could withstand the spidery web of electricity that would leave the globe and envelop his hand, while at the same time alarming the audience who generally expected him to burn up on the spot.

The ring would also glow, but it would not be hot to the touch, a fact unknown, of course, to the audience, adding a bit of suspense to the show.

He sat in the darkness and let his mind take its usual left-hand path down to a calculated outcome, and by the time he had finished a flask of his own special medicine, he had the plan fleshed out.

≥≤

"Samuel Esteban Aragon!" The tone of his mother's voice and the fact that she used his full name meant the dog was up to his old tricks.

"Come get this mangy egg-sucking excuse for a dog and tie him up. He's been worrying the chickens again."

The dog cowered in the corner, tail between his legs, ears back, and head down. Marcella stood holding a broom, threatening.

"We're going to end this crime spree right now."

"Don't give him a lickin', Ma. He didn't mean no harm. He was just playin' with 'em."

"Oh, well," she said, lowering the broom. "You know I couldn't take so much as an old milkweed to him, but maybe he doesn't know that—at least, not yet." Samuel ran to the dog, who licked his savior with gratitude, keeping one eye on the broom, then darted out from the corner and out the front door. Marcella heard the dog's barking recede into the distance, followed by the whinny of a horse. She moved quickly outside to get a better look, looking back at the shotgun she kept high on the mantel. It was the medicine peddler. She looked around the house, started to move back in, but it was too late. She stood behind the door for a moment and ran her fingers like a comb along the side of her head, gathering up any loose hanging hair, and flipped it behind her ears. By the time she stepped out onto the porch he was leading the horse up to the front of the house. He wrapped the reins around the porch rail, then smiled broadly at her, pulling at the tip of his bowler. His teeth and eyes sparkled in the midday sun. He was dressed in a black suit with a paisley vest. His shirt was freshly starched, and she thought she smelled some kind of musky lotion.

"Miss Aragon."

"Mr. Pettifog. What a surprise. I see you're up and about."

"That I am, ma'am. That I am."

She moved to the edge of the porch, leaning on the post. "What brings you out this way, Mr. Pettifog?"

"I wanted to thank you in person for everything you've done. Doc Garrity told me you were the one who washed all my clothes, brushed my boots, and brought the homemade stew and shepherd's pie that provided me with the best meal I've had this side of the Rockies. I'm grateful, Miss Aragon, or as they say back home, 'Much obliged'."

"It was the least I could do after what you did for Samuel."

Marcella looked around at the mountains, the fence nearby, anywhere but at those eyes.

She didn't want to get lost in them again.

"It was kind, nonetheless. Allow me to repay your regard with a token of my gratitude." He moved to the other side of his horse and pulled out a bundled bouquet of flowers.

He splayed them in one hand and brought them to her, bowing slightly as he presented them.

"Wildflowers," he said, "whose unexpected bloom I encountered in a most unlikely desert oasis. A reminder that delicate beauty can flourish in the most inhospitable places."

Marcella blushed in spite of herself, and again had to look away. "Samuel! Fetch some water."

Alexander raised his arms in protest. "I can get that myself." He moved to the nearby well and began winding up the rope."

"I'm brewing up some Mormon tea, Mr. Pettifog. Please stay and have a glass with us."

"*Ephedra Gnetaceae*."

"I beg your pardon?"

"Mormon Tea. The Latin name. The Chinese call it *ma huang*. They've used it for thousands of years to cure colds, fever, and headaches."

"I wasn't aware of that, Mr. Pettifog." She turned and motioned to the door. "Now, come in and share a cup of that Mormon tea about which you are a fountain of knowledge. Samuel and I gathered some branches this morning. It might help if you're still ailing from a headache."

Pettifog removed his hat and stepped inside. "I apologize if I sounded like a pretentious lout just now. It's just that most people consider patent medicine peddlers fakes who sell nothing but bootleg liquor disguised as medicine. I try to disabuse them of that notion as often as occasion permits."

He moved into the kitchen. It was small, but bright and clean and smelled of lavender. "To be perfectly honest with you, Mr. Pettifog, that thought had crossed my mind. You were, if memory serves me, hawking your syrup to Caleb when we met." She turned and shot him an accusing glance, smiled, and then turned and picked up the teapot. "I believe that particular syrup is strong enough to clean pistols."

"Touché, Miss Aragon. I will gladly take both the tea and your advice on clientele—one for the body, the other for the soul."

"I'm...I apologize, Mr. Pettifog...Alexander. That was inexcusably rude of me. It's just that Caleb nearly died of liquor before he was saved."

Alexander waved his hand in dismissal. "Don't apologize. Your chastisement is not misplaced. I will admit that a large cross-section of my clientele enjoy the side benefits of the tonics more than the medicinal qualities." He flashed an innocent smile.

Samuel burst through the front door with the dog in close pursuit, colliding with Alexander.

"Samuel!"

Alexander regained his footing and steadied Samuel, who stopped and stared up at him. "Samuel!" Marcella cried. "Watch where you're going." She put her hands on her hips.

"I believe you have something to say to Mr. Pettifog here."

"No need, ma'am. He didn't know I was here."

"I'm sorry for running you over, Mr. Pettifog."

"It's quite all right, boy."

≥≤

Half an hour later, his eyes were watching her across the checkerboard tablecloth. Samuel stood by him, asking impertinent questions.

"So when you gonna let me see the mummy?" "Samuel." Her voice was a warning.

"You have that nickel yet?"

Samuel scowled. "No."

"Perhaps," said Alexander, "a preview could be arranged." Samuel's face brightened for a moment, then his eyes narrowed. "I still gotta get you a nickel?"

"Samuel, why don't you go find that scruffy pest. Don't go out of the yard. And watch for that skunk."

After Samuel had left, there was an uncomfortable silence, with both of them smiling and looking around the room for a moment.

"I'm obliged for the tea, Miss Aragon."

She smiled and poured another glass for him.

"By the way, I'm afraid your friend the preacher does not share your charitable feelings. He came to me with a petition signed by the town council. I had to move my wagon out of the town."

"William is very zealous.I suppose that's the kind of person we need, living with those...well, you know."

"Miss Aragon. If I may ask, was that your husband's name?"

"It's my maiden name, Mr. Pettifog."

"I'm sorry, I..."

"No, it's quite all right. I've never been married." Alexander tried to look properly embarrassed.

"It's my family name. My grandfather helped settle this land before...well, before the war. Under Juan Manuel."

Alexander nodded toward a small pine bookcase overflowing with books. "I take it you're an avid reader, Miss Aragon."

She flushed briefly, then nodded.

"Yes, I was raised with those books, Dr. Pettifog. Cervantes, Dickens, the Brontes."

"Quite admirable. I never was much of a reader of fancy—not that there's anything wrong with it. I just find that the world is complicated enough without making things up. You have any family around here?"

"I have two brothers in San Francisco. And how about yourself? Where are you from originally, if it's not too forward to ask?"

"There's not much to tell on that account, I'm afraid. I was born and bred in Georgia."

"Is that where you became a doctor?"

"Yes." He gave her his standard "history," the one designed to impress. "Matriculated at the University of Chicago. Taught for several years. The war changed a few things, as you know, and I ended up out here, having tea with a beautiful Spanish belle."

"You fought in the war?"

Alexander's face darkened. "I did, ma'am."

"It must've been horrible."

He took another sip of the tea. "War is what it is. It's high in the telling, low in the doing."

He paused a moment, then added, "Like romance." He motioned at the books, then held her eyes for a moment.

"I'm not sure I follow."

"Well, what I mean is, when you first meet someone, someone you find attractive and exciting, you see nothing but roses and glory—the promise of a successful campaign. Then, as time wears on, and you experience the actual day-to-day business of the affair, you see other things, things you couldn't imagine until they happened."

"I see."

"The glory fades away, the roses wilt, and what you're left with is...well, memories—bad memories. War is waste...it brings out the worst in everyone. You have to give in to it in order to survive. Cowardice, betrayal, you see it all if you're out there in the field. If you survive, you can never look at anything the same way again. It changes everyone. It doesn't bring out the best in anyone, despite what they teach you. If you're not careful, you end up like those poor benighted devils that live in the storm."

"Regardless of which side you fought on, it takes principles to fight in such a conflict."

"I didn't know anyone who fought out of principle. We fought because that was what was expected. It's what we were told to do. Or all we could do."

He leaned back in his chair and thought for a moment.

"The good soldiers were the men that didn't care one whit about life. They enjoyed the killing. They reveled in the carnage. The ones with a conscience were at a disadvantage. Irony."

"Irony?"

"God's sense of humor."

"I can't imagine what you must have experienced, Alexander. But there are two forces in the world, and I might offer you the thought that the hell you all experienced allowed our country to grow stronger. It's not fair, but it's, as you said, the way things are."

She lowered her head in thought for a few moments while Alexander took another sip of tea.

"I don't know why I'm burdening you with this, Alexander, but you've been forthright with me. I'll be just as honest with you. Seven years ago, some men came out of the desert and stopped over in our town. They drank too much, and one of our people was killed."

"I'm sorry to hear that."

"For a while, they had free rein. None of us were spared."
Alexander remained silent.

"Samuel was born from that experience, Alexander. And even though I will curse those men until the day I die, I thank God for my boy. So, you see, Alexander, I know a thing or two about irony because the worst thing that ever happened to me gave me the best thing that's ever happened to me."

Samuel came running back in, holding the squirming dog.

"Tea for my health and food for thought, all served in one helping." He smiled.

"I'm sorry if I've offended you Mr. Pettifog."

"Not at all. Quite the contrary."

He drank the remaining tea and set his glass down, watching Samuel play with the dog. "I've taken up too much of your time. I should be going now, Miss Aragon."

"Marcella," she said softly.

"Marcella," he said.

Alexander put on his hat and stopped in front of Samuel.

"Stop by the wagon one of these nights. I'll show you the mummy. On me."

"Can we go tonight?"

"Samuel."

"Aw, Ma."

≥≤

Alexander turned down the lamplight on the table, leaving only a dim, flickering red glow inside the crowded wagon. Closing his eyes, he began repeating the Hebrew phrases he had learned in Chicago. "Barukh ata Eloheinu ha-olam..."

He rested his arms on the table, being careful to leave the opening of his sleeves hanging down off the edge.

"Thamiel...Chaigidel...Sathariel..."

The old couple leaned in expectantly. The lamp dimmed, then went out.

As the light extinguished he quickly pressed his foot down on the small lever beneath the rug. Wooden slats glided noiselessly out from underneath the table, sliding under his forearms, into his sleeves.

"The spirits are coming."

A red glow appeared once again in the lamp, thanks to the chemical preparation in which the wick had been soaked. Long swirls of incense wound their way up and around the table, diffusing the flickering light. A small device Alexander had purchased from an inventor back east, loaded with clock gears and levers, suddenly sprang into operation in the nearby sarcophagus, creating a knocking sound.

Elias and his wife both gasped, Henrietta crushing his hand. "Don't be alarmed." Alexander exuded calmness.

More gasps as the table began to rise slightly as Alexander lifted it with the wedges in his sleeves. His hands never left the table.

After a few minutes the table returned to the floor. The globe, resting on the "hands" of the staff, began to glow green. A hissing, barely audible at first, emanated from the table.

"My god!" cried Henrietta.

"Silence, please!" intoned Alexander.

He leaned once again on the lever and the slats slid back into their chamber while the knocking from the sarcophagus covered any noise from the lever.

Then whispers. Sighs. A steady din of moans and unintelligible whispers that caused the hairs to stand up on their necks.

A few moments passed. Alexander closed his eyes and creased his brows in a look of intense concentration while he "summoned" the spirits. The globe began to glow green.

"The crystal will act as both a lens and a means of speaking with the entities who are now present around this table. I must release myself briefly from the circle. Henrietta, Elias, please join hands." He guided their hands to each other. Then, slowly, carefully, he raised his hands and reached toward the crystal ball.

"Give me a sign of your presence."

Suddenly, a web of lightning shot out from the crystal, enveloping his hand. Henrietta screamed, and her husband cursed.

"Remain calm!" Alexander stood and moved the electrified hand toward the globe, while small bolts and dancing skeins of liquid fire danced around his hand and arm. His hand touched the globe as Henrietta and Elias re-found each other on the opposite side of the table.

They watched, mesmerized, open-mouthed, as Alexander's hair stood straight up and out.

His eyes rolled back in his head.

"Come into me!" His voice echoed across the room.

Henrietta whimpered. Somewhere nearby, a dog howled. Alexander withdrew his hand and stepped back. The electric tendrils dissipated, and Alexander's eyes opened once again.

"Please," he said in a voice that sounded different, lower, harsher. "I am Tomagwi. Your spirit guide..."

≥≤

The séance was successful. As were the ones that followed. He had honed the art back east, under far more demanding conditions. A combination of keen observation, educated guesses, and reiteration of what they had inadvertently revealed was quite effective.

Presenting his deductions and readings from an "Indian" chief lent it a certain mystique. He had learned the art well from an affair with a particularly lusty Basque fortune teller, who had made herself a small fortune as a spiritualist. The pièce de résistance was, however, the museum artifacts, the whispering urn, and the so-called Staff of Osiris. It was possession of these items that won him the prize. Of course, his fame might lead to an unhealthy interest from certain parties who collected rosters of wanted individuals, even though it was highly unlikely for anything like that to reach him this far out west. Regardless, his itinerant lifestyle allowed him a certain indulgence.

The whispering urn, set upon a palette, served as the table's base, and the jasper quartz globe from the Staff of Osiris was a convincing crystal ball. Alexander's ministrations with the globe coaxed out the whispers and the sighs on cue. The longer the sitting, the more urgent the whispers would become, punctuated, harsh, guttural and menacing. He had no idea why this was the case, but it was fortuitous, as it was all he needed to stop the séance, feigning concern for the participants. They were leaving the door between the worlds open for too long a time. Unwanted entities were trying to gain admittance.

After only a few nights, the groundwork of his plan was laid, his reputation secure. Now all that remained was to reluctantly offer his services. Of course, there would be a fee, one that he could collect and enjoy long before his newly-earned reputation was tarnished. Meanwhile, he could enjoy the fruits of his labor in a more accommodating location.

Then there was Marcella and Samuel. They would be disappointed, of course, but he had learned his lesson well enough a decade before.

≥≤

"I don't care what he's really like, Mary. And the Lord guided Samuel out of that hell and brimstone—not some two-bit huckster. Did he ask you for money?"

"Of course not, Bill."

They were in the church. The "House of William," as some of the more heathen elements of the town referred to it. It was spacious and tall, paneled with oak. The benches toward the front were furnished with felt pads, the ones toward the rear were more ascetic in design. Those who arrived early, those in good grace with the Savior, would find their seats more comfortable. Better to learn the lesson temporally than risk facing it eternally. A large wooden cross gilded in silver was framed into the wall behind the pulpit, to provide the proper backing for the reverend.

Samuel was shuffling his feet along a corridor between pews, stiff in his black suit jacket and hard shoes.

"Samuel! Sit down!"

He put his hands in his pockets and tried not to provoke a hickory switch from the reverend. "You're not to see him anymore, Mary. The townspeople will start their clucking, and loose mouths preach a devil's sermon." Marcella folded her arms. "Do you understand?" She remained silent.

"For all we know that infernal fog brought him along with it. A decoy, a Trojan horse, designed to cause us to forget the path. Straight and narrow. No room for stragglers."

He began distributing hymnals across the pews.

"Let him in again and you may as well put on lipstick and dress like the saloon women used to."

Mrs. and Mr. Olsen came in through the open door in the back, hats in hand. "Morning, Reverend."

"Frank." William's voice was soft.

"Sorry, Reverend," returned the reprimanded Mr. Olson in a whisper.

William leaned in to Marcella and whispered. "This isn't over. But I'm willing to forgive. Seventy times seven if I have to, darling."

Marcella took her place on the bench next to Samuel, who sat swinging his legs back and forth.

Half an hour later William began his fire and brimstone speech to a mere half of a usual congregation. He exhorted and chided, brought some to shouts and others to upraised hands. He spoke of the evils of liquor, the danger of bringing fire to one's bosom and expecting not to be burned, of the spiderlike qualities of wanton women, the fight against principalities and powers in high places, and how the Lord stands at the door and knocks while the devil barges right in. After the final hymn he stood and blessed the faithful.

"I would like to add one special note of caution today. I feel moved upon by the Holy Ghost to broach a subject that many of you will find hard to believe...but it has come to my attention that there are some among you who are dabbling in sorcery." He raised his hand to stifle the murmurs. "This last battle with the devils in the storm brought us a visitor, one who bears all the marks of an emissary of the enemy. Strong drink and peeping after spirits, corpses and strange devices that work by the power of darkness."

Marcella's eyes widened.

"Let no man be deceived. I have tried to drive the evil from us. I call all of you as witnesses. I have fought these creatures for years. It is only the intervention of angelic power that has spared us thus far. That, and our obedience to the word of truth. And as long as we are righteous we shall prevail."

A pause. "But now the enemy has chosen a different tact. A front door assault." Marcella took Samuel's hand as the crowd began to shout.

"I can do nothing. The council has allowed this agent of sin to operate just outside the boundaries of our town, but there are those of our kin, those of our loved ones, who cannot resist, who visit him under cover of darkness."

Marcella shook her head and looked at Samuel. "There is a time for the saint to become a warrior!"

"I'm with you, Reverend!" declared one of the men in the back.

"We have been united thus far, and the devils have not harmed us. But that will change. We cannot look upon sin with the least degree of indulgence. We must face it with firmness, with the sword of righteousness and the shield of faith. We must put on the armor of righteousness!"

The reverend was beginning to sweat, and he paused to mop his brow.

"Now, I know some of you have family who are caught in this web of delusion. But did not our savior say, 'I have not come to bring peace, but to bring a sword. To turn brother against brother and father against son...'?"

≥≤

When he finished his speech half an hour later, most of the congregation was on their feet, and Marcella and Samuel were gone. William sat down while the deacon brought him another handkerchief to mop his brow. He looked out into the congregation, at the empty seats in the first row.

He stood up. "Where is Mary?"

≥≤

Marcella had dropped Samuel off at the smithy's, where he bounded out, eager with the enthusiasm of liberation. She drew the buggy up to Alexander's wagon.

Alexander appeared at the door at the back of the wagon, holding an afternoon pipe in one hand.

"Good morning, Marcella. What a pleasant surprise."

"I have to speak with you for a moment."

"Of course..." He stepped down off the steps.

"I can't stay," she said, her voice quivering slightly. Alexander stepped back, puzzled.

"Bill...Reverend Wilkes is working the congregation up to a lather. I'm afraid there's going to be trouble."

"That's what preachers do," said Alexander, smiling.

"You don't understand. You can't stay."

"I'm not sure I follow."

"You don't understand what he's capable of."

"Actually, I'm well aware of just what a preacher can do."

"I don't want anything to happen to you."

There was a pause as she looked away from his gaze, out across the grassland beyond his wagon.

Alexander sat down on the steps and took a puff of his pipe.

"I appreciate the sentiment, Ma'am. I assure you, I can take care of myself." He flashed a smile at her. "Aren't you taking a chance coming out here like this?" he asked.

"I follow my own path," she said, "no matter where it leads."

"Wilkes strikes me as the kind of man that doesn't tolerate that point of view."

She lifted the reins back up. "Please, Alexander, Watch yourself." She whipped the reins and turned her wagon around.

≥≤

Wilkes rode in the lead, followed by two buckboards of parishioners on a crusade for God. The sun was just beginning to set when they saw the smoke from Pettifog's campfire rising from the Willow grove. Wilkes drew up on his reins and held up an arm.

"The Lord himself fashioned a whip and flogged the money-changers from Holy Ground. I won't countenance any killing, but I will purge my flock."

The sound of a horse whinny drew their attention. Wilkes turned his horse back around in time to see Marcella emerging from the tree line.

A few moments later, he pulled her forcibly from the buckboard.

"Jezebel. Harlot."

Marcella pushed him back, slapping his face. His eyes flared like two hot coals in a wind. "Jed, see to it she gets back to town."

"I don't need anyone to show me the way..." she said through her teeth, "ever again."

Alexander was standing in the shadows next to his wagon when they rode into the clearing.

He held his Winchester up to his shoulder. "That's far enough."

They stopped, fanning out in a semicircle facing him.

"Well, well," said Wilkes, moving his horse forward a few paces. "Haven't you heard what happens to those who live by the sword?"

"If that principle holds, then all I have to do is talk you to death."

"The time for talking is done," said Wilkes.

Alexander fired, sending the dirt flying, causing Wilkes' horse to rear up, nearly throwing him off.

"You going to send me to heaven?" asked Wilkes, settling his horse back down. "I'll have a cat bird's seat to watch you dispatched back to hell."

Three of the men brought their guns up slowly.

"I've killed plenty of rattlers," said Alexander. "I've found that after I cut off the head, the body squirms around a bit, even rattles. Makes a lot of noise, but that's about it."

A few moments passed while everyone stood silent, waiting.

"No!" Marcella came running out from the trees, stopping between Wilkes and Alexander. "Stop it! Go home, Bill."

Wilkes laughed as he dismounted. Striding over to Marcella, he grabbed her and pulled her to him.

She struggled, trying to free herself. "Let her go, Wilkes."

The preacher laughed again. "Or what?"

"Put the gun down," said Nate, raising his pistol up, aiming it directly at Alexander.

"Sounds like good advice," said one of the men in the wagon, raising a rifle.

Alexander pulled back on the rifle and threw it down on the ground. Two of the men rushed forward and each grabbed an arm.

"Nate," said Wilkes, restraining Marcella, who was kicking and struggling, "put the pine tar on the fire. And someone get her out of here."

While the others watched and Alexander tried to wrest himself from the grasp of his captors, Nate, large and ruddy, picked up two buckets full of tar resin and hung them by their handles on a long branch that he positioned over the campfire.

"The rest of you, get in that infernal wagon; fetch me those bottles of hellfire." He walked to the wagon and picked up one of the pillows that had been thrown in the back. He slashed it with his knife, releasing a stream of feathers.

"Wait. Leave them in there...the wagon will burn better. But first," he said, pulling out some of the feathers, "let's invite the medicine man to a little frontier costume party."

The hoots and hollers from the men drowned out the cries of Marcella as she was carted away in one of the buckboards.

Two of the men stripped Alexander's shirt off of him, then held him down on the ground.

Two others held his feet.

Nathan retrieved one of the buckets with a glove and sat it down next to Alexander. "One coat or two?"

"Go gentle-like," said one of the others. "I ain't in the mood to hear another woman holler."

"Shut up—both of you." Wilkes stood nearby, his eyes gleaming in the firelight. "I won't countenance mockery of women."

"Irony," muttered Alexander.

"What was that, heathen?" asked Wilkes, moving next to him, staring down at him in triumph.

"I was talking to your boss."

Wilkes laughed as Nate ripped off Alexander's shirt. "Don't tell me you're getting religion all of a sudden?"

"It wouldn't be the first time," said Alexander.

Alexander screamed as Nate and one of the others began painting the hot tar on his chest and stomach.

The pain was almost unbearable. Someone was making clucking noises. He closed his eyes and the sounds around him began to recede.

"Reverend! The marshal's coming. We gotta get out of here."

He was turned over, his face pushed into the dirt. The searing pain on his back was the last thing he felt before blessed oblivion.

Marshal Anderson and one of his deputies arrived just ahead of Doc Garrity and Marcella. They found Alexander lying unconscious next to the fire pit. His chest and back were smeared with tar, feathers, and blood. There was no sign of anyone else. Just two buckets of tar resin over the fire and a torn shirt.

≥≤

Marcella met Garrity outside his office.

"Well, I patched him up. He'll be fine, Mary," said Garrity. "I gave him something for the pain, but he's got his own supply of tonic. No need for you to worry."

Marcella was lost in thought as he took his seat on the buggy.

"Come on, now. I'll get Felipe to give you a ride down to the Mendoza's place. Samuel will be glad to see his ma again."

"Any word from the sheriff?"

"Nate and Paul were cooling their heels in jail, but your friend in there is refusing to file any charges. The sheriff wants to go ahead with it, get a judge up here, but I suspect Alexander will just leave town when he feels better. That's probably the best thing for everybody concerned."

≥≤

Three days later, Alexander sat with Marcella at her table. Samuel was spending the day with the smithy. He still wore bandages around his neck and moved a little more gingerly in certain directions, but he had used his mending time to prepare. Wilkes had been neutralized for the time being, and he was counting on a sympathy vote from the town council when the time came for his proposal.

He was chatting with Marcella, something that he had to admit was becoming a real pleasure. She had been moody since the incident, and he felt regret that she was even involved. She had saved his life, but things weren't going to be easy for her.

He watched her as she brought out some coffee, sweetened with honey. When she handed the cup to him, their hands touched.

≥≤

She had never been kissed like this before. Ever. It began with a silence. He held her close, gazing down at her, the moonlight gilding his silhouette in silver, those eyes fixed on her in the translucent light of a full moon. He leaned in as if to kiss her, and she parted her lips to receive him, but he moved by, brushing her face with his cheek. She caught a day's worth of stubble, a marked contrast to the subsequent softness of his lips upon her neck. He came back and again met her gaze, stroking her cheek softly with the back of his fingers. She swallowed as a tremor of anticipation seized her without permission. Then he kissed her, slowly, moving his lips back and forth across hers; she felt his tongue roll along the inside of her lip, exploring.

It occurred to her during those moments of passion, that this was it, this was what she had read about in the novels, the passion of Elizabeth for Mr. Darcy, the transcendent love of Heathcliff and Catherine, the dark fascination of Jane Eyre for Rochester. In Alexander she had her own Rochester.

≥≤

Doc Garrity took his seat in the front of the courtroom along with the rest of the town notables. Everyone but Reverend Wilkes.

"So, you've told us what you want to do, but just how do you intend to pull this off, Dr. Pettifog?"

Alexander stood before a table, a sheet covering a large object. "By trapping those...those apparitions"— He pulled the sheet off with a flourishing motion, revealing the whispering urn—"inside a prison, and then relegating them to the netherworld where they belong." The members of the town council glanced at each other.

"That's a prison?" asked one of the men."Looks more like a spittoon." There was scattered laughter.

Alexander wore as grave a look as he could while he shook his head. "Appearances can be deceiving, can they not?"

He paused in the silence.

"Are any of you familiar with the Arabian Nights? Aladdin and his genie in the magic lamp?"

"We may be without certain amenities, but we're not without books, Dr. Pettifog."

"Then you're aware that spirits are referred to as djinn."

"Gin is a spirit in these parts, too." More laughter.

"Not gin, djinn—D-J-I-N-N," said Alexander. "Or, genii, if you prefer. They could be trapped in containers of various sorts—lamps, bowls, jugs."

"They must have been tiny little fellers." Alexander ignored the heckler.

"But all of the legends so faithfully recorded by Sir James Bruce are but echoes. Echoes resounding from the magical workings that took place in the Temple of King Solomon.

"You see," he smiled down at Marcella. "Ladies and gentlemen...According to Talmudic legend, Solomon was able to command both man and demon—men by virtue of his wisdom, and demons by virtue of a ring."

He paused, pacing back and forth a few paces.

"A very special ring. Given to him by the Archangel Michael himself."

"I don't recall that being in the Good Book." A woman's voice from the back of the room. Alexander held up an old, thin book, embossed in silver lettering.

"The Testament of Solomon. Translated and annotated by none other than a former colleague of mine, Professor Theodore Neihbur of the University of Chicago."

"The document, dating to the time of the captivity in Babylon, tells of a particularly nasty demon named Ornias, who was feeding on the blood of one of Solomon's favorite servants. The King prayed for guidance and wisdom in dealing with the demon, and God answered his prayers with the ring."

He passed the book to a man in the first row.

"The ring allowed him to command the demons, to force them to obey. He used Ornias as bait to trap other demons. Eventually, he pressed them into service building the temple.

The deacon sat forward, one hand raised in protest.

"Are you trying to tell me that the Temple of the Lord was built by devils?" Alexander shrugged.

"Not me. Like I said—ancient writings."

Several people gathered around the book, trying to make out the small, arcane, and technical writing.

"After the Temple was built, Solomon couldn't just release the demons back into the wild, so to speak. So he had his high priest fashion a receptacle, a container...an urn..." He moved to the urn and placed his hand gently on the rim, "into which he banished the demon horde."

He paced up and down before the silent crowd.

"After this was done, the legends conflict. According to one source, he had the urn dropped into the Red Sea. But according to another, the urn was among the treasures sacked from Jerusalem by the father of one of his many wives, the princess daughter of the Pharaoh of Egypt."

He gestured toward his wagon.

"Laugh at me if you will, gentlemen, but this amazing artifact, standing here in front of your mocking gaze, is the very same device in which King Solomon imprisoned the demons he used to build his temple."

The deacon stood. "Oh, come on, I can't believe such a thing. Do you seriously think we would..."

"Three weeks ago," interrupted Alexander, "I would not have believed that a town could be terrorized by dead soldiers."

No one spoke. Alexander moved back to the urn.

"It's been nicknamed the whispering urn, for reasons that will soon become apparent to you."

He touched a finger to his lips.

"I need absolute silence."

Alexander stood directly behind the urn. Slowly, gingerly, he placed his hands on it, resting his open palms on each side of the neck.

He began to caress the urn. His fingers glided over the surface. He looked up at the audience. His eyes moved over the faces as he stroked the container. When they met Marcella's gaze, they lingered, then closed. She watched his fingers dance and glide over the gleaming surface. She remembered how they mastered the keyboard in her parlor, moving rapidly up and down the row of keys, striking all the right chords, coaxing the subtle vibrations with expert pressure. She thought of his shoulders while he played, the undulations of knotted sinews that joined together in his arm. She remembered how firm his forearm was to the touch when he was resting in Doc Garrity's bed, how hard his lower back was when she had wrapped her arms around him afterwards, how warm he was as he held her.

She could almost hear moans.

Moans! Her eyes sprang open as her surprise was joined with the gasps of those around her.

Voices, a multitude of voices, were coming from the urn. Sighs, moaning, a steady hiss of whispers rising in magnitude.

Alexander stood, his head down, his blue eyes glittered in the dancing light of the nearby lamp, shadows playing across his face. One of the corners of his mouth was raised in a smile. His hands came to a rest. Stepping back, he raised them in a supplication.

"Behold the Urn of Solomon. King of Israel. Man of Wisdom. Master Exorcist!" Doc Garrity stood up.

"Even if I accept that this...device...is what you say it is, you said Solomon controlled the spirits with a ring..."

"This ring."

Alexander lifted a small metal box from the inside of his coat and placed it ceremoniously on the table near the urn.

Most of the assembled rose to their feet to get a better look. Alexander held up a hand.

"Please, keep back. The ring is powerful, and, as you can discern, the spirits are not pleased."

He picked up the metal box with both hands and carefully opened the lid, letting it rest on its hinges. He carried the box across to the table, allowing the eager townspeople to crane their necks and gaze at the ring—metallic, set with a precious stone and inscribed with strange characters.

He snapped the lid closed and returned to the table. The whispers were beginning to subside.

"Ladies and gentlemen," he bowed slightly. "The process is difficult. Removal of a curse and exorcism requires a knowledge of the ancient rituals and tongues—acquired at great cost by myself at the University of Chicago, and supplemented by my travels abroad in the Holy Land. Fasting and prayer. Concentration, and need I say it, courage. I will need to rest. I'll have to interrupt my touring schedule—I was due in San Francisco two weeks ago.

"Besides," he paused, looking down, "I feel an obligation to repay the generosity and good will of the town in saving my life."

He continued.

"We have no guarantee that a storm will gather anytime soon. The price I'm asking will barely serve to offset the expenses I incur..." He motioned to his own head. "Not to mention danger to life and limb."

Doc Garrity rose to his feet and folded his arms. "Thank you, Dr. Pettifog. We'll have a vote and let you know our decision."

≥≤

Thirty minutes later, Alexander began preparations for his performance. A storm could gather at any moment, and he had to be ready. Five hundred dollars for a few simple theatrics and he could be on his way from this accursed town, and a few weeks later he could be on a ship bound for the Orient.

Something was pushing itself into his awareness, working its way through at the periphery of his consciousness. Was it regret? Surely not. He should feel elated. The money he would make from these bumpkins, and the small fortune he stood to make from the collectors in San Francisco would ensure that he would live in comfort for many years. He would lead the life of a gentleman, and everyone else could go to the devil.

He looked over at the urn, gleaming in its wooden support against the wall.

The devil. Funny, in a way he owed the devil, or devils, for his good fortune, just as he owed that preacher and the God-fearing townsfolk back in Illinois years ago for his misfortune. Again, irony. God did have a sense of humor.

Still, something niggled at him, pricked his sense of smug satisfaction, refusing to allow it an undisputed and peaceful presence. The woman. The boy, so much like his own son. But he was not his son. And the woman, in spite of her kindness, the force of her personality, the way she felt in his arms, was after all, just another woman. He had had so many. Why was this one so different?

Perhaps he was just getting old. No one wanted to grow old alone. But he would not be alone. He could buy a dozen women once he retired. Women who would do what he wanted, who would not question him or his plans. You die alone, anyway. No one escapes that fate, no matter how much money or power they have.

He thought of the Pharaoh, once ruler over all Egypt. Kingdoms fell at his command. He wielded the power of life and death over millions. And all that remained was this shriveled corpse, this dry husk, laying in its box in his wagon, forgotten to the world at large. The spirits in the storm, the spirits in his urn, the pharaoh in his coffin, the people of this town, all shared the same fate. Oblivion.

Still, the thought of disappointing Marcella gnawed at his conscience like a grave worm.

He thought of his son. He would have been a young man by now. He could still see his son in his mind's eye, catch glimpses of his mannerisms, certain memories were clear and persistent, but his son's face had grown indistinct. He could no longer see it clearly—only in his dreams did his son appear as he had been, but the afterglow would burn away in the heat of the morning sun.

He forced his thoughts back to the task at hand.

≥≤

"I will not allow this to continue."

"Evening to you as well, Preacher."

William sat on his horse, glaring at Alexander, who stood silhouetted against the dim interior of the wagon.

"You may have the town council fooled, but not me. And if you think I'm going to stand idly by while you drag all these souls to hell, you've got another thing coming."

Alexander stepped out onto the wagon steps into the moonlight. "I thought you'd learned your lesson, Wilkes."

"Oh, I learned something, all right. And so will you. I promise. I'm afraid, though, that your lesson will be brought home to you in the fires of hell."

"You know, Bill, we're both cut from the same cloth, you and I. You from sackcloth and me from silk."

"How dare you compare me to a fallen creature like yourself," said Wilkes. "You're nothing but a two-bit con man. A wolf in sheep's clothing."

"You're just angry because I'm better at it than you are."

"Have you seen Mary since I forbade it?"

"She doesn't answer to you anymore."

Wilkes started to raise his walking stick. Alexander reached into the darkness behind and pulled up a Winchester 73.

"Why, Preacher, I thought you were supposed to turn your other cheek." Wilkes shook visibly with the effort and lowered his cane.

Alexander sat the gun down and continued. "You peddle self-regard and a promise of future happiness, then charge everyone for their ongoing obedience. And not obedience to that book. I can find anything in that book. I can beat a child senseless, rape and kill according to your book—simply because I say God commanded it."

Wilkes laughed. "Forgive me if I doubt your ability to interpret God's word for Him."

"You prey on their fears; I simply pander to their unhappiness. I sell tonics for the mind and body, and I charge them a small one-time fee. I give them something that helps them now. The difference is, I don't require anything but money for my services. I sell happiness, temporary as it may be. Respite from the misery of existence. A few hours of relief from the pain, the pain of body and mind, all for the cost of a bottle. You charge far more for far less. I give them a reason, a rationale, all in the name of medicine and healing. Same as you."

"You are a threat to the flock. Nothing more. I've dealt with your kind before. We'll see if you're as smug when the fires of hell lap at your boots."

"My customers," continued Alexander, "don't have to go to church, give me a percentage of their hard-earned money for my salary. I don't require control. So, let's not talk about right and wrong. Save that for the Sunday sermon. And while we're on the subject, I've had experience with your kind as well, Preacher."

"You pathetic worm. Half the town's been taken in with your chicanery. I can't figure out why they don't see right through you. Even Mary, poor benighted soul that she is. But she's chosen her side, made her bed with the devil, and now she'll have to lie in it."

"You drove her into my arms, Wilkes, or don't you see that."

"Mary's blind. Half the town is blind. Darkness covers their eyes like scales."

"Mary sees what she thinks men could be. Not who they are. I suppose that's blindness in a way. You had it made, until you went and opened her eyes to who you really are underneath that frock coat."

Wilkes laughed.

"And she'll know who you really are, underneath those carnival clothes. Mary told me you fought in the war—on the losing side, I might add. I'll wager you weren't worth spit in a windstorm on the battlefield. In fact, I'd wager you weren't a soldier at all. It takes gumption, sacrifice to be a warrior."

"At least my enemies were real."

"And victorious."

"The war's over. I took my licking. I took the oath of allegiance. I never owned any person, never thought it was right. And I didn't need a book to tell me that. Come to think of it, maybe you can clear up some confusion for me, you being a preacher and all. Didn't God's chosen people practice slavery—at least until they themselves became slaves?"

Wilkes smiled. "And God delivered them from bondage."

"So, it was okay for them, but not for anyone else? Seems to me it's all a matter of who's writing the book. Or who wins the war."

"You're wrong, heathen. The war is still raging. And, once again, you're on the losing side."

Wilkes backed his horse away, shaking his head. "Vengeance will be the Lord's."

"Let him judge between us, and reward us accordingly," said Alexander.

"Oh, he will, devil. He will."

After Wilkes disappeared in a cloud of dust, Alexander rolled a cigarette and sat down on the steps of his wagon. The smoke drifted lazily up into the darkening sky. He allowed his thoughts to drift with the smoke, and remember.

Pettifog's son, would forever remain six years old in his memory. He would be a man now. He wondered if he would recognize him. Alexander had fought his way up as an orphan, had wanted his own kids to have the best. He'd spent too many days and nights on the road, or on the "medicine." So, he found a woman. Had a son. Slicked his hair back and went to church. Did all the things he saw good families do. The local preacher had always taken a keen interest in the welfare of his family, especially his wife.

While he had been out in the field earning his daily bread, sowing seeds for the future, the preacher had been doing some sowing of his own.

He had returned from a supply run one night to find his family gone. The preacher was gone as well.

≥≤

On a cool evening two days later, the bells of Redemption pealed across the valley. Clouds were gathering over Tulane Mesa like the spirit of Jehovah over Sinai. Crimson webs of lightning arced through the gloom, and the sun was sinking fast, repudiated by the angry sound of thunder.

Dr. Alexander Pettifog was ready. He had seen the halo around the previous night's moon and felt the electric air crackle in his clothes. He had prepared everything for his last performance in the forsaken town. His time had come, and if the lunatics let him alone he was going to give them what they asked for.

Doc Garrity and a couple of members of the council arrived ten minutes later in a delivery wagon.

"We didn't see your wagon. Thought you'd lit out."

"O ye of little faith," replied Alexander. He climbed onto his horse.

"I do hope our confidence has not been misplaced."

"Follow me, gentlemen."

"Where are we going?" asked Garrity.

"The cemetery."

And with that, he flicked the reins and galloped off.

≥≤

"Not so fast," said Sheriff Anderson.

Reverend Wilkes stood in the Sheriff's office, flanked by two gentlemen in dusty dark suits and bowler hats.

"I sent a wire to Tucson. Made some inquiries."

"Let me guess, Reverend," said the sheriff. "The medicine man, Pettifog."

"His real name is Granger," said one of the gentlemen.

"Do tell," said the sheriff. He took the toothpick out of his mouth, figuring his afternoon was going to be busier than he had anticipated.

Wilkes motioned to the man. "This is Inspector Halstead, from the Pinkerton Agency in Chicago."

"You picked a helluva day, Reverend. A storm's coming up. Fast."

"An apt metaphor, brother Anderson," said Wilkes with a gleam in his eye.

Halstead spoke. "Nearly three years ago, a cache of artifacts, including a priceless mummy from the 21st Dynasty era, was stolen from the storeroom of the Chicago Institute of Oriental Research. Artifacts on loan from the French government. The culprits were never caught, but they were identified. Anton Dupuis, aka Marcel Pelgrin, a burglar and thief, and one Zebulon Granger, a former Confederate Colonel. A couple of Dupuis's henchmen are already cooling their heels in our luxurious accommodations."

"Well," said the sheriff, rubbing his jaw, "I hope you've got an extra bed. It looks like you're going to have another guest."

The two men nodded. Halstead withdrew an envelope from his coat pocket. "Here's the paperwork. We'll accompany you, of course."

"You're welcome to tag along. You fellows want to freshen up a bit, I'll take you to the hotel. But we'd better hurry."

"I don't understand..." said Halstead.

Wilkes broke in. "Sheriff, he's out at the cemetery as we speak,"

"That he is," said the sheriff.

"We need to go now. He may have already left."

The sheriff motioned to the open door. "You do see the clouds out there. Them bells are coming from your own church."

"We're lawmen, Sheriff, just like you," said Halstead. "We can handle a little rain, and we don't need to dandify ourselves to pick up our man." Halstead's partner opened his vest, displaying a shouldered pistol.

"No reflection on either of you, gentlemen. But I'm not going out in the storm. And neither will either of you, if you have any sense."

Halstead looked puzzled.

The sheriff sighed. "Folks around here do not go out in the storm."

The sheriff sat down on the edge of his desk. "You want to explain it Reverend, or shall I?"

≥≤

The cemetery was located on a small hill outside of town, and crosses and tombstones stood silhouetted against the red and black clouds. Alexander's wagon stood black on the hill, next to a T-shaped pole crowned by a glowing green ball. The squat outline of the Urn sat nearby.

"The Staff of Osiris." Alexander was pointing to it from atop his horse. The other men, some on horseback, others in buggies, cringed at the thunder that bellowed. All of the horses were pawing the ground or rearing up.

Alexander stood, arrayed in a white robe that he had found in a tailor's shop in Tucson that had been used by the Freemasons. He had added some Egyptian hieroglyphs for authenticity. He wore a turban on his head, and he had placed the purported Ring of Solomon on his finger. It, too, began to glow.

"The weak and impure should retire now while there is still time. Those designated as witnesses should remain, but only under protection."

"And need I remind anyone to stay clear of the staff and the Urn. The transference will take no account of demon or man. Approach it only if you desire to spend an eternity within a demon prison."

A wind-driven spattering of rain began to fall as Marcella pulled back on the reins and her buggy came to a stop near the crowd of frightened onlookers.

Alexander called to her. "Marcella, go home. This is no place for you."

Doc Garrity rushed to the buggy.

"He's right, Mary. Get back home now. It's far too dangerous out here." Alexander appeared behind Garrity.

Marcella tied the reins and jumped from the wagon, calling Alexander.

"Marcella, wait at home," he said softly. "I can't do my job properly if I have to worry about you."

"I can't find Samuel," she said, panic in her voice. "I left him with the Potters. They said he went out to the barn to check on Scruff and never came back."

"Hell and damnation," said Garrity, "He ain't here. I'll wager he's out chasing that blasted dog at the Potter's place."

"No," said Marcella, crying. " They saw him leave on the back of a horse. Three riders. They don't know who it was."

"That don't make no sense. Who the hell would pick him up?"

Just then, a voice came out of the darkness behind them. "The boy's fine."

They all swung around. Reverend Wilkes stood holding Samuel by the nape of his neck. Another man stood next to them, Wilkes holding a rifle and the other man pointing a pistol at them.

Marcella ran towards them. "Bill. What are you doing..."

He waved the rifle back and forth, pulling Samuel up by the back of his shirt. Marcella stopped.

"We couldn't take any chances on Samuel being taken by this..." he pointed the rifle at Alexander, "this...imposter."

Everyone stood silent. Fog writhed around them.

"Zebulon Granger," said the man with the pistol. "Come on over here, and keep those hands where I can see them."

Thunder rolled across the sky above them. Marcella kept her eyes on her son. "Samuel!"

"And if you have any ideas about lightin' outta here, you might want to reconsider. Right, Hurley?"

A voice came from somewhere out of the darkness. "I got him in my sights, Inspector." All eyes turned to Alexander.

"Nice to finally make your acquaintance, Granger."

Alexander smiled. "I'm afraid you have me at a disadvantage, sir," he said, smiling.

"Don't you fret. We got plenty of time to get acquainted. The rest of you, get back home. Your own sheriff wouldn't come out here."

Doc Garrity tried to protest.

"Now, go on. Git," said Halstead.

The shadows lengthened as the wagon rolled away, and fast-rolling clouds covered the moon. A writhing mist began to flow through the gathering.

A sudden sound of angry yells echoed in the distance.

"Hurley!" called Halstead, keeping his eyes on Alexander. "What's going on out there?"

"Let Samuel go, Bill," said Marcella, holding back tears. "This is no place for a boy."

"But it is a place for a whore!" said Wilkes, grinning. Behind him the shadows began to writhe and move.

Everyone froze, all eyes on Wilkes.

"What the hell..." Halstead didn't finish. Marcella screamed.

A figure stood behind Wilkes. A silhouette with gleaming red eyes. Other faces appeared in the shadows. Spectral. Angry.

The sound of hooves. Screams.

"Samuel!" Marcella ran towards Wilkes, lunging at Samuel. Wilkes slapped his hand on her face and pushed her back, throwing her onto the ground. Alexander lunged at them.

"Stay where you are, Granger." Halstead pointed his pistol straight at him. "Blink an eye and I'll shoot it out."

Alexander froze.

"For God's sake!" Hurley's voice from the darkness was followed with a scream and a gurgling noise.

"Hurley!" Halstead backed away, holding his gun on Alexander. "Hurley! You out there?" Halstead glanced back around at Wilkes and started, a raspy noise escaped his lips.

"It can't be true."

Wilkes laughed, glaring wide-eyed at Alexander. "Time to pay the devil his wages!"

"Reverend, watch out." Halstead swung his pistol around.

The figure was a uniformed soldier, his form shifting in the shadows, his eyes continuing to glow. It was drifting closer to Wilkes.

Wilkes continued to laugh. "Take your medicine, man." Samuel turned and saw the creature, then yelled.

Alexander lunged towards Wilkes just as Halstead fired.

Alexander's momentum carried him into Wilkes, who was trying to bring his rifle up.

Samuel wretched free and ran to his mother, while Alexander stumbled to the ground.

Halstead brought his pistol back around and fired at the apparition.

Wilkes raised the rifle, placing the barrel against Alexander's head. "He who lives by the sword, dies by the sword."

Halstead fired two more shots into the shadows. The apparition vanished.

"Put it down, Wilkes," said Halstead. He paused, looking around, while the sound of hooves grew louder. "This can't be happening," he muttered.

Alexander wrapped his arms around Wilkes' legs, pulling him back with him as he fell. Wilkes fired, wretched free and regained his footing, just as two horsemen raced by, one an Indian, the other a soldier. Their forms dissipated into the fog.

"This...can't be..." Halstead held his stomach, blood gushing from Wilkes's bullet. He raised his pistol, aiming at Wilkes.

Wilkes laughed, then ran into the shadows.

Marcella grabbed Samuel, hugging him, shielding him. Halstead crumbled to the ground.

All around the battle raged. Alexander pulled himself up. Marcella and Samuel rushed to his side.

The sky flashed blue, and thunder rumbled across the sky. "You have to get out of here," he said.

"Alexander..."

"The crypt."

"What?"

"The crypt." He raised a finger, pointing to a small mausoleum that appeared through the mist.

On their way, Alexander pried the pistol from Halstead's hand.

They stumbled their way through the tombstones, keeping Samuel between them. The fog was thick, and they caught fleeting glimpses of forms running through the mist. The air was filled with the sounds of cries and yelling, the whiz of arrows, the sound of hooves. Skeletal figures materialized around them and fought, then collapsed into mist. Rain began to fall.

They reached the tomb. The door was latched to the adobe, secured with a heavy chain. He held out the pistol, aiming at the chains that held the gated door closed.

"Stand back."

Marcella wrapped herself around Samuel, their back to the door. She cupped her hands over Samuel's ears.

Alexander fired at the chain wrapped around the door. It took three shots from his unsteady hands before the chain split and coiled to the ground.

"Quick, inside."

He pulled the door open and peered inside. Three rotted wooden coffins lay in a row on the floor. The stench of mold and decay hung heavy in the moist air that came in with the fog.

Marcella started to lead Samuel in. Suddenly, a form rushed at her out of the mist. She fell into Alexander, and they both landed on the line of coffins, collapsing them, finding themselves lying amidst bones and congealed shrouds.

The door slammed shut, plunging them into darkness. Alexander stirred. "What the hell?"

"Samuel?" said Marcella into the darkness. Then again. "Samuel! My God, they've got Samuel!" She began screaming and pounding on the door.

She felt the door, desperately trying to find a handle, some way to open it, but the door was wedged shut.

Alexander joined her. He ran his fingers along the junction between the door and the wall. Marcella continued to scream, throwing herself against the door. She collapsed, sobbing. "We need a wedge, something like a knife."

Marcella rose to her feet again, holding her face in her hands. She could hear him moving around the chamber.

"I've got something."

She searched the darkness, found him. He reached out and took her hand, guiding it to something hard, jagged.

"It's a bone," said Alexander.

They both moved back to the door. Marcella took the bone and wedged it into the joint on the side that opened out, slamming her fist into it several times. Then she pushed on it sideways. The door began to move.

A few minutes later, they emerged into the rain and the night mist. They both called for Samuel. Marcella ran first one way, then the other.

Then they heard it. A wail. "Listen!" cried Marcella.

The wind carried the sound. "It's Samuel."

They followed the high-pitched cry to the edge of the graveyard, to the base of the small hill where Alexander had prepared his demonstration.

"Samuel! It's okay, son!"

Samuel stood at the top of the small hill, surrounded by grave crosses, still, shaking, his face wet with tears. Wind whipped his blonde hair.

Marcella saw him and cried out.

"Samuel! Oh my God, Samuel! Where have you been! I'm here!" She ran forward. Alexander caught her, gasping, holding his side. "You stay here. I'll get him. Something doesn't feel right about this."

"Samuel..." She ignored him, held to his waist as he stepped forward, making his way across the small precipice.

Alexander searched the darkness around the boy. "

Don't move, boy! Stay where you are. We're coming."

Samuel held his hands to his face and cried.

Above them, black clouds roiled by like the rapids of a river, while the wind drove rain into their eyes.

As he approached Samuel he noticed the rope that bound the boy's legs. He heard Marcella scream behind him as a large shadow moved out from the tree. He saw a flash of light, felt a searing pain in his side. He crumpled as a voice came out of the darkness.

"Well, if it isn't the peddler and his whore!"

A flash of blue lightning lit the landscape. Reverend Wilkes stood holding a pistol in his right hand, a ribbon of smoke being torn away from it by the wind. His left hand rested on Samuel's head, while Samuel held his ears and stood wide-eyed and wet...Wilkes wore a broad smile, his eyes shone black and shiny in the lamplight, like the carapaces of beetles.

Alexander, on his knees, pushed himself back to his feet, and stood in front of Marcella, blocking her. He felt as if his side had exploded. She tried to push by, toward Samuel, crying out for him.

"Stay where you are, Jezebel, or the boy dies!" Wilkes wore a crazed grin.

"Whoremongers and adulterers, God will judge...the whoremongers and sorcerers and idolaters and all liars shall have their part in the lake which burneth with fire and brimstone...Blessed are they that do his commandments, that they might have right to the tree of life and may enter in through the gates to the city. For without are dogs and sorcerers and whoremongers and idolaters, and whoso loveth and maketh a lie."

Wilkes stopped, his eyes blazed and he screamed. "Whoso loveth and maketh a lie!"

"Let the boy go, Wilkes. He's done nothing."

Wilkes brought the gun back up, shaking, while thunder rolled across the sky above them. "You said yourself that God commands the children of his enemies to be slain for righteousness sake."

"For God's sake, Wilkes..."

"Don't you see, the land is cursed," Wilkes spat. "Polluted with whoredoms. The cries of the afflicted have called out for vengeance."

Fog rolled in suddenly, a wave of cold wetness, rushing past them, enveloping them. Alexander made his move, his side exploding with pain. Charging forward, he struck Wilkes headfirst, knocking him back into the tree. Wilkes reacted. Something heavy hit Alexander's head, taking him to his knees.

Another smashing blow caught him in the chin, and he flew backward, rolling off the small plateau, down the incline, coming to rest flat on his back.

Marcella watched helpless as Wilkes dragged Samuel with him and stomped to the platform where Alexander had set the urn. He placed his foot against it, then kicked it over, watching it roll down the hill, coming to a stop at Alexander's feet. Grasping the staff, William rooted it out of its base, turned, and made his way down to the crumpled figure of Alexander, pulling Samuel with him.

The fog above swirled above Alexander like a pinwheel. A silhouette appeared above him. Wilkes. His eyes were wide and black—his mouth clenched in anger. Rain poured down his face.

He pushed Samuel down next to Alexander, then grasped the staff with both hands.

Marcella screamed.

William raised the staff high in the air above Alexander. "Vengeance is mine saith the Lord!"

The lightning strike happened in a split second, but it was followed by several more bolts from the clouds above. Wilkes's face was frozen in a hideous death grimace as he began to smoke. The lightning seemed to play with him, twisting him, jerking him one way, then another. Then, like a whirlpool, the fog around him began to swirl, and Wilkes's body, still frozen, holding the staff high in the air, began to spin as well.

Marcella ran down the slope, nearly falling, collapsing next to Samuel and Alexander. Hugging Samuel, she told him to move away, pushing him back from the dancing corpse of the preacher. She and Samuel both grabbed Alexander's hands and began pulling him back across the mud, out of the way of the gathering vortex.

Forms, diaphanous and threadlike, long streaks of luminous sheets, faces of soldiers and Braves began to appear, lengthen, and disappear into the center of the churning hole, as if a hole had been torn in the very fabric of the space around Wilkes.

The fog itself streamed into the whirlpool in great eddies, as the darkness at the center of the hole grew larger. Marcella pulled with every ounce of her strength, while the gathering force around Wilkes and the staff pulled at Alexander's shoes, sucking his scarf, pulling at his cloak.

"Samuel, get out of here!"

"No, Ma'am!"

"Mind your ma," said Alexander weakly, drawing his legs together and turning over.

Together, the three of them managed to move out of the main force of the whirlwind. They lay in a tight knot, Marcella shielding Samuel as Alexander watched the fog and clouds and apparitions stretch and wrap themselves into the vortex of the urn. Finally, Wilkes himself began to change. He began to glow, and his skeletal structure was etched in light, until it, too, began to contort, melding around the staff.

Then, one final brilliant flash of blue light and the column collapsed, sending the urn tumbling down the side of the hill, smoking, with webbed blue electricity still coursing around its exterior.

"Now, that was ironic," said Alexander, collapsing back onto the ground.

≥≤

Two days later, Alexander sat atop Marcella's wagon, holding the reins, bandaged and smiling. Marcella sat to his right, with Samuel and Dog between them. A short distance away sat the traveling museum.

"I'm going to miss it."

"Didn't Solomon say something about a time and season for all things?" said Marcella. Alexander smiled and flicked the reins.

"Do you think we did the right thing?" asked Marcella.

"I think old Solomon would appreciate our solution."

Alexander snapped the reins, and the wagon pulled away from the railings, away from the large, gaping hole, covered with a few thin planks and flanked by a sign: KEEP OUT— OPEN MINE.

≥≤

The thunder and rains come and go across the grasslands now, and the trees grow tall and sigh in the night wind. The town of Redemption is a ghost town, full of rattrap houses and rusted mine works.

The few souls who know the area have stories. They tell of a haunted mine a short distance outside of the old town, a deep shaft somewhere below the marsh grass. They claim that on certain nights one can hear whispers and moans, as if the shaft below extended all the way down to hell itself. Others chalk it up to an acoustical phenomenon, the wind whistling among the timbers deep below. Green orbs of light have been seen on some nights, and storm clouds seem to gather a little too often over the area of the former mine. Others claim they hear Bible verses being spoken.

Rune Lore
By Lynn Voedisch

≥≤

Lynn Voedisch is a Chicago-based writer who worked for many years as a newspaper reporter for a metropolitan daily. She also did freelance writing in print and online. She decided she liked fiction a lot more than reality, and upended her career to write urban fantasy from her home. Her novels include *Excited Light, The God's Wife,* and *Dateline: Atlantis*. She lives with her husband and three cats. Her son is an attorney in Chicago's loop. She has many hobbies, but really needs to get back to tennis.

From the author:

"I'm half-Swedish and was brought up in a family that reveres all things Scandanavian. I have been to Sweden three times and have learned a bit of the language. I've had a great interest in the Vikings of the past, especially once I learned of their religion and the occult magic of rune casting. To bring the world of runes into today's contemporary world, I invented a group of NeoVikings (which actually are popping up throughout the Scandanavian countries). As always, magic proves powerful, positively and negatively, and must be treated with care."

≥≤

Annabritta kicked the ground where the crabgrass met the mud in front of the double-wide. She didn't feel much like walking up those dirty aluminum steps to the front door.

Cousin. Ha! Who knew she had a cousin out here in this beat-down trailer park? She pulled her windbreaker tightly around her chest, even though it wasn't cold. She just didn't want anyone to see her there.

Mom set her up to this. Annabritta had been asking crazy questions to anyone who would listen about whether there was anyone in the family who did "voodoo" magic. Most people rolled their eyes in response. But Mom, who seemed to sense the deeper fears of her frantic daughter, sat her down at the kitchen table and put on those silly reading glasses that spelled "I Am Woman" on each temple. She wrote out Ragnar's name with care and the address out in the Fox Valley. Then she handed it over, squinting a bit, and not from the glasses.

"Ragnar is in a NeoViking group called Daughters of Freya," Mom explained.

Annabritta didn't understand what Vikings had to do with voodoo and started to open her mouth. Her mother never let her get a sound out.

"They practice the old religion with runes and things." Her mother looked amused, but continued. "Magic from before Christianity. Should be right up your tree."

"I guess..."Annabritta said, pulling the paper toward her as if it were an animal that might bite. "Rag-nar," she said putting the emphasis on rag.

"No, it's pronounced *rain-yar*," Mom said, putting a sort of Spanish ñ sound to the *g*. Mom had perfect Swedish pronunciation.

Annabritta tried again.

"Good enough," Mom said. "People have been calling her Rag Lady and worse all her life. "She'll appreciate the effort."

"And she is my cousin?" Annabritta asked.

"Pretty wild to imagine, but yes. On your Uncle Gunnar's side."

Oh, wow. That bunch.

She dashed out of the kitchen before Mom could say any more, but it was obvious the old lady knew why Annabritta needed supernatural help. Somehow things went wrong when she went out with that bastard Donny Blanchard. He convinced her to go out to the tent city that some kids had built up in the back of a closed factory. It's where the kids hung out and did drugs. He lured her into his secret spot, and they got too high for her to say "no" when he started pulling off her jeans. The truth was, she hadn't been out with too many popular boys, and Donny was a star baseball player. It was stupid, but she felt proud to have had sex with him. At the time.

Then, Annabritta wound up late. Pregnant. A small pile of pregnancy test kits all gave the same reading: a plus sign. Not so "plus" for Annabritta, especially since Donny said it wasn't his problem.

Normally, Mom, with her liberal ideas and hippie background, would have hustled her right over to an abortion clinic. But Dad made things difficult.

Over the years, Dad made a killing at his business and palled it up with North Shore Conservatives. Pretty soon, the former Democrat was spewing right-wing talking points. If his own daughter terminated her pregnancy and anyone found out, people at the Country Club would make life difficult for him. Bad for business.

Damn Dad, anyway. Annabritta fumed as she picked her way through the mud, trying to find the safest, less mucky way to Ragnar's front door. She thought about her other cousin, Howie Highland, MD, and how he wouldn't write a Plan B prescription that would have solved the whole mess. Two pills and she'd be over this. Mom was on the telephone line pleading, but Howie, Ragnar's brother, was too afraid of what Annabritta's father might think. Jesus.

Well, the darn little zygote, or whatever it was, was only week or two old, Annabritta thought. It shouldn't be that hard to dislodge. She had no concept that this could be a little human being. It was a parasite to her. She had seen all the anti-abortion garbage left around the ground at the local Planned Parenthood, but those people had pictures of fully formed fetuses that probably were viable on their own. This little thing in Annabritta's abdomen was nothing more than a problem to her. She had no maternal thoughts at all.

Mulling about her plight gave her enough angry strength to pull herself up the stairs and to knock on Ragnar's trailer door.

To her shock, the door swung to almost at once, revealing a tall, frazzled redhead (was it real?), all knees and elbows, decked out in clothing that Annabritta was sure were purchased at H&M, a Swedish fast-fashion company (Annabritta had memorized the entire H&M catalog, dropping hints to her parents when her birthday came near.) Yes, Ragnar was Swedish through and through. Probably what little furniture there was came from IKEA, too. Ragnar's blue eyes stabbed the frail visitor, taking in the dirty blonde hair, the gawky posture, the downcast glance. Still, under challenge, Annabritta stood her ground.

The stalemate lasted a good minute until a hound rushed up and began licking Annabritta head to toe. She giggled.

"Some watchdog," Ragmar muttered, peeling the dog off. "Whatta you want? Better not be selling nothin'."

"No, *Rain-yar*. I'm your cousin, Annabritta Hogland."

With that, Ragnar burst into fierce laughter, doubling over and holding knobby knees that stuck out of her Bermuda shorts. After a few last whoops of hilarity, she ushered her cousin inside the grim trailer.

Still snickering, she folded her skinny arms in front of her and barked, "Still holding onto that dreadful last name, I see? Uncle Bertil just couldn't let go of it."

Annabritta, shoved into a ratty bean bag chair that may or may not have harbored fleas, knew the whole story. Hogland, for immigrants such as her father and uncle, was a fine Swedish moniker. It meant "elevated place," and also denoted aristocracy. But in the U.S., well—land of the pigs. Uncle Gunnar saw reason and changed his last name to Highland. Ragnar, rebel that she was, went further and took on the old-fashioned name of Signesdottir, the daughter of Signe, her mother. Usually, Swedish women only took this sort of name if the father died or a mother was raising children alone. Ragnar didn't care. She was proud to be Signesdottir, and it was light years from Hogland.

"Well, Ragnar, I'm only fifteen, and I can't just change my name any time I want to."

Ragnar sniffed, and Annabritta felt ridiculous. The younger girl got the feeling Ragnar had been on her own since at least fifteen, and changing what people could call her was first of the alterations she made in her life

"Old Bertil is a fool to hold on to that name, making his family miserable," Ragnar said, turning to the kitchen to start making tea. "I'm sure your life was hell because of it. Right?" She didn't turn around, but her words pinned the girl to her seat. "Kids calling you Pig Girl from Pig Land. Oh, I went through that until Daddy changed the name. But you've been living through it at a vulnerable age. Adolescence." She pulled out two cans of an unmarked herb and readied it for infusion, all the while speaking of the evils of being left out of popular crowds at school. Pain eked out of her voice.

She splashed the boiling water into two mugs as her anger grew and slammed the herbal tea on the tiny kitchen table. She crooked a finger and demanded Annabritta to sit on a table bench.

"So, why ya here?"

Annabritta reached back and pulled her ponytail tight before answering. "Your brother wouldn't fill a Plan B prescription..."

"Pregnant! Well, we can fix that. We are the Daughters of Freya. Drink this. It's for strength."

It tasted like weeds pulled from her garden. To distract herself, Annabritta looked at Ragnar's fingernails—all purple with spidery lines drawn on each fingertip, each design different. Ragnar caught the girl looking and wiggled the fingers in front of her face.

"Runes. Rune magic will make the little unwanted one go away."

She stood up and grabbed a slim volume from the narrow hallway that served as a library. "Here." She tossed the book to her visitor, who barely caught it. *Rune Mythology.*

"Forget the 'mythology' nonsense. It's all true. This is the old religion. The true religion. Be here at eight on Wednesday for our meeting, and we'll put you right. Ending a pregnancy is no problem at all." She let out a mirthless laugh.

Before Annabritta could adjust her eyes, she was outdoors again, standing in the mud in the gray trailer park. Ragnar waved goodbye from her aluminum storm door, and the hound dog was moaning a sad farewell. Overhead, the steely skies announced a spring rainstorm that could only make the muddy walk to the car worse.

≥≤

Waking the next morning only brought misery. A small, bloody animal lodged itself in Annabritta's mouth. She poked at it with her index finger until she realized it was her own tongue. In her fevered nightmares, she'd been chewing her own insides. She ran to the bathroom to spit out the blood. Then her stomach roiled, and she heaved out more than blood.

She began to shake. This isn't supposed to be happening so soon, she thought. Maybe I'm further along than I figured. Then she remembered the horrid brew that Ragnar urged on her at the mobile home. She drank it down in her fear of the woman, but the stuff was nasty, and she could still taste the lingering bitterness. Probably was that toxin that turned her gut to goo.

Annabritta sat on the bathroom floor and leaned against the sink, closing her eyes. Images of the book she had been reading the night before came racing to her conscious mind. Viking women, clad in rags, stood around a campfire holding runes etched into wooden staves. They were colored with human blood. A leader sang incantations as the group murmured around her, then they pitched their runes into a giant pile, and the head runecaster sang her spell, calling on Freya to aid them. Then they all held up bowls of mead, the sacred drink of the gods, and drank it down.

Freya was not a benign goddess, it seemed. She had many guises and one of them was a warrior queen. As consort to Odin, she took one half his share of war dead and patrolled Valhalla like a monarch. She also tricked the Vikings' enemy kings and seduced them to their deaths. Freya was as much about death as she was about life, and the Vikings liked it that way.

There was imagery of brutality and cursing in the book Ragnar lent her. Poisoning. Ice. Freezing. Some of the runes promised torment and sickness for women. No wonder Annabritta didn't feel well on awakening. What kind of book was that?

Wednesday was tomorrow night, and she wasn't likely to show up and watch Ragnar take graven images that looked like kindergarten renderings and redden them with her own blood. Annabritta shivered for the second time.

≥≤

After a full day of looking up Viking legends in the library, Annabritta avoided dinner and drove out to Fox Lake again. Runes were an early alphabet and nothing more, according to the history books. While it was true that the Vikings were a rough bunch who lived by ravaging other peoples, they also had a fairly sophisticated religion and philosophy of life. One writer postulated that the Viking/early Germanic view of life and death was so complex that no society had come near to understanding it until psychologist Carl Jung created his cosmology of the Ego, Self, Shadow, and the Collective Unconscious. Even then, the Viking schema was far more complicated.

Writer J.R.R. Tolkien got the idea of Middle Earth from the Vikings, who projected that the world we live in was merely one of many inhabitable worlds, all connected by something almost looking like wormholes from science fiction. Valhalla was another world, and something called Hel (one *l*) was another. Hel, however was a place of total detachment, and not the fiery torment imagined by Christians. All the worlds of the Vikings when diagrammed on paper looked a bit like the arrangement of the Kabbalah. Or parallel universes. Annabritta had to admit she was intrigued. So, she changed her mind and decided to come to Ragnar's Nordic meeting.

Still lost in thought, she pulled up in front of the ramshackle trailer park to see a group of women just visible behind Ragnar's double-wide. She recognized Aunt Signe's ancient Volvo. So, she's a member, too. Huh.

Annabritta crept around the back of the trailer to see a group of women stoking a barbecue grill, all chattering, while one of them was fussing with an iPod in one of those adapter/speaker boxes. Some reenactment. It looked like a modern-day picnic. Annabritta was about to turn and leave when Ragnar caught sight of her and grabbed her by the arm.

"Look who's here, the guest of honor!" Ragnar pulled Annabritta to the middle of the circle. The women, most of them in their twenties, but a few middle-aged, stared at her as they looked up from the food they were preparing. Aunt Signe brushed her blonde-gray hair away from her forehead and let out a bashful smile.

"This here's Hildur," Ragnar said, indicating a mannish-looking woman with bad teeth. "This is Solveig." A blonde sprite bobbed her head. "Siv." A sweet woman with heart-shaped face gave a lopsided grin. "Then there's Margit and Marika. They're sisters." Twins with dark bobbed hair nodded and returned to slicing tomatoes. "My best friend, Annika." A woman with hair that was almost white-blonde looked down from nearly six and a half feet. "You know Mom. And this here's

Ragnhild." If anyone looked like a Viking, it was this lady. Muscled like a man with steely-colored braided hair. She didn't smile but stared with laser-like blue eyes. Annabritta remembered Ragnar's book again and gulped.

It took some time for the group to assemble themselves, but eventually, they ate and were ready to transform into modern-day Vikings. By this time, Annabritta had forgotten her fears and had lapsed into a comfortable conversation with her aunt about knitting. Annika joined in, and everyone was leaning back in their resin chairs laughing and drinking beer or Coke.

Ragnar called everyone to attention, and the fun stopped. Women shushed each other and put their drinks down. A few brought out some ceremonial-looking cups. Margit or Marika—who could tell the difference?—put wood on the barbecue and brought it to high flames. The smell changed from backyard charcoal to a searing bonfire. Cats and dogs that had been frolicking with the group backed away at the change in the fire and scurried down worn paths to their homes. The women formed a ritual circle. The light flickering up on their faces made them look mutated, grotesque, insane.

Ragnar took center stage and began speaking in a strange, lilting language. Signe, who managed to stand next to Annabritta, whispered in her ear, "Old Norse." Old Norse? How did Ragnar learn Old Norse? Her cousin knew Swedish fluently, but Old Norse?

Ragnar brought out a set of runes, carved into wood, just as the book had said. She indicated the one called Thurs, and Annabritta knew it meant "woe to women." She clenched. Ragnar also indicated several other runes, including one called Nauthiz, or "need," a rune that means both "need" and "salvation," and the Berkano, or birch rune, which governs all types of childbirth and death. Annabritta heard her name mentioned.

After Ragnar sang a spell, she took a sharp knife and scraped the blood-soaked runes off the wood into a rough pottery bowl. She also sliced the knife on her palm and let her own blood drip into the ugly jumble. She then poured the shavings and blood into a large bowl of mead and stirred the mess together. The group watched with reverence. Ragnar donned a crimson-colored robe and lifted high the bowl of mead. Annabritta expected to see lightning and the beginning of a hailstorm. Instead, she only felt a sharp, electric jolt inside her head, as if she were psychically attached to Ragnar's offering. Freya had spotted Annabrita, of that she was sure.

After getting Freya's blessing, Ragnar, as mistress of ceremonies, began to fill the participants' cups with the magical mead. Annabritta held her cup, trembling as Signe helped her stay steady on her feet.

"It's dirty, Aunt Signe," she whispered.

"Don't worry. It's just a speck of wood and blood by the time it reaches your cup. Ragnar believes it's holy. Go along with it. Let the magic work."

Everyone took a quaff, and Annabritta choked it down. But her stomach would not be quelled. She looked around at all the faces, the steely braids, the white hair, the strange names, the bad teeth, the piercing eyes. The fire was too hot. The stares seemed to be focused on her belly. Her poor belly with a tiny life that no one, not even she, wanted. She imagined the runes were going to work in there, dislodging the fetus from its hold on her uterus. She saw her insides begin to come apart, and the bloody tendons started to separate. Dissipating. She was leaning on Aunt Signe's left arm.

"Dear, are you...?"

Darkness fell like an axe to the head.

≥≤

Back at home, she woke to hear Signe talking to Mom in the kitchen. They spoke in hurried tones. She realized Dad wasn't home yet and prayed he didn't know where she'd been. There was noise on the stairs. She closed her eyes tightly, but Signe knew she was awake. The girl's eyes fluttered open.

"Ragnar said that if the runes don't work, she's going to try the herbs." She put a finger to her coral lips before Annabritta could react. "Of course, you don't want to try those awful things. You think you got sick from the tea! But, you know, that herb stuff works. It has worked for centuries, but we really don't need to use it anymore. There are more modern methods. I'm going to give you a sedative to help you sleep. Your mother and I will work on options when you wake tomorrow morning."

Annabritta forgot Signe was a nurse. Of course she'd have a sedative. Sure. Nice. Go to sleep. She felt the prick of the needle and was off to Neverland.

She awoke at dawn to blood. Blood everywhere soaking her sheets. Blood, blood, blood, down to her mattress. Its sticky sweetness made her woozy.

"MOM!"

Quick, off to the hospital. Dad still wasn't home. Poker with the boys must have lasted a long time. Who cared? Oddly, there was no pain, just blood. Annabritta lost her grip with reality again. She swooned into Mom's warm arms.

≥≤

The nurse woke her in a hospital room as the sun reached high over budding trees. To her shock, Ragnar stood above her bed. Mom, Signe, even some of the Daughters of Freya were there.

Annabritta dreamed of a great dragon that came and took the fetus away in its vicious teeth, ripping half her abdomen with it. Yet when she looked down, everything was fine.

"Miscarriage," Mom said. "You could have had it at any time. Stress. Bad diet. Even if the baby wasn't fertilized correctly.'

"Dad?" Her voice was so feeble she could hardly get the word out.

"I let him go on that golf trip he was hankering after," Mom said, nodding her head the way she did when she made smart decisions. "I forgot to tell you. He'll just think you had a bad period."

Annabritta smiled and felt the muscles in her chest release. She dared look over at Ragnar. The redhead wore the three runes she used at the ceremony on a necklace over her tank top. She wore a smug smile.

"Thanks for seeing me," Ragnar said. Her expression locked on Annabritta and wouldn't let go.

Annabritta averted her eyes and began to review how she got to where she was. That pulling, crawling feeling after she drank that tea in the trailer. A sedative (what kind? Was it really a sedative?). Signe was a member of Daughters of Freya. Who knew what she could have injected into Annabritta's arm? That necklace of runes on Ragnar's neck—the sight of it made her let out a great, pathetic sigh.

"The runes?" She asked no one in general.

Ragnar merely smiled again, and Annabritta could swear her sharp teeth looked like those of a feral beast.

Cut to the Cross

Mary Marcus

≥≤

Mary Marcus grew up in Louisiana at the turbulent end of the Jim Crow South. She is the author of the novels *Lavina* and *The New Me*. Her short fiction has appeared in numerous literary magazines including *The North American Review*, *Fiction*, and *Karamu*, among others.

From the author:

"I was writing a series of stories I called my 'nasty man stories,' and Stanley is the most awful of them all. After many drafts, I gave him redemption at the end, but it didn't make me less angry with him. To this day, when I read 'Cut to the Cross,' I want to punch Stanley out."

In the Japanese restaurant on Sunday evening, Stanley Waxman rips open the paper cover of his wooden chopsticks, pries them apart, and immediately gets a splinter in the painful quick under his right thumb. Nothing, Stanley thinks peevishly, not one single thing is made the way it used to be, even fucking chopsticks. He holds up his thumb, and looks at it from the bottom part of his bifocals. Sure enough, a small bit of wood is sticking up right in the place where, if he was being crucified, he'd be nailed to the cross. Stanley, who was raised a strict religious Jew (though is absolutely nothing now) is always getting crucified these days, or at least thinking about it. He's never before had the problem of footage repeating itself like this in his head. But now, ever since he completed the project about Ancient Rome, the footage keeps playing back to him. He can be driving to work, reading the newspaper, or be in the middle of a conversation when, without warning, he'll see the actors in their loincloths up on the cross with the Romans hurling spikes at their hands and feet and hear the horrible groans of agony. When you work on something you know isn't real, you put it in the work slot in your brain; but this isn't what's happening anymore, not with the crucifixion footage, it's not. Scenes of human carnage are now such a commonplace for Stanley that he's gotten in the habit of thinking to himself, "OK, Stan, cut to the cross."

Death and devastation can scare the shit out of you and also make you unusually hungry. Indeed, the smell of teriyaki sauce is tantalizing in his nostrils, even the pinging of cutlery against plates from the neighboring tables is making Stanley hungry—he had a nothing sort of sandwich for lunch today. Stanley looks sidelong at his wife, Barbara, thinking resentfully that there's never anything to eat around the house unless he shops for it and cooks it. For better or for worse, he's the homemaker now.

The splinter, meanwhile, is really making Stanley's mouth water. He longs to get at it with his teeth and pry it out but refrains because Liza, his friend Barry's wife, is sitting across from him. Liza, who has red lips and sparkling eyes and who designs clothing and has just breezed in the crowded restaurant—late as always— has a very young body for someone her age. Stanley admires Liza, though would never say out loud, "You look great tonight, Liza." Though he has broken down a couple of times and asked Barbara if she thinks Liza is sexy.

Stanley knows if he were his son Drew's age, he would have a crush on Liza, one of those torturous crushes where you can't wear your shirt tucked in and which always causes you to say the wrong thing. Or spit involuntarily, or worry about a bit of something caught in your nose or front teeth. As it is, Liza looked so tempting when she glided into the room that Stanley fantasized standing up when she got to the booth, throwing his arms around her, and telling her: *I love that shirt, the way it clings to you, the way I can see your tits and your nipples underneath the thin material. Sit down and tell me one of your stupid stories, Liza, so I can stare at them and pretend it's your fucking mind I'm interested, in which, P.S., I'm not...*

They always sit the same way here at their Sunday night dinners in the same booth Stanley reserves as soon as the restaurant opens at 5. Barry sits across from Stanley, and Barbara across from Liza. Barry and Stanley talk about work (both are in film) and world events (both are liberals, read the national edition of the *New York* Times, and refer at dinner to its Sunday morning op-ed pages). Stanley doesn't know what the women talk about; he supposes they talk about things women find interesting, though Barbara and Liza aren't the same kind of women at all and probably do not think the same things are interesting. Barbara is a social worker at the Veterans Administration. Liza works downtown in some garret she calls her *atelier*. Stanley is sure Barry subsidizes Liza's business, and he would like very much to have his suspicions confirmed, but still would never come right out and ask Barry this. Tonight, Stanley and Barbara's son Drew, who is home from college for the summer, sits between Stanley and Barbara. Drew looks quite a lot like Stanley. Both of them have the same low hairline, the same dense, dark hair. Stanley felt distinctly bereft when Drew left for college three years ago, furious at him for growing up and leaving home. Now, having grown used to it, Stanley finds these visits home somewhat trying; though he knows he shouldn't feel tried by his own flesh and blood, nevertheless, he does. If Barbara hadn't decided that Jim, the marital and family relationship specialist they had gone to for years on Saturday mornings, was a waste of money, Stanley would have mentioned it there, this feeling of being put upon, having his space invaded, even by Drew who has a face remarkably similar to his own and who usually does whatever he's asked to do, up to a point. And, of course, whom Stanley loves. Whom else would he love? Barbara never questions the existence of love as Stanley does. Especially not love for Drew. Barbara and Drew are always showing that they love each other by hugging and kissing each other in public, and at home, too. Drew has never gone through that stage where he rejects his mother's hugs and kisses; in fact, he appears to welcome and reciprocate any physical advance Barbara makes, which are, in Stanley's view, constant. Though, perhaps Drew makes the advances; it's hard for Stanley to tell. In any case, Stanley watches them going at it right next to him and wonders what Liza makes of their closeness. Stanley has never seen Liza and Barry's son kissing and hugging Liza in public, though it has been a while since he's seen their son at all, at least a couple of years. Stanley tells himself he's quite sure he'd remember if he had seen their son behaving as Drew behaved. Stanley believes it might reassure him. But maybe not.

Liza says, "You are such an affectionate family," in that soft, way of hers that Stanley finds very attractive. He wonders if Liza really means this, or is she being sarcastic? It's hard to tell; she has such a nice, soft voice, not like Barbara's voice at all, which is more like the bleat of a sheep. Stanley does not know exactly what a real sheep sounds like, though he had on a couple of occasions used a sheep sound effect in his work. Does a sound effect count? Thinking about it further, he concludes, within his parameter of reference, a bleat is the sound Barbara's voice most resembles. With her curly hair, she even looks a bit like a sheep. A sheep with eyeglasses and earrings.

Though Barbara is always telling Stanley she's sure he doesn't love her, or is worried he doesn't and needs to be told once in a while, he is reasonably sure he loves Barbara. Haven't they lived together for many years, owned a house together—one that has nearly tripled in value from their original investment? Don't they also share a bed, a joint checking account, a son, and many friends in common? Friends like Barry and Liza. And don't they always give an annual party every year, where at least fifty people stop by? At dinner every night, don't they also tell each other about what they had done that day? Obviously, this means love. Stanley had told Barbara, "I love you." He had told her on more than one occasion in their twenty-five year association. He had said "I miss you," as well—he is quite sure he had said "I miss you"—when they had been separated for periods of time when Stanley was on location. Admittedly, it was rough going, and he did not like saying it—always felt distinctly put upon, invaded, bossed around, told what to do, when he did so, even when he said it all on his own, which had happened, he knew it had happened at least once, maybe even twice. His trouble with saying "I love you" had taken them to Jim and taken them away from Jim when Barbara hadn't gotten what she wanted from therapy. Stanley never minded discussing the fact that he doesn't think it's necessary to say "I love you" just because Barbara wants him to. He does not mind discussing it at length, for years at a time, incurring considerable expense. He does not even mind admitting there is a problem, it being, notably, Barbara's problem more than his own. What he minds is saying "I love you." He'd much rather say "I miss you." Saying "I miss you" isn't as hard as "I love you." But he doesn't like saying "I miss you," either. Stanley and Barbara have talked about it and talked about it; several years have gone by talking about this and also about the fact that Stanley does not want to take her hand in public, put his arm around her, or in any way whatsoever tell the world he has affection for her. Certainly not the way Drew can. Drew, who is at this very moment quite affectionately rubbing Barbara's neck, which just lately has begun to jiggle a little. Barbara's neck often gives her trouble, causing her to don the neck device, which is unattractive but at least covers up the jiggle when it's on.

Stanley coughs and at the same time draws the afflicted palm up to his mouth and neatly—and he hopes in a recondite manner—extracts the splinter with his teeth. He then rubs his thumb over the spot and discovers, to his dismay, a bit still imbedded in his flesh. How long does it take for an infection to happen? A day, probably. A full week to possibly lose the use of the hand; quite a bit more to lose the hand itself. In the movie he can't get out of his head, a metal spike severs the hand of the poor devil who is being crucified. A terrible way to die; in fact, a terrible way to earn a buck, having to hang from a cross like that, even a simulated cross. Stanley feels his heart distinctly racing. He calms himself now by imagining what he'll do when he gets home tonight. The hydrogen peroxide, the antibiotic cream, and band-aids he'll apply. Across from him, Liza's red lips are curling. Barbara can't have said anything so amusing as to make Liza laugh. It must be Barry. Liza is always laughing at her husband's jokes. Stanley finds that very attractive. Also attractive is the booth quivering with her laughter, her pert breasts shaking. Liza often wears peasanty shirts and colored brassieres that show off her high breasts to great advantage. Compared to Liza, Barbara looks like a full grown hedge next to a flower on a stem. What kind of hedge, he wonders, what kind of flower? It's unusual for Stanley to make such comparisons. Now that he has, he feels amused, though unnerved. He hopes the comparison doesn't show on his face. Though he knows it to be technically impossible, some part of him wonders if Barry, or Liza, especially, could actually read his mind. Stanley knows Barbara and Drew can't read his mind; he would have found out years ago—both would brag about it. The film he'd worked on before the one about Ancient Rome had been a science fiction thriller for the cable network. The subject was mind control and telepathy, and in the movie the actors read each other's minds at will. Stanley knows it isn't really possible, but there was always that slim chance that it might be. He imagines Liza taking his hand, looking deeply into his eyes, and asking, "Do you think we have the power to read each other's minds?"

Here comes the food. Stanley notes that he's being served last. Liza, who always arrives late, after the rest of them have had a sake or two, fresh from her after-fitness shower, is, as usual, being served first. He watches the young waiter, solicitously positioning her sushi dinner down, placing the cup of extra ginger with a careful bow directly in front of her bust line. The waiters always anticipate Liza's whims, like the cup of extra ginger and bowl of lemon wedges, and ignore Stanley's standard salmon teriyaki; though Liza doesn't pay the bill or tip them, all she does is smile and say, "Thank you."

Drew, who these days is talking of going to culinary school in Italy is chastising the waiter for the lack of something Stanley has never heard of on the special rolls he created here on the spot, with much ado, so much ado that Stanley felt embarrassed in front of his friends. He's quite sure Barry and Liza's son would be straightforward in his ordering, though you never know.

Stanley watches his son pointing to the roll and declaring, "I want it to crunch." Barbara is always telling Stanley that Drew is creative. Stanley supposes talking about "the crunch" can be categorized as creativity of a sort. Though Stanley is quite sure he saw a dark look pass over Barry's face that he knew had to do with the waiter, and Drew, and the crunch, or lack thereof. Barry and Liza's son, who is just a year older, is already in law school at a prestigious university. Stanley wishes he could refer to a prestigious university, or maybe just a state university, which would be cheaper and still worth a lot. Nevertheless, Stanley is all set to go along with the culinary school plan; he's set to go along with any plan Drew might care to come up with—he just wants a plan, one his son will stick to. But he does not want to be like his own father and mention this aloud to Drew as Stanley's father had done so many years ago, forcing Stanley to settle in the film world when he knows very well he has no business being in the film world; it's a wonder he can make a living at all. Yet, he's making a very good living and has a reputation as a talented professional in his area.

Liza reaches for her chopsticks.

"God, I hope you don't mind if I start. I've just come from Yoga-Lattes, and it's a killer. I'm famished!"

"Yoga lattes," Barry laughs. "What the hell is that, yoga with coffee?"

Liza laughs. "You're so funny, honey."

Stanley watches her dump on her plate the entire bowl of extra ginger the waiter has given her without asking, as if he read her mind.

"God, they are always so nice here," she says between bites. "I hope we give them a good tip."

Barry says to no one in particular, "We?" Before he can say anything else, Barry's sukiyaki arrives. Then Barbara's black cod dinner. The waiter refills Liza's tea for the third or fourth time tonight, and still Stanley hasn't gotten his salmon teriyaki plate.

Drew's redone rolls arrive. Still no food for Stanley. Stanley raises his arm and snaps his fingers. When the waiter arrives, Stanley says, "Bring my dinner." He purposefully does not add, please. Or thank you.

"Here, Stanley, have a piece of sushi," Liza says. "Which one would you like?"

Stanley shakes his head. What he'd like is one of Drew's rolls, which look delicious, but he does not ask for this. They are expensive, made-to-order rolls, and Drew, who has never held a real job and who does not value money, will order more if deprived.

Stanley waits.

"Aw, come on, Stanley, I'm giving you the yellowtail, my favorite."

Stanley doesn't care for yellowtail, though he doesn't tell Liza this. He's pleased Liza wants to share with him. Especially her favorite fish. He doesn't see Barbara offering any of her cod.

Drew raises his arm in a gesture identical to Stanley's. He snaps his fingers.

"I'll get them, Dad," he says.

Barbara dumps half her bowl of rice on her plate and hands the rest to Stanley.

I don't want your fucking rice, he thinks. But he takes it and starts to eat. He'd eat anything by this point.

Stanley watches Drew tenderly taking his mother's hand and kissing it.

Liza stares. Stanley can sense that she's amazed, perhaps offended by the gesture. She does not say anything now about the Waxmans being such an affectionate family. She probably thinks Drew is gay. Instead, he can see her looking across at Barry, trying, Stanley knows, to catch his eye. Will she tell their other mutual friends that Stanley's gay son Drew was kissing his mother's hand in public? Come to think of it, who in their right mind kissed his mother's hand in public, anyway? And this is what Barbara would like for Stanley to do. And come to think of it, that's exactly why he wasn't going to—because it didn't fucking look right, that's why. If they were still going to Jim like they were supposed to, Stanley would mention it there. As it was, he wasn't going to bring it up unless Barbara brought it up, though they didn't fight about it, really; they didn't fight about anything. That was another one of their problems: they couldn't really fight, neither one of them did. They didn't fight with each other; they didn't fight with Drew—why then did Stanley feel so aggrieved and angry at Barbara and at Drew, too, now? Drew, who was kissing the top of Barbara's curly sheep head.

Stanley's stomach growls with hunger. In his mind's eye, he sees the familiar spike—this time driven into the stomach cavity—and the guts spurting out all over the penitents who sit below the cross, lamenting.

Just then, their waiter arrives, empty-handed. Drew lets go of his mother's hand to point it at the waiter. His son's voice is harsh, testy.

"My father would like his food, and I would like two more, this time with just a little *less* crunch. Do you understand what I'm saying about the crunch? Or should I come talk to the sushi chef myself?"

That's it, Stanley thinks. *I'm not going to stand for another second of this.* He gets up from the table. They'll think he has to use the men's room. The restaurant is full of Sunday night diners.

He hopes nobody they know will be here, but this is the West Side of Los Angeles. He has to be careful not to make himself too conspicuous; Drew and Barbara have made him conspicuous enough already. People he might work with could be sitting here; normal people with their absolutely normal families could be right here. People he could end up in a meeting or working with down the line. He doesn't know exactly where he's going, but in a vague way he knows to head for the back of the restaurant where there's an exit sign.

He pushes open the door. Outside, the sun is blasting—it's still only seven o'clock on a Sunday night in July. But with all he's been through, Stanley's exhausted. The unrelenting sun beating down makes it feel like high noon in hell.

A busboy is leaning against the building a few feet down, smoking a cigarette and looking out on the pitiless sun on the horizon. Stanley goes and leans against the wall near him. The man is small and compact, and his pure black hair is greased into spikes on top of his head. Stanley can't decide if he's Japanese or Mexican. He's certainly something.

Once his eyes are adjusted to the bright light, Stanley opens up his palm to examine it. It's still tender where the tiny bit of wood is embedded in his flesh. He rubs his left thumb against it, but instead of frightening him as it did inside, the pain soothes him. He worries over it for a moment and tries to get it between his top and bottom row of teeth but can't budge the stubborn bit of wood.

He gestures to the busboy with the afflicted palm.

"Chopstick," he explains.

The busboy smokes, looking straight ahead.

"Chop-a-stick-a," Stanley says again in what he knows isn't a Japanese accent, or a Mexican accent; what he sounds like is a jerk talking English in a peculiar way.

The busboy takes his last deep drag from his cigarette. Horrified, Stanley watches him flicking it out into the parking lot where pools of oil are standing, ready to set off a conflagration.

In a second they could all be in flames. Stanley had read about just such a thing happening: one goddamn cigarette had burned down an entire city block.

Nailed to his spot at the wall, Stanley watches the cigarette land. Just as it might burst into flames in its pool of grease, an inhuman sort of growl comes from the bus boy. Stanley glances in his direction. Are his eyes deceiving him? A preternaturally large wad, the size of ping pong ball, is coming forth from the busboy's mouth, landing exactly at the tip of the cigarette, putting it out—a miracle of perfect projectile spitting. Is this a nightly miracle or just a lucky hit? Stanley's relieved, of course, though at the same time vaguely disappointed they all haven't gone up in flames.

The busboy glances at his watch, then mournfully touches his pocket. Meanwhile, Stanley's back on the cross: he sees a bloody spike, a limb breaking loose from its socket, and can hear as if it's happening right now, the pitiful moans of the poor bastard actor putting in his hours. Fifteen or sixteen takes for that crucifixion scene alone. The director was a joke. Most of them are. *Everything's a fucking joke,* Stanley tells himself. *And people say there's a god.*

The busboy is making his way to the door. Stanley knows now's his chance. If he doesn't take it, there'll never be another one like it. Not here. Not anywhere.

"I'm not sure about love; it's not something I understand," he says in an ordinary voice, but one that feels amplified a thousand times. "Maybe I don't love Barbara or Drew. Maybe I don't know how." Then a little louder, he almost screams, "That's why I'm being crucified!"

Without so much a glance back in his direction, the busboy disappears inside. Stanley once again stares ahead at the parking lot, the sky dusted brown by pollution, and the orange-red sun glaring in the horizon. West LA looks like what it is: a giant parking lot with a few low trees plopped down here and there. No mystery, very little shade, a place where you don't want to run and there's nowhere to hide.

A blue Prius enters and parks. Many of the top industry players now own the Prius. Stanley is thinking of purchasing one himself, though having to pay sticker price or even above is quite offensive to him. *This very car,* Stanley thinks, *could be filled with people who matter.*

By now, he's turned to push the exit door open. He's making his way through the crowded restaurant to their booth. He can see the back of Barry's head. Liza has her compact out. Her wide, red mouth is puckering up in the mirror as she applies yet another coat of lipstick.

His salmon teriyaki plate, though, has finally arrived. Beside it is a new packet of chopsticks, ready to tear open.

Just then, Barbara looks up at him and shyly gestures toward his plate as if to say, "See, it's OK, Stan, help has come, your food is here. I'm here too!" Their eyes meet for a moment, and Barbara's pale lips form a little smile.

She's still in there, all these years later, hoping I'll love her one day. Stanley recognized this all at once. He did not call it a blessing—such words or even the concept of blessings were not in his lexicon. But to himself, he acknowledged that her love was a good thing, and such as he could be, he was grateful. He sighed to himself almost contentedly.

Yes, Barbara obviously loved him. She had her hand in the air and was waving at Stanley with a modest little fluttering of her fingers. Stanley gave her the briefest of smiles and made his way toward her.

Drew and Barbara got to their feet to let Stanley slide in. Sitting himself down, Stanley sees Liza still going at it with her lipstick. He gingerly removes the paper cover and carefully pries his chopsticks apart. Stanley's right thumb is bleeding just a little. He studies his palm for a moment, letting his fingers curl over the stigmata, his shoulders hunched, waiting for the sights and sounds of crucifixion...

But he's no longer nailed to the cross, at least not at this moment, he isn't. What a fucking relief to be free of it. Stanley closes his eyes for a moment and sighs again. The world, he thinks, isn't so bad after all.

Without thinking, Stanley leans over and kisses Barbara's cheek, which is soft and smells faintly of cod.

"Dad," Drew is saying. "No way, Dad!"

Liza's red mouth is hanging open.

Oblivious, Barry is babbling on, thank God.

Well, that wasn't so bad, Stanley thinks. Barbara's eyes, meanwhile, have gone wide—even sidelong, he can see how wide they are, and terrified. Her hand is reaching out towards him for a moment, then she catches herself, and it falls lifeless to her knee, like a dead bird shot down from the sky.

Good, Stanley thinks, *that's enough.* She could have slobbered back, and she didn't. She contained herself. *Maybe it's all going to be okay.* Securing a piece of fish between his two chopsticks, he dips it in the special teriyaki sauce he loves and brings it to his mouth. His dinner is, by now, of course, already cold, but all in all, things could be a lot worse.

The crowded restaurant, his successful kissing of Barbara in public, even the busboy's miraculous spitball—all of it feels pretty good. Stanley secures another bit of fish, dips it in the sauce, and then tries the rice. It, too, is cold. Everything should be sent back, but he's not going to do that; he's hungry. And down off the cross, that's the main thing—at least for the moment, he is. Maybe if he's lucky, for a while.

Hide-and-Seek
By Christopher Slater

≥≤

Christopher Slater was born, raised, and continues to haunt Middle Tennessee. His love of history led him to teaching that subject, which gave him the opportunity to hone his storytelling skills with a captive audience. Once he thought he had sharpened his abilities enough, he decided to start writing for a more voluntary audience. When not writing, Slater enjoys historic reenacting, playing airsoft, and converting oxygen into carbon dioxide. He teaches middle school in Tennessee where he still lives with his entertaining son, very patient wife and a cat that won't get out of his seat. Christopher's first novel, *Pup*, won the initial AuthorsFirst novel contest and became a national bestseller. "Hide-and-Seek" features the main character from that novel.

From the author:

"Life can be very confusing for any eighteen year old, but the boy that everyone calls "Pup" is dealing with more troubles than most. Drafted into the US Army, he is forced to deal with one of his biggest problems—himself. Pup

> is clumsy, socially awkward, and has a unique ability to say or do the wrong thing at the worst possible time. Before he gets deployed overseas to fight in a war that he struggles to understand, he must first survive his training in the States. His fellow soldiers hate him, his instructors want to hurt him, and all that Pup wants to do is go home. Now he is partnered with a brooding soldier for special training and has to wonder if he can still push himself through another difficult lesson on life. Some heroes are born brave—and then there's Pup."

≥≤

I managed to pull my little subcompact into the parking spot with ease despite being surrounded by much larger pickup trucks, SUVs, and a spattering of sports cars here and there. The fact that none of them ran me over just for sport was a good sign, as far as I was concerned. I put the car in park and engaged the hill brake.

"Seriously, Pup? We aren't even on a hill," my passenger grumbled. He had been complaining for the entire drive to the facility. "At least we can finally get out of this Altoids tin that you call a car." Flinging the car door open, I watched Private Brian Wallace stand up and stretch until his crackling joints could be heard over all other noises. I knew that my car was small and had about as much power as a slug on a salt bed, but it was paid for, and Wallace didn't have a car at all. That means that I won.

I opened my own door and found myself stretching as well. It had been a long two-hour drive from the base where I was going through infantry training to this facility. The truth is that I'm not cut out for this army stuff. If I hadn't gotten drafted, then I would have been in a college class or sitting in a dorm room trying to figure out how to make ramen noodles. Instead, I managed to survive basic training only to find that the Army wanted to "challenge" me some more. I screwed up quite a bit in the initial infantry training because I was all thumbs, had two left feet, and couldn't find my butt with both hands. That's a direct quote from my father. Still, the instructors kept pushing me. I had just started showing some improvement when my and Wallace's names were chosen at random to come to this facility for an escape and evasion exercise. I pointed out to an instructor that I had never won a single game of hide-and-seek as a child. It didn't matter. I learned that once the Army told you to do something, you got your camouflaged butt in gear or you started peeling potatoes, cleaning latrines, doing push-ups, and all the other things that made up most of my basic training.

It took a while to walk to the building where we were supposed to sign in. Neither of us spoke. Wallace didn't like me much. Honestly, most of the people I trained with didn't like me much. I tended to be a little bit hazardous to those around me. Grenade training was an especially lonely time for me. Still, my traveling companion seemed a little bit more irritable than usual. Right now, he seemed to be determined to make certain that I didn't even look at him. Naturally, that forced me to keep glancing at him to see if I could figure out what the problem was. That continued until he wordlessly reached over, grabbed the top of my head, and made absolutely certain that I was facing forward. I fought the urge to look at him after that. His grip wasn't exactly gentle.

Once we arrived and signed in, we were told to wait for our instructor. Wallace and I walked over to some uncomfortable folding chairs and sat down. As soon as we were seated, Wallace looked over at me with an unmistakable glare. Without asking, I picked up my bag and moved over so there was one chair between us. We only had to wait in awkward silence for a few minutes before a female sergeant entered the room and walked over to us. Wallace and I both came to attention and saluted at her approach. She returned the salute before looking both of us over. I was used to the disappointed look NCOs gave me every time they did that. I knew I was pretty scrawny and didn't look "military," so I wasn't shocked when career military came to the same conclusion.

"At ease," she said in the no-nonsense tone of voice I believe is issued to every person who reaches the rank of sergeant. "The two of you follow me, and I'll brief you on the exercise."

Maybe I was in too much of a hurry. Maybe I wanted to be first in order to make a good impression. Regardless of my motivations, my body moved more quickly than my mind. I picked up my bag and tried to follow directly behind the sergeant. Wallace didn't have a chance to pick up his duffle, and it was sticking out into the floor a little bit farther than mine had. My right foot caught on the duffle bag, and I stumbled forward, falling directly into the sergeant. Tangling up her legs, I forced her to fall forwards as well. The racket of our combined fall was quickly replaced by the sound of the sergeant's curses. I jumped up from the floor and looked down to find her cradling her wrist and giving me the Glare of Death as she muttered curses. Doubting that she would take well to the idea that she got injured because I wasn't watching where I was going, I decided to fib just a bit.

"I think someone needs to put up one of the Slippery When Wet signs here, ma'am." I heard Wallace chuckling quietly as I ran off to find a medic, the sergeant still muttering curses as I practiced my ability to retreat.

Twenty minutes later, I sat in the briefing room along with Wallace, watching as a medic wrapped the sergeant's wrist. She had stopped cursing, but the Glare of Death hadn't quite subsided yet.

"Well, Sergeant Dickerson," the medic said after double-checking his work, "it isn't broken. It just looks like a sprain. Take it a little easy over the next couple of days."

"Not a chance," Sergeant Dickerson replied. "I'm going to lead this exercise personally." The medic looked at the sergeant and then at me. He raised his eyebrows a bit and then beat a hasty retreat. After stretching her arms back and forth a few times, the sergeant decided to proceed with the briefing. "The two of you are going to be the targets of a manhunt by my squad and me . Your job is to try to escape and evade us for forty-eight hours." She pointed at a small pile sitting on the table in front of us. "That is all you will have with you. The rest of your gear will be locked up for the duration of the exercise."

I looked at the pile. There were some hydration packs, a few field rations, a compass, a map, and a couple of survival knives. It seemed like a pretty skimpy selection of things to live off of for two days.

"A truck will drop you off somewhere in the exercise area. It will return to pick you up at a location marked on your map exactly two days later." She stood up and walked right in front of the table. "We will start looking for you two hours after you are dropped off. Pray that we don't find you." She looked back over at me. "What do they call you? Pup?"

I nodded wordlessly.

"Well, Pup, if we manage to catch you, I might also turn this into an interrogation exercise." She leaned in close to me. "I know that I can break you."

My eyes went wide and I swallowed a lump in my throat.

"Get going. Your ride is waiting."

Wallace and I gathered up the meager gear we had been issued and hustled out of the room. I felt like I was rushing to get to my own funeral on time.

It never ceased to amaze me how many trucks the army seemed to have. The funny thing was that they all seemed to have the same engine problems, the same exhaust system that put out enough black smoke to choke a horse, and no shocks. I had never ridden in an army truck that was comfortable. Every pebble felt like a boulder, and it was amazing how many actual boulders this truck seemed to want to drive over. I didn't comment on it, though. Wallace and I were the only two in the truck, and he seemed both angry and fidgety. I never would have pegged him for someone who got nervous before an exercise, but I'd been known to get things wrong before. I didn't want to speak up and have a fellow private wanting to kill me when I already had a sergeant prepared to turn me into a shish kabob. The rough ride lasted around twenty minutes before we came to a screeching halt. It wasn't that we stopped suddenly; it was just that the brakes screeched a lot. The tailgate was dropped, and Wallace and I were left in the middle of nowhere without a word and without any indication of where we might be. As the truck pulled away, I noticed that Wallace didn't seem to want to make the first move towards ascertaining our position, so I took the map and the compass from our small collection of gear and began to take some rough readings. It took me a couple of minutes, but I was eventually able to figure out our approximate location.

"Well, isn't that something?" I said mostly to myself. Unfortunately, when I talked to myself, I talked out loud. I had to stop doing that.

Wallace snatched the map from my hands and looked at it, but he couldn't seem to figure out which way was "up." He also looked around us a lot, but he couldn't seem to focus on what he was seeing. Finally, he just threw the map back at me. "What are you on about, Pup?"

I thought about showing him where we were on the map, but with the way he was acting, I doubted it would mean anything to him. Instead, I pointed at a rise to our right. "Let's go to the crest of that hill. I can show you what caught my attention; plus, we can look around for good cover to hole up in." Wallace didn't seem thrilled, but at least he didn't complain. Once at the crest of the rise, I pointed out to the left, where we could see a good chunk of the exercise area. There was a dense, wooded area about a half mile away. "I think that is where we should go. The trees can prevent us from being spotted from the air, plus the limbs, leaves, and hopefully some underbrush can be used as a hiding place."

Wallace took a deep breath as he looked in the distance. The breath sounded a little bit shaky to me, but we had just climbed a pretty steep hill, and I had to admit that I was a little winded, too, so I didn't think much of it. "Sure. Whatever. Looks pretty good to me. Was that what made you so excited when you were looking at the map?"

I pointed behind us. "I wasn't excited, just surprised. After all the walking we did, they ended up bringing us back to our car." We both turned around and saw that at the bottom of the other side of the hill and past a fence was the parking area. I could clearly make out my car from where we were standing. "Seems like they made us waste a lot of energy."

"Yeah, I guess they did," Wallace replied absentmindedly. He was chewing on his lower lip and thinking pretty hard about something. He obviously didn't have his mind on the half-mile march we would have to make before we could get concealed, hopefully without the search team finding us first. He was still looking away when he asked me, "You don't have your car keys on you, do you?"

I patted my left hip pocket. "Yeah, I do," I answered with an oddly proud tone. "I have this really strange habit of—"

"I don't care," Wallace cut me off. "Come with me," he commanded. His tone was so demanding that I didn't even think about not going. We double-timed it to the bottom of the hill. Wallace looked around to make certain no one was watching; then, he removed a multi-tool from his pocket and began removing one of the clasps that attached the fence wire to the post. "We'll have to crawl under," he said without looking at me.

It took me a second to understand what it was he was doing. Once I did, I nearly had a panic attack. "Wait! We can't! You're talking about going AWOL. I don't want to wind up in the stockade. I annoy people! I'm a wimp! I look terrible in orange!"

Wallace reached over and grabbed me by the collar. He swung me around so he could see me while he continued to work on the fence. It resulted in my hitting the fence post. My shoulder ached. The fence post didn't budge. It was like playing Red Rover in grade school. "Listen to me, Pup. I really don't care if you *want* to come with me because you *are* coming with me.

It's your car. Plus, if you get caught by the patrol and I'm not with you, then you'll tell them what happened, won't you?"

I had to admit that I would have. I'd never been good at being sneaky. "But how is it better for me if we both leave the base?" I figured the steel trap of my logic would stop him in his tracks.

"We won't get caught because we will both return in time to get picked up from the exercise," Wallace explained through gritted teeth. My logic trap must have been made by Acme because he had broken right through it. I heard the fence wire break free from the post, and Wallace put his multi-tool back into his pocket. Once he had done that, he was able to grab my collar with both hands and pull me forward until I was nose-to-nose with him. "It will also be better for you because if you don't crawl under that fence now, I will have to beat on you until you start to think it is a good idea. Don't you find volunteering to be easier?"

I was on the other side of the fence twenty seconds later.

Leaving the base was a lot easier than I thought it would be. I expected to see flashing blue lights and the MPs coming out of the woodwork. It turned out that my imagination was a lot more dangerous than reality. The guards at the gate didn't ask for any papers or orders. I guess it never occurred to them that someone would decide to leave the base as a way of evading an escape and evasion exercise. Twenty minutes after I had shown the parking lot to Wallace, we were on the highway and headed into town. I was going to ask him where we were going, but the words caught in my throat when I glanced over at him.

I had already seen Wallace angry and annoyed. That was spooky enough. Right now he looked ill. His face was pale, he was trembling, and there was a sheen of sweat on his forehead. I wasn't sure if he was about to pass out or puke up his breakfast, but I really didn't want to experience either. I know I was training to be a soldier, but I was drafted, not a volunteer. I wasn't born with that natural, take-charge instinct that some people had. My first impulse was to drive back home, curl up in my bed with a book, and hope that my mom might take care of my under-the-weather companion. However, since home was an eight-hour drive away and since my mother gave me explicit instructions when I was younger to stop bringing sick friends to the house, I did the only thing I could think of doing. I just kept driving straight forward.

Although he didn't look any better, Wallace eventually started to give me directions. Once I started following them, I started wishing that he had just let me keep driving straight. The part of town he led us into was one of those areas in which you rolled up your windows and locked your car doors. I started to wish that we had been issued weapons for our training exercise because I was worried that I might need one soon. The looks I received from the few people who dared to be walking along the sidewalk were not just unfriendly; they were downright hostile. It seemed like everyone wanted the chance to kick my ass. I felt like I was back in my high school gym class. The only thing missing was an overweight coach yelling at me about how bad my physical condition was while he ate a jelly doughnut.

Just before I was about to drive out of this place as fast as I could, Wallace told me that I needed to pull over. The car hadn't even stopped moving before he jumped out and onto the sidewalk. He ran up to some guy who just seemed to be standing around with nothing better to do. I couldn't hear anything they were saying, but I guess who they must have known each other because after a few seconds, they shared some kind of odd handshake, and then Wallace got back into the car.

"We're good. Let's go," he said with obvious anxiety.

"Is your friend coming with us?" I asked. "If so, I'll have to clean out the back seat."

Despite his continued shivering and sweating, Wallace still managed to look at me like I was an idiot. "Move it, moron!"

Even I could manage to follow that order.

Unfortunately, he didn't lead me into a better part of town. We seemed to be sinking further into the depths of urban hell. After about a mile or two, he pointed to an alleyway. "Pull in there, Pup." A voice in my head was yelling at me not to go there, just like people yell at the screen during a scary movie, but I turned into the alley, anyway.

I came to a stop in front of a dumpster. We sat there for a couple of minutes in silence. I was silent because I didn't have the first clue what was going on. Wallace was silent because he seemed to be looking to see if there was anyone else around. I guess he was finally satisfied that we were alone because he opened his door and said, "I'll be right back," before closing his door and going farther into the alley. He disappeared behind another dumpster, leaving me in the car alone.

It's pretty hard to describe my concerns at that point. I was worried about Wallace. He looked really bad, and his behavior seemed a little erratic to me. I was also worried about myself. I was in an alleyway in a bad part of town with no means to defend myself. I might have been wearing a uniform, but I was still scrawny even after basic training and looked like a kid playing in my father's clothes. I had the word "target" painted all over me. I decided that the only way to deal with both of my concerns was to get out of the car, find Wallace, and stick with him. I found that people tended to take care of me whenever I was around, even though it was just to save their own butt from getting into trouble. I'd take help any way I could get it.

I walked down the alleyway quietly. I didn't know who or what I was trying to hide from. Maybe I didn't want to disrupt any rats. I felt like I would get the plague if I even looked at one. I thought about calling out for Wallace, but that would have been the same thing as sending up a flare and telling everyone in the area that I was lost. Instead, I walked quietly and tried looking for where my wayward companion had hidden himself.

I found Wallace, though I'm certain he wished I hadn't. He was kneeling next to a dumpster. I wasn't looking down at that moment, and I tripped over him. I managed to catch myself on the wall of one of the buildings. Wallace wasn't so fortunate. He tipped forward, off balance and shocked at the unexpected interruption. Something went flying from his hands and into the air.

"No! No!" I heard him shout. A clear plastic bag and some substance that I couldn't recognize headed straight for a storm drain in the middle of the alley. Wallace tried to dive to catch it, but he was too late. Whatever it was landed right on top of the storm drain and fell through the grate. I watched Wallace attempt to collect some of the substance off the grating, but it was a lost cause. I could hear him sob a little and wondered if I should check on him. When he turned towards me with a murderous look in his eyes, I realized that his sobbing was the least of my trouble. "Do you know what you've done?" he snarled at me.

"No," I answered honestly. I really should have known better than that. Honesty may be the best policy, but most people have no tolerance for ignorance, no matter how honest it is.

"You signed your death warrant, that's what! I'm going to kill you!" Wallace lunged at me with his hands outstretched towards my throat. He was still off balance, so I was able to dodge to the side easily. "Get your scrawny neck over here so I can wring it!"

Several training officers had threatened my life. I seem to bring that out in people. This was the first time I truly believed the threat was real. Wallace was angry in a way that I had never seen. I knew he wanted to kill me. I also knew that under normal circumstances I wouldn't be able to do anything about it. These weren't normal circumstances, though. Wallace was still trembling, sweating, and not thinking clearly. I had the advantage in a fight for the first time in my life. When he came charging at me a second time, I just took one step to my left and held out my right arm. Like a perfectly executed wrestling match, Wallace clotheslined himself. He hit the ground hard, his head bouncing off the concrete. I dragged the unconscious soldier to the car and strapped him into the passenger seat. I couldn't get out of that part of town fast enough.

Wallace woke up the next day. He was still trembling and sweating, but his eyes were just a little bit more focused than they had been before. He tried to speak, but his throat was dry. I handed him a bottled water. He drank it down in one long pull, then tried speaking again. "Pup, where are we?"

"Still in my car. I found a parking lot that was empty in a better part of town. Figured we could sleep here."

Wallace checked his pockets and then started to look panicked. "Pup, what happened to my stuff?"

"What stuff?"

"I'm serious, Pup!" He was looking really worried now. "Where is the meth I bought? Did you take it?"

"So, it was drugs." I guess I should have known that. I think I probably did. I just didn't want to admit it. "It all went down the storm drain, remember?"

I knew he remembered once I saw his expression fall into absolute despair. "I don't have any more money, Pup. How am I supposed to get more?"

"You don't," I responded matter-of-factly. "You shouldn't be doing that stuff, anyway. It's bad for you."

"This isn't health class. Don't give me that just-say-no crap. I really need some! I don't think I'll make it another few hours without it." The trembling was becoming more pronounced, and he was sweating enough to moisturize a small desert. "You've got to have some money on you. You can buy me some, can't you?"

I did have a little money on me, but no matter how bad Wallace looked, I couldn't make myself use it to buy him drugs. "Let's go get you some help."

"No! The army will throw me in the stockade if they find out!"

This gave me an opportunity to look at Wallace like he was the idiot. "We're AWOL from an army training exercise! I'm pretty sure that the stockade is in our future whether you're on drugs or not!"

Wallace put his hands on his head and scrunched his eyes closed in frustration and despair. "Just help me, Pup. Please." It was said in the most pleading tone I had ever heard. "I don't want to go to the stockade. I don't want to keep hurting, either. Just get me through the day."

I thought about the situation. I couldn't get him drugs. I didn't care how much he begged me, I wouldn't feed his problem. I didn't want to turn him in like some kind of snitch, either. My mind raced through all I had seen in the last few days, and a way to pass the time occurred to me. An hour later, Wallace and I were at a ruby and sapphire mine that I had seen billboards for on the interstate. Wallace couldn't have looked more confused as I purchased us bucket-loads of dirt and sifters.

"Pup, what the hell are you doing? Unless there is meth hidden in this dirt, I don't see what you hope to accomplish."

"We have to be back at base in twelve hours," I pointed out. "It'll take roughly an hour to get to the base and park, at least another hour to reach the extraction point, which leaves us with a lot of time to kill. I figure this will give you something to focus on. Tourists do it all the time."

With fire in his eyes, Wallace pointed to himself and said, "Do I look like a tourist to you?"

I had decided that I would fight fire with fire if he chose to be stubborn. "No, you look like an out-of-control addict to me! You look like someone who just got their butt kicked by the scrawniest man in the army! Now use those trembling hands to shake the dirt out of those sifters and find us some rubies or I'll knock you on your ass again!" I don't know if I could have followed through with that threat. Wallace had every advantage in a fight against me, but I was hoping he was too strung out to realize it. I guessed correctly. Wallace and I spent the next eight hours at a sluice box sifting for rubies and sapphires like some sort of old-time prospectors.

Getting back onto base was a breeze. We reentered the fence at the same place we left it, and I used my map-reading skills to get us to the extraction point with twenty minutes to spare. Wallace was still looking terrible, but his trembling had subsided a little. He hadn't spoken much since we started panning for gems, but that also meant he didn't yell at me, either.

I wasn't sure what to expect from Sergeant Dickerson when we returned to the headquarters for debriefing. Whatever happened, I decided to be honest. Wallace and I hadn't had an opportunity to practice a cover story, so I didn't want to get tangled up in a bunch of half-baked lies. Better to just get it over with. Wallace and I snapped to attention when Sergeant Dickerson entered the room along with a lieutenant and two MPs. I started imagining myself in prison-orange, and it wasn't a flattering sight.

"Lower your salutes and explain how you two worms evaded us. No one has evaded my patrols in three years."

The sergeant was obviously unhappy with being on the losing end of this exercise, and my explanation didn't make her any happier. "We were in the hills at a tourist trap panning for gems, Sergeant."

The lieutenant's eyes got wide. The sergeant's eyes got narrow. Neither response indicated an easy path for me. "You were where, Private?"

"We were in the hills at a—"

"I heard you the first time, Private!" she yelled. Why did she ask me, then? I'm glad I didn't ask that out loud. I was known to do that. "You went AWOL during a U.S. Army exercise so that you could play in the dirt?"

I pulled a bag out of my pocket that contained a large stone. "Actually, Wallace found the largest uncut sapphire in the history of the mine. Once it's cut and polished, it'll be worth thousands."

"I don't care!" I don't know why I showed her the sapphire. Perhaps I thought a shiny object might distract her. Maybe that only worked with me. "What made you think you could leave this base?"

"You didn't say we couldn't, Sergeant."

Dickerson sat there sputtering. I'd pushed her to the limit. What happened next didn't help. The lieutenant took a look at some papers and whispered, "He's right, Sergeant."

Sergeant Dickerson may have been a lower rank than the lieutenant, but she was older and had more experience. She had no problem turning her anger on him. "How in the hell can he be right, Lieutenant?"

He placed the papers onto the table in front of us. "These are the written orders for the exercise. Nothing here says that the participants must remain within the containment area. This would not hold up in a court-martial."

It was the final straw for Sergeant Dickerson. "You two maggots get the hell off my base and never come back again!" Wallace and I both saluted and started out of the room. We had almost made it out the door when Dickerson stopped us. She walked over to me and snatched the bag out of my hand. "This was obtained during participation in an official Army exercise and must be turned in to your immediate superior. That's me."

"But Sergeant, we—" I stopped when Wallace stomped on my foot. "Yes, Sergeant."

I hobbled to the car with Wallace in tow. I didn't say anything as we buckled in and left the base. We were about ten miles down the road when Wallace spoke up. "Drop me at the base hospital when we get back."

"You know you'll end up in the stockade."

Wallace's voice gained some of its determination back. "I've been hooked on that stuff since my junior year of high school. Maybe I deserve to spend some time in jail. I'm just tired of it controlling me. Besides, I would rather be in the stockade than have to deploy overseas with you." I wasn't sure if he was joking or serious. Probably a little of both. "I thought you were being creative when you had us spend hours panning for gems. That really forced me to focus, by the way. Still, I'm surprised by how you came up with that argument about those orders. That was ingenious."

"It'll only work once," I admitted. "They're probably rewriting those orders as we speak. As for where I came up with the idea, you know those ridiculous warnings you see on products, and you wonder why they're on there?" Wallace nodded. "I caused two of them to be written. Today makes number three."

Wallace smiled and went to sleep. He slept for the rest of the drive to base. It was the first time I managed to win a game of hide-and-seek.

Two O'Clock Train
KJ Steele

≥≤

KJ Steele writes about the characters and events that will not otherwise leave her alone. She is the author of two novels, *No Story to Tell* and *The Bird Box*, several short stories, and is currently fascinated with bringing her imaginings to life on the stage.

From the author:

"Fresh spring days and childish play. Best friends Mara and Jimmy are anxious to push the doldrums of winter away. An unexpected event lurks upon their horizon however, and it will take their young lives in vastly different directions, irrevocably altering the path beneath them."

≥≤

The town itself is small and dirty. An insignificant gray dot joined to a myriad of other insignificant gray dots by an iron scar of railroad track that crosses the vastness and connects a country. Trains thunder through six times a day, and the town's children grow up with the shrill of its whistle embedded like a song deep within their hearts. For the rest of their lives, no matter where or how far away they roam, a train's frantic calling will pull them back with a loneliness that is instantly traceable to their northern Canadian roots. And yet, growing up, the children are blankly unaware of the train's influence. The trains are like night and day, and the seasons. Winter, spring, summer, fall—always arriving, always leaving. But unbidden, like breath. And like the seasons and like breathing, they have a silent role to play, giving rhythm and measure to the children's days.

For the most part, the original houses of the community had sprung up within sight of the tracks, clustered tightly together as if for security. Practical rather than pretty, they had been built by the rough hands of rough men who'd arrived a half-century earlier to open up the region, eking out a living from the trees and metals that filled the surrounding hills.

But one house stands out from the rest. Placed on a knoll at the end of the street, it seems to preside over the block like an old queen over her court. With a touch of paint and a few repairs, the house could blossom into a splendid little place that would elicit cries of *Charming!* or *Quaint!* from passersby. Having received no such encouragement, however, it sits wan and listless, sagging under the weight of its own decay.

The boy trots across a path of hard-packed snow dissecting the backyard, red scarf flapping, boot laces working themselves loose. Entering the back porch of the house, he works his way through a maze of cast-off stuff. Smelly bottles, lopsided chairs, and a broken refrigerator, its door yawing open like a paralyzed mouth. In the light of day the porch is just messy, but by nightfall it transforms into a terrifying place, full of all sorts of things that can get you.

He raps on the door, the sound muffled by his frayed, woolen mittens. Untucking a pink ear from under his toque, he leans carefully toward the door and listens for any noise or movement coming from inside. Clues. He's never been inside the house. Not once in the whole time that he and Mara have been best friends has she ever invited him inside, and the unyielding forbiddenness of it has fueled a great, galloping, unbearable curiosity that has agitated his imagination into fantastical conclusions. Maybe Mara's family had found buried treasure. Or had a two-headed dog, or maybe even dead people were buried in the basement.

Hearing no movement inside the house, he raises his hand to knock again, his red-mittened fist falling through the sudden air as the door yanks open.

"Hi," Mara says, bright squirrel eyes squinting in the light. She's beaten him once again. Like so many of their games this one invented itself. The boy crosses his eyes, then rolls his round face into a goofy mask, sending them both into a fit of giggles. This is the penalty for losing. A moment's humility between the best of friends.

"Wanna come play?" he asks with wide green eyes, the color of the king cob she covets but can never seem to win from him no matter how many games of marbles they play.

"Okay, but I have to get dressed first. Wait here a sec," she says, but he presses his hand against the peeling yellow door as she starts to close it.

"Can't I come in and wait?" he asks, eyes unblinking, as if blinking itself could give her a reason to refuse.

She sees that flakes of paint have rubbed off onto his mitten and the sight of it annoys her somehow.

"No," she says. "Just wait here. I'll be quick."

"Please?" he begs.

She shakes her head tightly.

"But why can't I?" he continues, his voice rising up in a nasally whine. "Just this once? Please?"

"Shhh!" the girl hisses, eyes darting quickly as she looks behind her, body tight as a spring.

"But *why?*" he whispers, this time vapidly, the set of her jaw making it clear he will not get his way.

"Because...because my mom's sleeping," she whispers back, resuming her pressure on the door.

"Sleeping?" he echoes, eyebrows burrowing into a question.

"She's sick," Mara says quickly as she begins to remember how long ago it was since she'd heard the noon-time train go past.

"But..." he starts as she closes the door on the too-many questions, which are forming across his freckled face.

The inside of the house is wrapped in false night, shades and curtains drawn. Mara pads quickly into the living room, soft bunny slippers almost soundless on the carpet. She stands in the darkness and listens to her mother's first awakenings. A sofa propped up against the far wall offers out a vague outline, and Mara directs her voice to this as she speaks.

"Can I go play?"

"Who's at the door?" her mother asks thickly.

"Jimmy."

"Why doesn't he come in?"

"He doesn't want to."

"How come?"

"I don't know. He just likes to wait outside."

"Weird kid," her mother replies, yawning herself awake.

"Can I go play?"

Mara waits like a shadow, following the sounds of her mother's hands across the debris of the coffee table, knocking over a can, pushing aside glasses, rummaging along until they find the soothing square corners of her cigarette package, and she fishes one into her mouth. A burst of light explodes across her mother's face. Mara quickly looks down into the glassy questions that swim in the black eyes of her bunny slippers.

"Can I?"

"Can you what?"

"Can I go and play?"

"I don't care what you do. Just don't be playing around here. I have a headache."

Mara slips across the hall into her bedroom, her thoughts already leaping forward into the fresh day. Grabbing jeans and a daisy-flowered sweater off the floor, she shakes them to life and shrugs them on. She can't tell if she has one black sock and one blue sock or a matching pair, but she pulls them on regardless.

≥≤

Outside the sun is brilliant, slicing toward them with the first promise of warmer days. The touch of its lengthening rays seems to stir a lightness and freedom within the children and sets them off down the slushy street in an impromptu race to the stop sign, which the girl easily wins. She bounds up a massive gray snow bank and fires a few loose snowballs at the boy's head. She misses with every one, and he laughs gratefully. They both know she could easily pick him off even with one eye closed. She watches triumphantly as he clambers up toward her, the sun happy on his face.

He collapses beside her, and they sit for a moment in communal silence, smiling at their own delirium. Suddenly, unable to abide by winter's constant constraints, they struggle free of their parkas and send them flying back down the hill like great, boneless birds.

In the distance a car starts up the street and, almost instinctively, they begin to pack an arsenal of snowballs. But when the car passes below them they throw without conviction, and it escapes unscathed. Winter is no longer fun. The snow itself has grown tired and old, as uninspiring as last year's Christmas gifts.

The boy jumps up, a flash of defiance sparking in his shiny eyes, the red toque that tames his cowlick slipping toward his face.

"Let's go down to the river," he proclaims, already sliding down the snowbank toward his coat.

She is not supposed to go near the river, nor the railroad tracks they have to cross to get to it. But the sight of Jimmy's fleeing back fires a strong, competitive alarm inside her. The cheat! He knows she is a faster runner, so he has invented the game of the unfair start. Flashing a quick look toward her house, she sees the drapes are still drawn. She bolts like a rabbit down the hill and up the street, arms and legs pumping like pistons, singular in her purpose until she sees him falter in the heavier snow where the path ends, and his legs begin to give way.

"Cheater," she accuses as she comes up behind him, and he stops to laugh at her.

They continue walking along together side by side across the vacant lot, the crisp crust of snow snapping beneath their feet like communion wafers. Taking a package from his pocket, he unwraps two cookies—peanut butter—and hands her the biggest one. They smile at each other, and she stares enviously at the gap in his teeth and the knobby white wrists that his sleeves can no longer cover. These changes don't sit comfortably with her. She doesn't like the fact of his growing up before her.

The railroad tracks are not far off now, and Mara walks along beside him, munching on her cookie like she couldn't care less, but inside she's wondering if he is bluffing or if he really means to cross them. But as they approach, Jimmy doesn't even slow down, just marches straight across. Mara matches him stride for stride. Slipping down through the snowy trees to the river bank, she slows her pace, and when he steps gingerly onto the river's icy face she hangs back on the shore.

"Chicken," he needles.

"Am not."

"Am too."

Mara looks up and off into the distance. They stand quiet for a moment and listen, feeling the two o'clock train long before they can hear it.

The boy jumps a bit, tentatively, testing the ice beneath him. Its solid strength seems to embolden him, and he jumps some more, harder, until a satisfying crackle, like the breaking of a gumball in his mouth, sounds beneath him. They look at each other and freeze; he poised to jump back to shore, she with hands raised to cover a silent scream. Then, when nothing further happens, they explode with laughter, and he jumps some more.

By the time the train cuts through the edge of the horizon and is hurtling by above them, the boy has taken on its primal rhythm and is working frantically to keep time. "Look-at-me, look-at-me, look-at-me," chugs the train, and it is impossible not to look at it as it fills the world above them, blocking out trees and sky, shaking the very air surrounding them. Its whistle begins to blow, loud, deafening, drowning out thought, and Jimmy joins it, hollering furiously as he jumps upon the ice with a terrible urgency.

"Whoo-whoo-whoo," he screams, arms flailing, red scarf licking around him like a flame.

Fascinated, Mara begins to shriek and laugh too, not knowing what she feels, but just erupting with a wild joy that surges up inside her with the pounding of the train and this beating back of winter. And then she stops. Jimmy is gone. A jagged black circle in the ice is all that remains. She starts to ask a question, but no one is there, her words vaporizing into the roar of the train. Hurrying to the hole, she is met by green eyes filling with fear. The red toque is gone, stolen away by the current, his cowlick remaining subdued by this dousing of frigid water. Soggy-mittened hands seize upon an icy outcropping, but it gives way when he attempts to pull himself free. Desperately, he grinds his elbows into the ice around him and hoists himself higher. For a second Mara can see the red of his scarf against his coat, but then the ice buckles and lets go of him again.

"Jimmy!" she shrieks. "Oh no, Jimmy. Oh no! Here, give me your hand," she cries as she lowers herself onto her knees and reaches for him. "Is it cold?" she asks vacuously.

The boy tries to nod but is caught by a convulsive shiver that deforms the movement, almost causing his hand to jerk away from hers. His face has taken on the grayness of the ice, as if it has already laid claim to him. His hollow, muted eyes frighten her. She grasps his hand tighter and pulls with all the strength her small body can give. But this is not a fair game, and her efforts are not enough. Not nearly enough, and the river pulling below at his parka and snow boots and nearly inert body merely laughs at her as it keeps swallowing him up, then begins to pull her in as well.

"Let go, Jimmy! Let go!" she screams, and whether his hand slips free of hers because of her pleas or because he simply has no strength left to hang on she cannot tell, but she scrambles quickly away from him, watching as he flounders helpless as some damaged, half-dead beetle. She fears them both now, the horrible blackness of the hole and the strange, waxen mask that has become his face.

"Get a branch," he whispers, his voice old and thin.

Relieved to get away, she leaps up and dashes toward the trees, but there is nothing. Winter still binds the land, a thick blanket of snow shrouding the earth.

She turns instead to the passing train, running after it, stumbling and falling in the unforgiving snow, getting up and carrying on again. Running, running, running. Running until her legs give out and her lungs blaze. She can see the shape of a man standing outside the caboose, and she yells and screams and waves. Slowly he raises an arm into the air and slowly, slowly, slowly, he waves. Waves until the hoarse voice of the train sounds only as a dim memory.

When she returns to the hole, there is only emptiness. Jimmy is not there. He has left her alone and gone home by himself. Anger pushes tears from her eyes as she throws down the stick she has finally found. This is not right. This is not what a best friend is supposed to do.

A sudden thought rearranges her face, and she smiles. It is the smile she smiles when she beats him at a game. Or remembers a secret that they share. Her eyes search among the still, vacant trees, and she runs swift as a fox up to the closest one, peers around it, and is startled to find no one there. She dashes quickly to the next one and then the next. She knows he is there. He is hiding there somewhere. Hiding behind one of those trees.

Howard and Pablo

Earl Javorsky

≥≤

Earl Javorsky was born in Berlin and immigrated to the US. He has been, among other things, a delivery boy, musician, product rep in the chemical entertainment industry, university music teacher, software salesman, copy editor, proofreader, and novelist. His Story Plant books include *Down Solo* and *Trust Me*, and a sequel to *Down Solo* will come out in 2017.

From the author:

"'Howard and Pablo' is a traditional short story that pits the industrialist Howard Hughes against the musician Pablo Casals. Hughes, hostage to his inner demons, can only find solace in Casals' rendering of Bach. A command performance becomes a battle of wills."

≥≤

Howard Hughes sits in a chair that is covered with a plastic sheet. He's wearing a white silk robe over white pajamas. With his long silver hair and beard, he looks like a Sufi ghost, an Imam apparition with the curving claws of a Mandarin, only this dervish isn't whirling, at least not on the outside. It's his mind that spins like a Great Plains twister.

"Bob, I'd like you to turn on the Hi-Fi and then sit and join me."

"Why, thank you, Mr. Hughes." Bob doesn't express his surprise. He has never been invited to join his employer in this private ritual. He goes to the phono console, a state-of-the-art assembly of electronic components designed for power and clarity by one of Howard Hughes's many companies.

Bob sets the recording on the turntable and reads the label as the platter spins: Bach Cello Suites, performed by Pablo Casals. The same music today as yesterday, and the day before, and every day for the past six months. He engages the tone arm and walks over to settle in a chair facing Mr. Hughes, who sits erect, fingers steepled against the bridge of his nose, thumbs at his chin, already in a state of fixed concentration.

The music begins: Bach's Suite #1 in G, the prelude, starting with an arpeggiated chord, building immediately to the next chord and the next with inexorable power and logic. The pattern reaches a plateau and now changes: a deep bass and a higher middle note, an alternating of bass and melody increasing in tension as the melody climbs in pitch, a sweet vibrato on a long, sustained note as the tension releases.

Bob looks over at Mr. Hughes. He sees tears streaming from the man's pale blue eyes. Bob looks away, focusing out the window on the nighttime view of Los Angeles shining brightly below as the next piece begins. He ponders the strange, cold man for whom he has worked so long.

After a silence, Mr. Hughes speaks. "All the work I've done, the things I've built, and still there's a hollowness inside me."

"This is a question of religion, sir?"

"Perhaps. My mind is an untethered kite. These moments with this music are my only relief." There have been days recently when Bob has been summoned into the room ten, even fifteen, times to start the recording at its beginning. "Do you know that this man Casals refuses my invitation to play for me personally? I offered him more than he makes in a year."

"Yes, sir; I made that offer, if you recall. Mr. Casals said that his music is for the people."

Hughes moves in his chair and brushes something invisible from the plastic cover. "I've come to a decision. I want this man here, and I don't care if he consents to it or not. Handle it. Discreetly, of course."

"You want me to kidnap him?"

"I want you to escort him here. He will be compensated."

≥≤

The abduction is fairly straightforward: Pablo Casals is tricked in a limousine switch after a performance of the St. Matthew's Passion at Carnegie Hall. He is transported by private train car to the West Coast, then, over his vehement protests, brought to the Hughes mansion and given a wood-paneled room on the top floor of the south wing. The room overlooks the city and the ocean. On a small, round table at its center are a bottle of Armagnac, a brandy snifter, biscuits and cheese, and a single red rose in a slender vase. By the window, a single bed with a quilt. A door leads to a small bathroom. There is no other exit. His instrument case lies on the floor by the bed. The door has been locked from the outside, and the window is far from the ground.

≥≤

The following morning, Casals wakes to a polite knock on his door. Furious at his imprisonment, he does not respond. On a normal day, he would begin with an hour's walk from his villa in San Juan. Next, he would play Bach on the piano in order to give his house the appropriate atmosphere for the day. He hears receding footsteps and tries the door; it is unlocked. A simple breakfast tray of croissants, fruit, and coffee has been placed outside the door. He sees a red-haired man in a gray suit standing at the end of the hall. The smell of coffee lightens his mood as he carries the tray to his table. He notices a note wedged between the coffee pot and the cup.

"Your presence requested at 8:00 a.m. My man will escort you." The signature is a childish scrawl that seems to say "HRH." Suddenly his circumstances become clear. The limousine driver, Bob, who accompanied him on the endless train journey and brought him to this hilltop mansion. The invitation, long forgotten, to play a private recital for the reclusive—some called him mad—billionaire.

Now doubly enraged, he is at the same time fascinated by the extent of the effort involved. He finishes his breakfast, and there is another knock. He is not surprised, when he opens the door, to face the limousine driver. The man is in his early fifties, wears a crisp gray suit, and bears the same wary, no-nonsense expression that discouraged conversation during their previous time together. He does not even protest as the man bends to grasp the handle of the cello case.

They walk down the barren, uncarpeted hallway, past the red-haired guard, who nods slightly. Casals notices that the other rooms are unfurnished. In fact, the whole house has a feeling of being long-unoccupied. Descending a grand stairway, he sees what appears to be another guard, also in a gray suit, by the front door. They continue through the foyer, down another hallway, through an enormous kitchen, and finally enter the servants' quarters.

They stop in a small room. The lighting is dim, and heavy drapery covers the window to his left. Against the wall on his right is a couch, badly in need of reupholstering. In the middle of the opposite wall is another door, closed, next to which is a desk, behind which sits yet another gray-suited man. In the center of the room, facing the door, is a wooden chair with a cushioned seat, which Casals is directed to take.

He sits. His escort raps lightly on the door and then opens it, revealing another room, totally dark, from which emanates a medicinal smell, like that of rubbing alcohol. Gradually, Casals is able to make out the figure within. Seated facing him, not more than eight feet away, is a wild man, an emaciated creature of indeterminable age, with shoulder-length hair and a long, wispy beard. He is dressed in boxer shorts and an undershirt. He sits on the end of a chaise lounge, next to which is a small table. The room appears to be otherwise empty.

The apparition speaks but makes no effort to stand. "Good morning."

"A *good* morning," Casals replies, "begins with freedom. I demand that you have me taken to the airport directly!" His speech, thick with indignation, is ignored.

Hughes brushes at his lap as if smoothing invisible trousers. "Mr. Casals, we've been through a good deal of trouble to bring you here. As you may recall from my request last year, it is my desire that you play for me."

"Impossible! Absurd! I would as soon play for Franco himself." In his anger, the musician pushes his jaw forward, his lower lip thrust out like a bulldog's. His shapeless tussore shirt lies rumpled over his paunch as he leans forward in his seat. "You," he points his finger at Hughes, "belong in a dark room. Yes. This fits very nicely. I, on the other hand," he taps his breast twice, "enjoy the light. I must have it. You will not hear me play." With that, he gets up from his chair and leaves, followed quickly by Bob, who escorts him to his room.

The day passes. Lunch is brought. The afternoon wind sweeps across the Pacific, then dies as the sun meets the ocean. Casals receives dinner. Later, a fine claret and a book he has requested, a collection of Lorca. By midnight, his room is dark.

The next morning, after breakfast, the musician is again escorted down the grand stairway, but this time he is led through a living room filled with covered furniture. A piano with a sheet over it catches his attention. Beyond it, louvered doors open onto a tiled patio, from which a path leads across a wide lawn, through a garden, and into a grove of orange trees. "Will an hour be long enough, Mr. Casals?" Bob has been unfailingly courteous, and the old man finds himself grateful. "Yes, an hour, thank you," he says, and he follows the path.

An hour later, exhilarated by his walk, Casals meets Bob on the patio. When they enter the living room, he sees that the piano, a Bösendorfer, has been uncovered. Aching to play, he smiles instead and shakes his head. They proceed to the servants' quarters.

"You think," he says, facing Hughes, "that if you free me from my little cage I will sing in your larger one?"

"I only hoped you would find comfort in your morning routine." Hughes scratches at his beard as he speaks, then shakes away the long white strands that have come off in his hand.

"And how is it that you know my morning routine?"

"Because I am so interested in you. For example, I heard your speech on the radio: 'A special appeal to my fellow musicians to put the purity of art at the service of mankind in bringing about fraternal and enlightened relationships throughout the world.' You see? We share a revulsion for the atomic bomb."

"But you profit from the making of the planes that will deliver these bombs. I share no more with you than Schweitzer shares with the Krupp family."

"We share a love for Bach."

"And so I should play for you? Dios, sálvame de los tiranos y tontos!" Casals removes his eyeglasses, shaking his head in exasperation, and cleans them on his shirtsleeve. *God, save me from tyrants and fools.*

"Que dios?"

"The God, my friend, of love and compassion that you have so carefully shut out."

Hughes' hooded eyes seem to be looking inward even as he gazes out from his dark room. "You also proposed," he says, "that Beethoven's Ode to Joy be played in every town that has an orchestra and a chorus, on the same day, and that it be transmitted to all corners of the earth of the world by radio."

"Yes. A prayer, through music, for peace."

"I can make that possible."

"You hold me hostage and then bribe me? Your participation would make a mockery of the event."

"You are very clear in your contempt of me."

"I am sure what you have done with me is how you conduct your life. You run roughshod over the simplest rules of human transaction." Casals stands, impatient now and ready to leave.

Hughes replies, "I am interested in results. To your fine playing I hold up airplanes that transport people and goods around the world, films that entertain millions, and tools that make entirely new things possible."

"I say," Casals declares, "that the world is going backwards. That it is the simple things that count, and the world has forgotten the most elemental things, and that you"—he makes a gesture of dismissal with one hand—"are a leader of the charge in retrogression." And he leaves the room.

The day passes, and the night. On the next morning, and the next, the musician takes his walk through the garden and the orange trees, declining to play on the Bösendorfer, and returns to his room. Occasionally, he speculates on friends' and authorities' reactions to his disappearance.

On the evening of the fifth day, after dinner, Pau Carlos Salvador Defilló de Casals is again led to face his captor. Hughes speaks first. "We have something else in common."

"Eh?" The musician is unwilling to put effort into the conversation.

"You are in self-imposed exile from your native Spain. Only several months ago I chose this room for my own state of exile."

Casals snorts. "Bah! It is Spain who is isolated, not I. There is nothing at all the same about it."

"But I feel a kinship. I feel it when I hear you play, and I feel it now." Hughes seems to be pleading from the dark room.

"That is because music speaks past your sick mind to your soul," Casals replies. "Meanwhile, I have had enough. You are a very sad man, Señor Hughes, but this is criminal and ridiculous. You must let me go."

"There is nothing I must do," says Hughes.

"But you must hear me play."

"Yes."

"Ah, my poor Mr. Hughes." They sit in silence for some time before Hughes reaches out and swings the door shut.

≥≤

Seen from above, Los Angeles by night seems an almost endless expanse of stoplights and headlights, of stadium lights and rows upon rows of little box houses with their window lights. To the west, the display stops abruptly at Doheny Drive, the street that divides Hollywood from Beverly Hills. From Doheny Drive to the Pacific Ocean the terrain seems, by contrast, to be in deep shadow, sprinkled here and there with the reading lights of the sleepless rich. In the middle of this long shadow, at the end of a long and winding hillside road of massive mansions, overlooking the canyon below, the darkened hills and flatlands beyond, and finally, a half-moon slung low over the Pacific, a single window shines with a warm yellow glow.

A neighbor from the canyon below is awakened by a sound that spills out from the window. Another hears music that floats on a wind of its own, taking over his house, playing on his lawn like an earthbound spirit.

The notes jump out and march down through the hillside brush. Children awake and press their faces to windowpanes; an aging diva stands on her balcony in the night breeze.

In the servants' quarters of the big house, a man wakes from his fitful sleep. He crosses the room, grasps the handle of the door, and strides out, donning a bathrobe as he quickens his step through the kitchen. He seems weightless as he ascends the stairway. At the end of the hallway, he pauses, uncertain. He lifts his hands in the darkness and stares at them, wondering how the nails have become so long. There is a sudden welling up in his eyes. If he opens the door, the music may simply be too powerful, but the door is ajar, and he pushes it. Casals sits at the window, looking out at the first ember of dawn glowing in the clouded darkness over the sea, his left hand quivering on the neck of his instrument as the right bows the final sustenuto of the prelude.

"No," the bearded man thinks, his breath caught high in his throat, "it can't stop now." The musician turns, eyebrows raised as he regards his captor. For a long moment they stare at each other in silence, then the seated man nods once. He gestures for the other to sit and then returns his hand to the instrument. As the bearded man sits, the silence is broken by an exuberant double-stop, followed by the deep singing of wood as the cellist moves into the allemande.

ZEC

Roger Bagg

≥≤

Roger Bagg is a science fiction novelist, passionate about writing and the great outdoors of his home Colorado. His work draws on the scientific process of observation in creating character composites. An expressionist writer, Roger composes experimentally, playing on futurist and surrealist ideas. He enjoys hunting, fishing, skiing, hiking and camping. His breakout novel *Expedition Beyond* explores the realm of an inner-Earth discovery. He enjoys working intricately woven plotlines and develops engaging multidimensional characters.

From the author:

"Life never turns out quite the way anticipated and, sometimes, this is also true of writing. Usually, I'll write the beginning, then the piece's end. I'll retrace to the start and sequentially work toward the conclusion, not allowing the characters to wander too far off course. After completing the outline for this monograph, I found sharp deviation from the intended direction. I could either fight the flow or run with it. I decided to run with it. That is when the words floated off the pages, stood, and faced me."

≥≤

They're coming to shock me.

I hear them in the clean corridor—past the continuous and dull, low vibrational hum of the sound wall. I survey my cell. Three walls of windowless concrete-block surround me, the fourth facing this plainly visible corridor. Once again, as I have a hundred times, I inventory my meager belongings to cast aside thoughts of the coming voltage.

I have three books, nothing current or political, that I have read dozens of times. The wall-less bathroom has a red porcelain stool, sink, and small shower. My bunk bed lacks an upper twin. A single blue towel hangs across the footboard. Thin bed sheets are torn, the quilt tattered. A wooden chair and small table stand along the south wall. My entire space is twenty-by-twenty feet. The floor has embedded circular patterns fashioned into the concrete.

Still, I loathe what is about to happen. When they arrive, one Tasers my arm, the volts race through my body, and I'll immediately be down against the patterned concrete. Men in tan federation uniforms with trifold hats standing above, laughing at me. Blood will be dripping from my nose, oozing into the floor crevices, and flowing away from a swelling head wound.

But they are stupid—they will learn nothing. I've been in this solitary confinement cell for four years, and today's procedure will be the same. To me, it's inconceivable that this torture would continue, as they have gained no new knowledge. Yet, each time, the same regimen is repeated, almost choreographed. They dope my morning meal, the drugs designed to tire and relax me. I hear the metallic click of a door opening and closing in the clean corridor, past the sound wall, and then the Taser jolts me down.

They'll wheel me to the basement, strap me onto the electric chair, and threaten electrocution. They'll stuff the rubber mouthpiece in and strap a wired helmet on my head. In monotone voices, they'll ask the same questions over and over. Then they'll shock me, and each time again demand answers. I never respond.

They are criminals. I have committed no crime. Instead, I should be considered a political prisoner, or an adversary to their military structure, and treated with respect and dignity. Since they have decided otherwise, I have every intention of fighting them when they arrive and can yield a pretty nasty blow from my muscular 245-pound frame.

My mind wanders to my love for outer space. Nothing I've experienced is more soothing than traveling through deep space with time spent in the dead bed. I awaken refreshed and looking forward to the coming adventure. Many times, I've imagined the explorers of old in sailing ships experiencing similar elation while on route to distant lands — the unique smell of salt water, the creak of dry wood and ropes, the sound of sails unfurling, and the exhilaration of land found.

During awakened time, the vast emptiness of space is reminiscent of the sea, except the associated movement is more gliding than repetitive waves. The electronic instrumentation clicks and beeps, an occasional hull impact from small meteorites creaks and groans: these are the sounds of home to me. Thoughts of my previous travel and, of course, meticulously planning freedom from my captors occupy my mind and keep me sane. I believe it's the right and duty of every prisoner to struggle against oppression, even violently, and to devise an escape plan.

But, for now, the federation jailers are in the corridor. One holds his Taser high and motions me to the bed. They look pathetically stupid dressed in their uniforms—six men in all. I know they are following orders from misguided commanders, but I will show them no mercy.

I stand tall, grin, and in defiance dump the contents of my food tray to the concrete floor, tossing the empty tinfoil at the sound wall where it ricochets back across the cell. I have not tasted their drugged food.

As soon as the hum abates when the sound wall is turned off, I charge, blocking directly into them. The first shock folds me to the floor. I think I landed one face punch before everything went black.

≥≤

I awaken, straining against chains and fetters. Warm water washes over my face. Someone has his hands on my cheek, and I bite his finger until he yells. Blood mixes with the shower water. He explains he's shaving me. I see lights flashing, flares that stream upward while bubbles float over my naked skin. I howl and growl. Another has his hands on my head. I feel the vibration of the clippers as my hair melts into the water, flowing away.

This man is talking to me in a rhythmic, calming voice, mentioning how he is especially fond of my tattoos. I explain they are the lion, the lamb, the eagle, and the snake, representing the four Earth seasons and the life stages of a man.

He seems impressed. He says that I am scheduled to meet the council of judges for the first time in four years.

I break out in goosebumps. This is the beginning of my escape chance. If only they'll allow me to show instead of tell.

All of my previous preparations come flooding back. I have every intention of standing my ground and setting the record straight. They need to know, so when the time comes, we are all on the same page.

≥≤

Of course I took the kid. This I readily admit. The bombs that killed my family were raining down near him. They were indiscriminate in their murder, and we barely made it out alive. Besides, he had no life staying with commoner parents. His full capacity as commander of the universe could only be achieved through me. Now the council understands his power, and they want him back. I hate them for what they have done.

And now they shock me to find him.

I have the child stashed in space. By now, he must be larger than I remember, but I'm sure he still thinks of me as his father. He's not human, but Mauritian. He doesn't breathe oxygen and needs little nutrition, most of which can be sensitized by chemicals. The meager amount of food he does consume allowed me to leave more than ample supplies. His long, gangly limbs, ghostlike face, and cobweb matrix give him frail, wispy creature appearances of more form than substance. When he walks, it's like a dance, floating graciously from step to step with skull gliding merrily to and fro, and his gravity-defying body gracefully moving silkily around the room with arms swinging high. An apparition to most, I consider him to be my son and intend to keep him from this federation who will exploit him for their own purposes. In the short time we were together, we bonded. The young supreme commander they can't find, the future of the universe, calls me Papa. He holds the key to magnificent power, and when I return, we will most certainly rule.

I am lonely for him. The separation is sometimes unbearable. This loneliness is a contagion of the mind that leads to physical illness. I try not to think of him while in solitary confinement. Yet, I know he's alone, too. And so I fill my hours with physical exercise to embolden me and strive to concentrate on planning for the future.

Still, I feel the butterflies deep beneath my sternum of longing for him. This is an incarceration worse than physical confinement. To be with him, to hold him, the tragedy is in this separation. He is my son.

The water turns off, and they wheel me into an anteroom, placing a towel and clothes in my lap. They release me from the chair, but the chains and fetters remain. Then they are gone. I zipper on the clothes designed for shackled criminals.

They sit me upright in an elevated, short, wall-enclosed stand across from where the three judges will enter. I am level to my court-appointed attorney, who is standing nearby talking to me. I pay no attention to what he says. His jurisprudence is embryonic.

I do notice his appearance. The handlebar mustache is something new; his white-and-red-striped suit is amazingly insane, especially juxtaposed with matching bowtie. He's an idiot. I motion him closer and warn him to never tell me to shut up again.

The pathetic creature appears hurt.

The judges enter, and we stand. I can't control an amused grin, so I look to the ceiling. Acting refrained and noncommittal, I sit. My mind wanders, and I constantly try to concentrate. This is my chance. This is the beginning of the revelation. They will be putty in my hands.

My lawyer is arguing some kind of compromise. A judge retorts, noting my less-than-perfect behavior. I decide to study my oppressors.

They are old. The witch of a woman to the left is frail and ugly. Maybe once she was young and wholesome; she is now boney with pale, thin skin. Her white blouse and scarf cover her neck. She attempted to encircle her powdered, deeply wrinkled face with curled, thinning silver hair. A red lace shawl is draped over her shoulders.

The central figure is equally disgusting. His vitality left long ago, and his suit covered skeletal remains.

The justice to the right is new to me — not one that had sentenced me to life without parole four years ago. He has an interesting face with eyes that followed my every move. I wondered if the woman he replaced was dead or simply incapacitated.

My attorney drones on. To his astonishment, I stand. He stops mid-sentence. I announce I will lead them to the one they seek in exchange for more freedom.

The new judge, with cautious eyes, asks if I demand my release for this information.

I couldn't have asked for a better lead-in to my carefully constructed and rehearsed speech. I ask if I can approach the bench, at least halfway, to stand centrally for a demonstration of the location of the boy within the cosmos. And as to what I expect from this hearing and fulfillment of my obligation, even though I am innocent of any wrongdoing, I ask only for banishment.

The universe appears, surrounding me as I stand centrally, and the lights are lowered. Its stellar beauty briefly overcomes me. I weave my tale, ensuring all become engaged. My attorney appears awestruck. He never could have fashioned such a defense with his puny brain. Even the witch's wrinkles were deeper farrowed. I am an amazing speaker, and, by the time I finished, pointing to the sector where I had hidden the child, the room was completely silent. Time stood still, as even the guards were statuesque.

Cautious Eyes exhales. I shuffle back to the box. The judges adjourn.

≥≤

The jailers approach my cell. I hear muffled voices, then see them standing outside. I show them my empty food tray. They smile, thumbs up, no Taser in sight. One holds shackles; I sit on my bed.

Sunlight falls on my face in stripes through the slotted metal prison van window, and the warmth is glorious. Outside, it appears to be spring—the trees have fully-bloomed flowers in red, yellow, and peach colors; the bushes are adorned in purples from light to royal. Dark green lawns within parks pass by, along with a glimpse of the ocean with magnificent waves.

The scenery is completely oppositional to the cold twilight of space. Yet, I miss my home base, and the boy.

The van stops twice: once at the perimeter gate and again at the launch pad. We ascend by gantry elevator and board the ship. They unshackle me, still treating me like an animal, vetting me into the dead bed with needles of tranquilizers and tubes while a jumble of voices in sanitized uniforms read off checklists.

I smile, not so much excited about the impending space travel, but knowing all three judges and probably my punk-ass attorney will all die before I return. Such is the way with space travel and time.

≥≤

I awaken to the sound of spaceflight. This constant whisper of otherwise silence is generated by resonance of the eardrums. An eerie quality to many, I actually enjoy the monotonous emptiness, the biorhythm of the ear searching for fulfillment through sound where none exists. To compensate, there's a background of auditory white noise that the brain perceives from a blank screen effect, and I search for ways to test if my hearing exists. Then I hear the tinny, echoless sound of movement, or voice, or instrumentation that has a particularly flat quality. Added to this resonance of the eardrum is the suspension of the cochlea in the inner ear, affecting balance and orientation. This occurs even with artificial gravity, and the sensation is momentous.

Temporarily blind, I search for the eye drops. As my enclosure comes into focus, a nearby soup steamer beeps. I sit alone and enjoy the warm meal.

I'm a loner by choice. Surely, incarceration in solitary confinement would frustrate or infuriate others needing interactions to combat loneliness. But I was content, spending time body-building and planning the future. That future is now.

A captain appears on screen. He asks which asteroid. I tell him. This knowledge doesn't really matter—they will need my boots on the ground to find him. It is my second home, my base, and cannot be probed. My ship is there, deep inside but ready to launch with only minor preparation. Sensors are on. They will be unable to recognize any tunnels or subterranean rooms, sensing only solid rock. And the gateways are well hidden.

Two weeks pass by my calculation. I act restless; I know they are watching. Within the next week I will act submissive, beaten, and broken.

A captain reappears on screen. Where is my son? He can't find him. Perhaps I have mistaken this asteroid for another? No, no, no! I will show you where he's waiting.

A cunning plot requires an accomplished actor, and I am the best. After all, if the motive is true, then it's not really a lie but an act of achievement.

He resigns to take me on reconnaissance. The spacesuit is left for me to don. I've done this many times alone before, no problem. Even the helmet fits snugly.

My feet are shackled and my hands cuffed behind my back. I'm led to the lander where five federation soldiers are already suited and ready. We depart the mother ship.

The asteroid is six miles long by one across, and a half-mile deep. I hear over my headset a voice that describes a peculiar, knife-shaped vent on one surface, too narrow to enter. I direct them to land on the other surface.

It's not a vent. It's a well-camouflaged launch tube leading to my ship.

After landing, I lead them, hopping across the barren rock. I'm good at this pogo stick bounce, and twice I'm told to slow down. I do; they are grouped six feet away on each side and behind. They are well armed, and I know I will have to act fast. The landing craft is a half-mile behind us, the lip of the crater maybe a quarter-mile ahead. I hope they are tiring as I again test going slightly faster.

Then, three successive hops over four feet high and I fall over the crater's lip, rolling. I bring my feet through my cuffed hands, reaching under a nearby rock, pulling the hidden zip gun out. The first shot blows the closest guard's backpack clean off. His shoulder is exposed with bone and blood showing. He attempts to reach for his weapon, but his arm is obviously broken. He has only seconds to live without air or protection. Two comrades stand lamely by, seemingly consoling him.

My second shot blows the chain of my shackled feet in half, and I'm bouncing away, heading toward the manhole cover to my lair.

Two shots zip past me. I turn and fire, blowing the helmet and head off of another man. Blood shoots across his white spacesuit before his body crumples to the ground.

I'm at the entrance typing in code, then unscrewing the air-tight cover. I place my feet on the top rung of the ladder inside, close and tighten the cover above me as two shots narrowly miss. I flip a toggle, and lights in the room below glow. Quickly, I descend one floor and cross the foyer to the control panel, flip the switch to turn on the sound wall that separates vestibule from the remainder of my den. Next, the ventilator pumps chug to life, and oxygen floods into my space. I remove my helmet and laser the chain off that binds my hands.

The room is warm; I chuckle, thinking my son doesn't need oxygen, but he does need warmth. He's here, somewhere, but I haven't got the time to find him.

The sound wall ripples with a deafening roar, and I know my captors have blown the hatch above.

My ship is down two floors of metal ladder stairs. I descend. Only a second wasted noting the ship's clean and neat appearance before I board and climb to the flight deck. I toggle on all systems; each one begins with a caution light that quickly turns green. I electronically retract the neutron absorbing beryllium shields guarding the reactor core, and the engines heat.

Fifteen minutes.

Back up the ladder, I search for my boy. To my surprise, the federation soldiers are climbing down inside the vestibule, still fully-suited, separated from me only by the sound wall. The first to reach the floor turns, and I see he is not one of the men that had accompanied me. Across his helmet are the letters NUCLA, a member of the dreaded federation vexillum. I give him the finger. They can't stop me now.

Ten minutes.

I'm running from room to room but find no one. Back in the main room, the military elite concentrates on some kind of boring tool affixed to the stone. They can't shoot through the sound wall; the projectiles would only ricochet back. But this drill... there's a growing pile of grit and dust on the floor.

The sound wall hums normally. They're drilling on the wrong face to affect its operation.

Five minutes.

I must get back to the ship. The decaying uranium can only be exposed for so long before overheating. The men on the far side seem dedicated to achieving something. I must leave.

He appears, and I almost faint. He is tall and handsome and floats gracefully toward me. He's talking! To be sure, mostly in grunts and moans, but his happiness when he says "Papa" can't be mistaken. The force field surrounding him is stronger than I remembered and belies his featherlike weight.

And he hugs me with long, thin arms, holding on tightly. No man, not even my own strength, is a match for him.

The lights darken. The bastards in the foyer must have turned them off. They have their headlamps on. Two are manning the auger while the third passively watches, holding a metal cylinder.

High-impact explosives.

The sound wall hums. Never mind the lights; we must run, or we will be dust. How dare they be so ignorant to endanger the life of my son again!

I tell the boy we must go. He holds me dearly, forcefully. I try to break away and then attempt to lift him. His grasp is firm.

The blast of a stun grenade. The sound wall warps inward. The elite soldiers are climbing back to the surface. Ventilators fail. Only wisps of oxygen emit from the wall grate. Those sons-a-bitches!

I'm weakening fast, panting for the remaining airflow, sucking at the grate. The room churns. My son looks confused and scratches his chin. I reach for my helmet and fasten it over my head. The rich oxygen flows.

Headlamp on. With all my might, I pull the lad toward the stairs to my ship. Finally, he seems to understand, and we climb down furiously. Above, there's a concussive explosion. The idiot savants are the most uncaring creatures in the universe, only knowing how to kill! Rocks are falling all around, one wall collapses. A virtual landslide is cascading down the stairwell as we head toward the ship, ducking inside.

Boulders boom as they crack around the ship. I'm on the flight deck with the boy next to me. I harness him in, then me. Engines flare, the craft shudders, the tube lights above pass quicker and quicker as we accelerate and blow through the camouflage curtain into space. And we are free.

I feel total elation. I now have everything. My ship. My son. My freedom. We will begin immediately to invoke the revelation, the renaissance that awakens the universe, the ascension of good over evil as plagues are conquered and Armageddon avoided. The spirit of the cosmos will live forever as the beast is chipped away into oblivion. This is the prophecy we will fulfill.

Space glides in front of us. Two federation Star Fighter ships bear down from above. They menacingly pass then lock on their weapons. The loud, shrill noise from my headset confirming this speaks volumes.

Again, they threaten my son! I would have fought them into oblivion if not for his sake. The beryllium shields cone cover the core as I flame out my engines.

≥≤

They're coming to shock me.

I hear the clink of metal doors past the sound wall, outside my cell, past the clean corridor.

They have shocked me hundreds of times—they will learn nothing. These beasts are pathetic, scabs that need picking, maggots that chew at my flesh. The scum of the universe needs to be cleansed.

They have searched but cannot find the instrument that allows the embodiment of pure power, without which the boy, the supreme commander of the universe, can't effectively rule. The staff is the means to the end.

I have the staff, hidden within my royal sepulcher at the edge of eternity, and someday I will show it to them. And with one wave, they will all die. With this staff, I will find my boy, and we will become one—the Father, the Son, and the Supreme Command.

Legions will fall at our feet. Through extreme introspection, I will achieve divine intervention. The Earth, the sun, the stars, and the other worlds—the entire cosmos will be mine. This is my destiny.

For I am the Almighty Zec.

Twenty-Seventh Street
Robert Herzog

≥≤

Robert M. Herzog's debut novel, *A World Between*, an "extravagant and unputdownable" adventure mixing science and politics, was recently published by The Story Plant. Robert has had his stories and poems published in *Solstice Literary Magazine, Toasted Cheese, Downstate Story Magazine, Straylight Literary Arts Magazine*, and *South Jersey Underground*. He was a physics major until he read Nietzsche, a political philosopher turned entrepreneur dealing with the major issues of our time, a CEO of energy, environment, technology and health care companies, a Brooklyn boy who climbed Mt. Kilimanjaro, and he remembers the taste of the first great wine he drank.

From the author:

"For every Google and Facebook, there are thousands of startups that struggle through each phase of their lives (and deaths). The experience is intense, with constrant pressure, clashes of hope and ego, uncertain outcomes that mean success or failure, personal as well as professional. I've been through all sides of these equations, and "Twenty-seventh Street" distills some of those experiences."

≥≤

Riding down the elevator, I wondered what I'd say to Jack Devine. I'd gotten him so pumped up, and now—it was just putting things off, I would say, not shutting them down. But momentum is a quirky thing, more easily eroded than sustained. I walked to the informal line that waited for cabs at the Lex and Forty-third entrance to Grand Central. One of the little nooks of New York where unsupervised people cooperate, letting you feel you're in a community, distinct from most experiences in the surrounding office buildings.

Yes, I'd vowed I'd never take a full time job again. At this stage, consulting was fine with me; I was content with being an uncle, rather than absorbing the pressures of parenting. But... this was a real opportunity. After all those times. The Internet markets were so hot, we sizzled. It would be a short ride, ending in final freedom. I grew up when it was all about commu-ni-tee, liber-tee; now it was about annui-tee, equi-tee—not the kind that had to do with fairness. I wanted creativi-tee, and this would set the table.

Two cabs filled in an orderly fashion, both kids in suits on their cell phones. I helped a straight-backed, gray-haired woman out of the third, an actual traveler looking like she was already halfway to Greenwich, and got in.

"Perry and Washington," I said. The cabbie nodded, made possibly a concurring sound from under his turban. That was enough impetus.

"Take Lex to Twenty-seventh, across to Fifth, down Fifth to Eleventh, right on Eleventh to Washington."

You could catch all the lights with this route. I'd perfected it in the weeks spent working there. I'd first done the strategic planning, translating the founder's interesting but vague ideas into a real business concept, then helped him through the first round of financing, some hires and deals. Got a solid slug of stock for it. Vested. I signed on to advise for the second round, happy with the deal, a success fee in cash and stock, and time to do other things. But the founder—the Founder—wanted more.

He took me to a Four Seasons power lunch, to his usual table, as he had when we first met. Forty-four bucks for sea urchins over lobster tails—when else would I order that? Overcharging to create the insulation of exclusivity; I had to admire the marketing scheme. The F walked in talking and walked out talking; sometimes I went to the bathroom just for a break. Over a fifty-eight dollar, half-eaten Dover sole with a few more sea urchins slathered on it, waving to the next and the previous UN ambassadors and an assortment of Trumps and Murdochs, he made his pitch: I'd created a robust business model—that's what I do. His skills were visionary, he said, not managerial. He'd watched me in action, the company needed a CEO, he wasn't right, not a people person, not enough time. I was needed to bring our ideas to fruition.

He offered more cash, more stock. I thought about his Rolodex, the helicopter, staying on solid terms with him, his hints that he'd be helpful in the future of my choice. The challenge of implementing a viable Internet business model.

CEO, it had a ring to it.

At seven-thirty at night, the ride down Lex was quick. I'd defined this route after some experimentation: crosstown on Thirty-first was out—it backed up from Penn Station; Thirty-third tied up at the Empire State Building. Cross further north, you'd get caught going past those road blockers. Twenty-ninth was the first outlet that cleared, but therefore most of the cabbies took it—cabbies tended to be straight-line guys, not into vector analysis. Seventh Avenue was out, with construction around St. Vincent's jamming everybody above Fourteenth Street, plus the double-parked ambulances. Twenty-fifth didn't go through to Fifth, plugged at Madison Square Park. Twenty-third was too crowded, people starting to bail out before Lex ended at Gramercy Park, which also thoroughly clogged Twenty-first, where everybody had to turn right. That clearly left

Twenty-seventh to Fifth, and the rest of it. They'd try sometimes to take Fourteenth across to Ninth, but the peculiar geometries of the West Village made that a longer route, two more clicks on the meter. I wouldn't let them get away with that.

Home.

≥≤

Danielle was surprised, something that didn't often happen after eighteen years married.

"But you'd been talking so much to Jack about—"

"I know."

We'd gotten intense about getting funding for developing interactive learning programs, so kids could develop at their own pace; no more of the constant failure experiences I'd seen when I briefly taught fifth grade years ago. Use that to move on to producing original content. Jack Devine, an old friend, was in that world, and receptive; we'd started some script development. It didn't have to make it big—although the consultant part of me kept running scenarios into billion-dollar market caps, much as I tried to squelch it—more than anything, it was the chance to start relating to the world built around my ideas, again.

"And me," she said. True. Everybody trusted her taste and judgment; she got people to see problems as assets. She'd be great at developing sales, and the slight accent definitely helped.

"It'll just be ninety days, one-twenty tops. We close funding, find a real CEO, I get a big fee. This way I protect my position; we'll be better set up."

"And you run the show again. Is that what you want?"

I didn't answer quickly enough for the rhythm of this conversation. "Just so long as it's not like last time."

"No way."

"Promise?"

"Promise."

≥≤

Jesus, the place was a quagmire.

We'd leapt from five people to fifty in 127 days, overwhelming Chuck, the chief operating officer, who really had to go, but I'd brought him in myself; we had mutual acquaintances; it wasn't that easy. So I stepped in, the reasons I had declined other CEO positions nipping like flies that slipped through the netting—org charts, project planning, staffing descriptions, contract reviews, more org charts, nothing could be pinned down, all was Heraclitan flux. The funding environment was strong, so I figured I could get the ops stuff in order and still close soon. Retain a hot search firm for the permanent CEO; had to get that underway ASAP. I'd figured the commitment would be two days a week and priced the work accordingly, but being totally involved 24/7, waking up with ideas, e-mailing at two in the morning, living and breathing it, I'd forgotten how enjoyable immersion could be.

"Heading south?" a young girl wearing Lennon-like glasses asked me. She had a sweet, open face, reminding me of someone I'd dated, or wanted to, years ago.

"Sure," I said, although I would have said the same thing had I been heading north. She was going to Third and Thirty-first, dinner plans, which was only slightly out of my way. I told her, the way you do sometimes, about my decision to serve as backstop CEO for this company I'd been consulting to, how it would set me up for doing what I really wanted to do. I thought CEO sounded pretty good. She asked if I was waiting for my life to start, but she was too young to get that answer. As she turned towards me, the city lights, street lamps, store signs, restaurant neons reflected off her glasses. She said she worked nearby, often split rides. I felt I'd see her again; the stars were aligning. I liked the idea of sharing a cab—eco-friendly, another blow struck for urban humanity.

Fifteen years ago I'd ridden the last tulip boom, environmental work, owned pieces of companies doing clean-up—doing it the best way possible—in five states. Only it turned out everybody hated having to pay for anything, and then local people beyond-hated having a facility within conscious distance of them, and legal fees and permit fights ate up more money and energy than we could ever invest. So, finally, I turned in the keys to the money-people, who'd put me on a pedestal when giving it to me and wanted to bury me with the hazmat when things didn't work out. As if there was no risk associated with those high projected rewards. I bagged the startup mode, began my consulting biz. When I meandered into the tech area, I loved that here was stuff people wanted, got pleasure from, would uncomplainingly pay for.

≥≤

We made the turn and, as projected, we hit all the lights to Fifth. I called Danielle to crank up dinner. Then I called Marty, which I'd been doing since college.

"You know, I'm beginning to think you only call me now on the ride home," Marty said. He hated cabs, mocked my directions as futile. But I had my route.

"Now a right on Eleventh," I said to the driver. "Okay, good."

"Take a right; keep it moving," Marty said. He was on to me. I was too wired from dialing for dollars, revving the PowerPoint presentations, all the operational issues, to detox straight to downtime. I needed to keep the action going, before home, a glass of wine, dinner, talk (Danielle asking what I did today—sub-text, why?—but it was hard to describe, so I diverted into her day, the latest in Japanese antiques or conceptual sculpture), late night TV—I felt desperate for entertainment, watched *Star Trek: Voyager* reruns, especially the ones about the Borg and Seven of Nine, a cosmic caricature piece of ass in the flesh, then read, then I'd find myself at the computer, e-mail, replying, planning, directing, revamping the lines of the org charts, crying out to the chief technology officer for when v2.0 of the new website would be up, seeking schedules, milestones, perk charts, Gantt charts, critical path charts, measurables, deliverables, performables, any 'ables, trying to bring order to chaos, I who at heart believed in the creativity of chaos.

"Over here, on the right," I said.

"On the left, table for two," I heard in my ear. I paid.

"There's something I don't quite get," Marty said. "Weren't you planning something else?"

Good friends can remember you better than you can remember yourself.

"I was thinking about short-form content multi-media production, exploit the broadband roll-out, huge market in a few years." My ideas, my creativity in action. I explained why I was deferring that plan, all my good reasons.

I went inside, checked the already-empty mailbox, walked up the stairs. I kissed Danielle, careful not to hit her with the phone, said goodbye to Marty as I walked into my room, checked for e-mails, and headed towards the wine.

Shit, I hadn't called Jack Devine, again. I really needed to give him a heads-up about that temporary change of plans.

≥≤

Pissed me off. The search firm we wanted to find the CEO said they didn't have the bandwidth to do the job. Even with an equity kicker—which everybody was asking for. The lawyers want equity, and the landlord, and the website developer, and the coffee-machine people. Over a month wasted. They said they'd "drilled down deep" into the business plan. Fucking arrogance. Bandwidth availability was a fine euphemism...but if they didn't get it, not my problem; on to number two, more of a big body shop than the boutique we wanted, but we had to move it. I had to move it.

≥≤

For the first time, I noticed what looked like a cool place on Twenty-seventh Street, between Park and Madison. Its front was a big window parsed into squares by rust-colored rails, dark interior, hip. Inside, lots of candles showed only themselves and the alluring darkness between them,where all the possibilities resided. The entrance had a small velvet rope with a guy sitting there, even though at eight-fifteen the place seemed empty. It looked interesting, the kind of spot I never had the patience or the pull to wangle into. Filled with movie people. We went by quickly, traffic just the way it should be, too fast for me to catch the name. No downtime. A lawyer I shared with down to Twenty-third Street gave me his card. Everybody wanted in.

My phone rang.

"Mikey, the man on a bikey, my main man, I am on the plan." It was Jack. We had outlined a script a couple of months ago, over cigars and Ukrainian vodka martinis at Pravda, sinking in the old leather chairs and puffing like we would own the world; still flush with that night he'd just about finished it.

"Listen, oh fruit of the vine, just a little change; I've taken this assignment, and it's turned into full time, then some..." So we would have to put it off, but just for a couple of months, and then we'd be even better off because I'd have this big fee, and we'd be really ready to pop. And all the contacts I would have. Positioning.

"So that's the Pin-the-Tail-on-the Future sale?"

Yes, I can do it; I've never failed; I wouldn't this time. "Hang in there, buddy," I said. "Just a couple of months, we'll be off and running. There's nothing more important to me."

"It's already on the shelf, Mike. Let me know." I thought of more reassuring words but didn't say them.

≥≤

We were getting pushback from the VCs on valuation. I argued with the F: start low, get some heat going, nail it, do a price reset if we got overcommitments. "Like at Sotheby's," I said, searching for some context he understood. But he was looking for "market validation" of his idea, insisted on starting high. Based on one conversation he'd had with a lawyer friend who said he was seeing deals done at numbers far higher than we were looking at.

"Then let him fund it," I said, but that was too direct for the Founder's sensitivities, which were essentially social, and the lawyer was part of the set. Hell, maybe they knew more than I did. It was a hot climate; higher values meant less dilution. I'd been happy with my stock position and deal for the financing, but with these kinds of numbers even the little incremental stock I was getting each month for the management work looked like big time value.

So I floated the terms he wanted, and we didn't get called back. That infuriated the F—it wasn't polite not to respond. I had warned him, that *was* the VC response. Repricing downward is bad news, shows weakness, creates a spiral; my potential millions were collapsing to hundreds of thousands, but there were still a bunch of places we hadn't approached, a few top tier I'd kept in reserve, and some West Coast firms. They were usually too parochial, but I started fishing there as well.

≥≤

"I'm going to Washington and Perry. I usually go down Lex to—"

"I know where this is, no need."

He did my route. We made every light, but he sulked the whole way. Perfect—a pouting cab driver. The same as work: I was right, and everybody snipped. I took my vindication as it was served and added my own sauce.

≥≤

Fosette. That was the name of the place. I stayed off the phone till we got to it, to make sure I caught it. Lots of people dressed in black—hip, young, younger. Through the dusky windows I could just make out a few shapes, lithe beautiful shapes, amidst the flames of votive candles invoking the prayers of the young and the fearless. If I looked hard enough, I knew I would see the girl with the Lennon glasses, her clear wide eyes staring, wondering why the cab kept gliding by. "Where's the sharing in that?" she would ask. I checked as soon as I got home. It wasn't listed in Zagat's. Really new. Even cooler.

≥≤

It was after nine: after the California calls, my eyes half-closed. A lot of fuckers, even East Coast, don't call till seven-thirty or eight, thinking they'll catch you not there, so they can question your commitment. I put on a late-shift receptionist and a total protocol to get me on cell phone if I was not in the office, lots of luck. It was hard to get financing without a permanent CEO in place, especially with the F mouthing off at every meeting how he wasn't going to be doing it; he didn't have the skills—wink wink wink—a malignant streak of honesty amidst presentations drenched with hyperbole, claims delivered with a "Frankly, I was amazed at how great..." kind of intros that required wrenches to keep my eyes from rolling. The VCs maintained they invested in people, not companies, a platitude ranking only with "We want to be your long-term partner" for lack of verisimilitude. That led to "We want to look the new CEO in the eye."

They'd have to use a telescope.

But there were still tons of money chasing deals; if we'd priced it right we'd be done, or close, although I hadn't spent as much time on the actual financing as I should have, still recasting the org charts, searching for an I Ching pattern foretelling good destiny. Plus all the time spent like this morning. Vishnay comes into my office, his eyes large white spots against his dark skin. I'd hired him to develop Web marketing strategies.

"I will not be treated like this." He mustered his twenty-four-year-old dignity. He moved in quantums, turning his head and arms as if they were jerked by strings. We'd had to pay him 90K, plus options; Internet hiring was through the roof.

"What?" Although I guessed, I'd heard the fall-out. First the F had asked him to spend hours doing filing, since his latest assistant had quit as had the three before, threatening to sue, letters the F displayed cheerfully that would have humiliated me. Then he'd gotten yelled at for not passing on a message from the nanny about the F's son being sick at school. This was not what Vishnay went to Harvard for, not how he'd been treated when analyzing Internet companies at Morgan.

I joked, cajoled, praised, reminded him of the prospective value of the company. "But you are not treated like this; you don't know." His head veered up sharply, then towards me. My Special Relationship. I smiled, shrugged it off, got him to re-focus. My door was becoming a passage for the walking wounded, scalded and stabbed by their encounters with the F. The CEO has to be a therapist—I had no interest. But there was this special component to my position that hearkened for the future—even if this venture failed, the connection would endure, and that was a place of infinite possibility.

"Hey, you've got that stock," Marty said. He was the deputy director of an urban policy institute, referred to himself as a wage slave. "Not much equity in a not-for-profit," he moaned, and while I said good words about his good works, I believed I trod the golden path. He had one whopping retirement plan, though; all I had was promises of paper that was supposed to morph mysteriously into the currency of a newly-discovered land. The last business I started had turned into a not-for-profit, just not-on-purpose.

I needed to concentrate on the financing. I had to bump Chuck as COO; his idea of management was to be a shoulder to cry on, hence my disastrous operational inheritance. He'd made a ton of money before; his not being hungry enough was part of the problem, he could go back to doing seed round investing in between rounds of golf. Moved the CFO, Brad, into that slot, work on strategic alliances; although I had my doubts, Chuck had brought him in. I'd just bought a software company that could get us to market quicker, but that also accelerated our pace towards zero cash, which the VCs would try to exploit. The F had a hard time understanding the ramifications of lack of money. Each day hurdles were cleared, but each night the bar shot higher, and it was all going stale.

Marty was more sympathetic than understanding—I forget how rarefied this shit is—when the phone beeped at me. I hadn't figured out the Nokia's system for call waiting, so I ended up dropping Marty and took the call.

"How can you not have included a—what is it?—a cap table in the documents you sent out?"

"You don't send out a cap table with the preliminary docs. They're just to generate interest; then you follow up, show you're prepared."

These were docs I'd sent to prospective investors on his Rolodex. And one of them, a former director at an investment bank, had asked for the table. Everybody has their own questions—no initial documents can answer them all; it's a waste of time trying, but the F didn't relate much to my time. So fine, interest piqued, mission accomplished, we'd send him one.

My unacknowledged words echoed. I was getting tired of it—not a good trait for a consultant. "I see these people every day. I can't tolerate mistakes." As if they were okay by me.

"It's not normally done, but I've already prepared it; I'll get it to him."

"These people have the highest expectations. I won't have anything affect my reputation. We have to have a zero defect environment."

Fuck. I forgot to check out the restaurant. I'd noticed it yesterday, closer to Fifth. I moved the phone and looked up, noticing some Philippe Starck-like protuberances glowing white, hanging off the front of a building past Fosette. I turned my head to see what lay under these tusks, some sort of coffeehouse or a hotel lobby—it wasn't clear. I put my head back to the phone to explain our strategy to the F, for what that was worth. Home, wine, Star Trek. Zero defects. Fuck the e-mails. Sleep.

≥≤

I dreamed I was on a train. We were nearing where I had to get off. I went up front to say goodbye to some co-workers. The train reached my stop sooner than I expected. I ran to get my bags, just two cars back. But I started feeling heavy—I was wearing too many clothes, a bright yellow rain jacket over dark bulky sweaters, and could only move very slowly. I had to push past people who were getting off. I ran, but the distance hardly shrank. I went through a car where an old-fashioned black porter was standing, his face sad and understanding, and the mail door rolled shut. I got to my car; the doors were still open, but it seemed impossible to get to my bags, I felt so heavy. I finally did, but the doors had shut and the train was moving away.

≥≤

Christ. Dot-com stocks crashed, and the VCs freaked over portfolios aromatic with vapors and fumes emanating from: "Build community, get mindshare, we'll monetize it later," odors that now carried the stench of reality with them, nauseating a generation of entrepreneurs whacked up by Netscape's model, and a few billion following them, down tubes so obvious that when the bubble burst the oily residue just sped the slide. I had a revenue-producing plan from the start, and we were implementing on plan, but we didn't have a CEO and we didn't have liquidity and now they wanted traction and what that meant even I didn't understand and we didn't have...

One of the prospective investors, now dropping out from the next round, went through the herd's mantras. "It was all B2C, business-to-consumer, ride the Amazon, last fall. Then that cratered, and we all went B2B; that was a good fit for you."

"Great," I said. "We're all about business services: less cost for customer acquisition, clearer products—"

"Yeah, but now it's all about P2P."

"P2P?" I tried to say, my voice wrestling with adolescent squeaks.

"Path to Profitability."

As in, Hello, we just realized these were businesses we were funding. I had no problem with being buzzword-compliant; it was like my bad handwriting: a word could be read as any number of words, but they were all the same. I needed to catch up to take a P2P, however. And this from a guy who attended our last Board meeting and said, "There are too many suits for a dot-com." They'd funded children, then got surprised when the kids didn't think about profits and organizational structure.

"It's awfully quiet here," he'd said on the way out.

"That's because people are working," I said. But he was on his way to where decisions were made over the company ping pong table and gongs resounded every time fifty new people visited the website.

Now their values had nose-dived, and we were getting hammered.

On the way back from one of our VC meetings, sitting in the back of the F's chauffeur-driven Mercedes—doesn't every start-up have one?—I suggested, casually, as I had planned, that we have dinner that night. Extend the relationship to the next level. Plus part of me, I wouldn't really express it, thought that if his wife, Morgane, met Danielle, and they talked art and the latest auctions and the gossip on all the people Danielle somehow always knew about, it would further cement this next elevation of ties to him, a rare moment when I thought about actually doing the networking thing, laying some groundwork, planning for myself for a change. Consultants were like doctors: dispensing care to others, ignoring medicine for themselves.

≥≤

The phone rang. I pulled it out of my pocket, but it was the cabbie's. He chattered away, sitting behind a bus in the right lane by Thirty-third Street.

"Get over left," I said.

"What?"

"Get over left. You're talking on the phone and not paying attention to the traffic." It's as if once you told them we were going to turn right, the lane became a magnet pulling them over regardless of traffic conditions.

He muttered goodbye into the phone, muttered at me that he had to make a right turn and would not make it from the wrong lane; he'd already gotten a ticket for that.

"If you get a ticket, I'll pay for it," I said. He pulled into the left lane, and we jerked our way downtown.

I felt shrouded by the antiseptic stench emanating from the plastic green-pine air cleanser hanging from the rearview mirror, barely disguising the driver's rich colloquy of garlic and body aromas. I pushed the window button, but it didn't operate. Coughing, I asked the driver if it was broken. He must have pushed his child-guard button, for he said "Please to try it now," and I got the window halfway down, the air washing me in its burnt tang of breeze, exhaust and the traces of a million dying cut flowers. The city air confounded the foreign atmosphere of the cab; my air, home-court air; I could breathe again.

≥≤

I called a restaurant where we knew the owners, young alumni from Bouley. We would walk in, eat, walk out, no hint of payment. I went home to change out of the Levi's that were subtext dress code, enjoying putting on a jacket and tie, dressing like a grown-up. We walked to the restaurant, Danielle looking great as always, downtown perfection. I brought some wine with me, a rare Turley Zinfandel I would open with a flourish suitable to its unobtainability. We waited, had a glass of the house red. My cell phone rang, Danielle giving me that look when I was déclassé. It was the F. What had he been thinking? Tonight was the opera benefit, then a reception for some Norse ambassador; he was sorry. He was always recounting the previous evening's benefit, the important conversations, holding court on matters of great estate, except that none of it ever led anywhere. The F might have been an opener, but he wasn't a closer. That required specificity in a relationship, and specificity could engender dispute, so better to avoid that sordid part of the process. We opened the Zin anyway.

"Let's plan," Danielle beamed. "Your birthday's in a couple of months. Any ideas?" I used to wheedle extending the celebration to a week; now it was the two of us at whatever we thought was the best food in town, so long as it was south of Fourteenth Street. Our best times together, the talk exhilarating, no recriminations about cleaning up.

≥≤

We had to cut our burn rate. Stop paying bills for a while, extend breathing a bit. Fire people. Fun stuff. We needed more money, but we were carried to the bottom along with everyone else. The numbers portrayed our prognosis. Less than two months, at best. You run out of fuel, you stop. Then you die.

≥≤

Unable to convert a problem into a solution, the F sat in the big corner room, emerging only to spew venom, what hadn't been done, by whom. He'd made a pile of money in private practice, married richer, helicoptered to the polo matches now. He wanted to be admired in the right circle for a new triumph. He had vision, but it was an unpopulated landscape.

"Walk the floor," I said. "Talk to people. Make the connections."

"Don't even go there, Michael." The cords of his neck turned red. "I used to be at that level; now I don't care about them—trust me, they'll see through it. I'm too honest to pretend."

"Well, maybe if you didn't have four people working on matching the color of one of your shirts to be the cover of the business plan."

He'd started getting his hair cut and coifed in the office, further endearing him to the staff, who could never get any face time with him. His assistants were expected to be immediately perfect, to be mind-readers, to absorb abuse that sapped the office like an infection. No amount of shares could keep them. Going to and from our kitchen to get the special soups his driver brought in each day from his favorite uptown restaurant, the F quickly strode down the hallways, arms darting in front of him, with such determination it looked like he was muttering to himself. Nobody interrupted.

"Hey, that color on the website really stood out. My instincts are terrific for things like that, I don't know why. Did I tell you, Morgane wants to buy in Palm Beach—don't get me started. Fine with me to rent there; don't we have enough houses?" I sometimes tried to calculate their monthly expenses, but it was beyond me in all ways. Except I suspected it could float the company for months. "We're flying down there for Saturday, then over to Italy." He mentioned some telecom mogul, who got a new boat—four hundred feet—wants us all to help christen it."

"That sounds like fun." Christ, four hundred feet, owning an ocean liner. Why?

"Uh, sleeping on a plane two out of four nights, if that's your idea of fun." Well, it was the helicopter to the private jet; indistinguishable limousines meeting, dropping off, hovering like motorized maids. It didn't sound all bad.

"That's rough," I said.

≥≤

I tried to explain to Danielle, all the shares, protect value. She'd nursed me through the last flame-out, a near breakdown, all the years of lawsuits. I'd sworn I'd never get in that position again, she reminded me, prodding me to connect my actions to my memories.

"You don't have to learn only through suffering," she said, a relic of her Sufi Scribes. I agreed, but it was as if I'd lost text from the book of my life: I had a set of answers but no longer remembered the questions.

"Besides, I said I would do it. I gave my word," my image puffing up with echoes of Bogart, of Cooper.

"I'm sure Custer's men were loyal too." My French wife nailing me with American history. Perfect.

≥≤

I had enough of sharing the fucking cab. Got caught once having to inch across Thirty-first when, if my fat fellow traveler had just been willing to walk four blocks as I suggested, we could have made much better time across Twenty-seventh. Besides, the charm of people contributing to the fare had also faded. Most of the time I didn't take any money—"Hey, I was going this way anyway"—and didn't want to bother slowing up for the calculation; let 'em jump out while the cab was still moving. Then I felt compelled to give the driver a bigger tip than usual because he'd made the extra stop, and why should I be providing free transportation for all these people?

And where was the round-faced girl with the Lennon glasses? When cities make promises, they should keep them.

≥≤

I don't know how I hadn't spotted it before, but just when you make the turn from Lex onto Twenty-seventh, there's a little

Turkish place that looked good. I remembered my first encounter with ekmek kadayifi, Marty with his wife, me with my then-girlfriend before law school claimed her, a large amount of dope, and an overwhelming combination of apricot paste and thick sweet cream. What tastes!

The phone rang. It was Jack. He was bailing. A shot at doing an hour series in L.A., they were hot now. After hearing for the *n*th time it would be just a couple more months, he couldn't put it off any longer. I no longer had the energy for the arguments; we hung up, and I went for a ham sandwich from the deli downstairs, which I ate while revising the PowerPoint presenting our business plan, deleting last month's wonderwords like B2B, vertical trading community, portal. Into the night.

≥≤

Into the morning. Valuations had cratered. CEO candidates wanted more cash, cared less about stock. The F wailed that we had missed the market; he wasn't about to settle for the even-lower valuation now being discussed. Close to the dread down round, less per share this time out of the gate than the last. None of the VCs were old enough to have been through a cycle before, seven years of upside, and my seasoning was not welcome to their sauce. Four months as "acting" CEO, a lifetime of limbo culminating in this purgatory. All I wanted was out.

The search firm had a couple of candidates, but without a clear next round financing, no one would come on board, and without a CEO you couldn't close a financing. The VCs kept asking me what my plans were; I kept mumbling I'd do what it takes for as long as it takes...and they were gutting my equity value. Four fucking months. For the first time I'd had a goal, a time frame, a reason. I'd put flesh and organs on what was barely a skeleton, created an infrastructure and made it viable for funding; I had, in effect, acted as a founder, but the F had eleven times more stock than I did, and when I broached that perhaps I deserved some bonus for being so instrumental in creating this company, he opined as to how fair my deal was.

≥≤

Saturday morning, Danielle said, "The Met has two private collections, modern to contemporary; got great reviews." I knew; the F had been to the private opening, which he described in excessive detail. "Shall we go?" Danielle had worked in one of the tonier uptown galleries; no one ever questioned her taste or advice, but she'd gotten tired dealing with the tantrums of her clients. I didn't understand the problem at the time.

"I'd love to, but I've got to get back on questions from some of the first round investors, wondering what's going on."

"Well, I'm going to go myself, okay?"

"Sure, of course, yes."

"I'd rather go with you." For a girl from Paris and a kid from the Bronx, we had remarkably similar taste in art. We'd often noted that, with enjoyment. She got her coat.

"How do you want to celebrate your birthday?" she asked.

"I don't."

The door shut behind her.

≥≤

I came down the elevator with the VCs *du jour*, who hadn't fully finished raping us upstairs. I left them in front of the office and walked to my cab spot. The phone rang, a Board member, Slade Watkins. His company had raised twenty-seven million before the crash; he could afford to be compassionate, full of ideas from a bygone world. There was nobody in front of me, so I half-held up my free arm while talking. A cab stopped; I waited for the woman inside to get out. As she did, out of the corner of my eye I saw a guy running from farther up Lex, and before I moved he cut in front of me to get into the cab.

"Hey, there's a line here. I..." I talked softly, moving the mouthpiece above my head so Slade wouldn't hear.

"I was waitin' up the block; too fuckin' bad," the guy said. He was shorter than I, stocky in a barely-post-Neanderthal way, holding a shiny briefcase more cardboard than leather.

"That's not the way it works here."

He sat down. I threw a kick at him, half-assed that hit him in the side. And I used to swear by non-violence. I could hear my pulse in the phone.

"You wanna go at it over this cab, let's do it," he looked up at me. I was ready to bash his flat face in, but there was Slade on the phone, and maybe the VCs were still down the block—not good behavior in a marginal environment. I stepped back, hoping for the sound of an immediate crash, but the cab pulled safely away, injustice unpunished. I hate that. Slade had more ideas.

≥≤

Seven-thirty a.m. Bleary, I picked up a phone my caller ID told me I should let ring.

"Do you know," the F screamed at me, "why I stayed late in the office to finish reviewing the revised presentation? 'Cause that kid Vishnay kept bugging me about it, and I cancelled going to the ballet opening where I could have talked with the head of banking at Credit Suisse. Trust me, I'm at this all the time; have been for months, 17 hours a day. I've got no life. Morgane says she just wants me back, and then I learn that Vishnay has some fucking class, and what did I do it for?"

"He's studying for the GMATs," I said. The F actually knew this but had no memory for other people's obligations. "I arranged for Susan to input your comments. What's the..."

"The point is if I'd known he was leaving early, if anyone bothered to tell me anything relevant around here, then I could have not lost an irrevocable opportunity to be meeting with someone important." He screamed beyond hearing, with the rage I had seen directed at others. "You're the one who told me I should pay attention to the staff, so there I was, Michael; I was doing it for him. This fucking kid kept checking up to see if I was done."

The F had sworn he'd finished the review that morning, then went off for some personal meetings, which remained shrouded in ambiguity; at best he spent a few hours a day in the office, which was just as well. Except it was impossible to download everything to him, so the definition of relevance became that which he was not told.

"You weren't doing it for him, you were doing it for the company. Once Susan made the changes I got it out to several people, including the CS analyst, so—"

"I gotta go—our designer's on the other line; trying to reach him for days."

I stared at the phone, trembling with the anger of the words I had not spoken and the question of why I had not spoken them. I was just another form of driver, maid, decorator. Like the assistants, I'd go, and there'd always be someone new on the pile, snared by Four Seasons lunches and the possibility of rubbing shoulders. There would be no opening of the Rolodex, there would be no invitation to the Tuscan house, or evenings on big boats or intimate shores, or introductions to studio heads. There would be only more of this exhortation and disinterest, bouts of wit and conversation the gilded contours of anger and blame, of expectation without absolution. I saw now my hubris, my idiotic pride that let me take on this job thinking I could overcome the F, with the staff, with the VCs, with a focused implementation of a plan. Now I faced my next move like a Chinese executioner, after all the other bodies were done for.

On my way out I saw some guys doing street repairs and looked at them with envy. The pulse of the jackhammer followed me up the block. For I had measured out my life in metered fares.

≥≤

Marty was encouraging me to keep at it, think of all that could happen if it hits, remodel the cabin upstate, fly first class, flat-panel TV, fund my start-up, run the script in which I became parent to my own plan, my core passions behind it, not reciting eighty times to MBAs younger than Danielle's children what it meant to develop a real business. I didn't tell him about Jack, and the others I had gotten psyched; it would be impossible to reassemble them, like putting together a watch you take apart as a kid.

I negotiated a bridge loan to keep us afloat, got yelled out by the F for being too conciliatory on conversion terms, got pounded by the VCs for all we had done wrong in failing to propel the next round of financing, held up contracts and deferred bill payments. My back spasmed during a vain attempt at a round of golf in a place the cell phone wouldn't reach. Danielle had seen this before; she was sympathetic, but I could tell it made her tired. My reassurances to her clanged in the dim lobe of my ahistorical brain. There was no discriminating; nobody trusted value, nobody wanted to step up to the table; somebody mean had snatched the VC's comforter, and they weren't happy any more.

Markets don't just die. When they crumble they carry people to unexpected fates, like a cabbie who doesn't know your address and won't listen to your directions. We drowned in the cries and tatters of businesses going under, pulling down with them the people, mostly younger, still shocked by being fired, just more resilient, more options, more time ahead to recover and to forget, remember when that bubble burst, they'd laugh at the hopes they had then because they'd overlaid them with newer ones, and when any were realized, the others didn't matter. And pulling in with them me, but I had less time, more hopes lost in the past, less generated for the future. I had to make this ride work, because when you get older it hurts more when you fall off.

≥≤

Fuck it. We made the right turn on to Twenty-seventh.

I told Marty he might be right, but there was a point you got so burned that the logic fried until even the smoke vanished. As we turned off Lex towards the warm candles and iron-bounded square windows and people in black not worried about cycles, I started dialing Danielle to come meet me and leaned forward to tell the cabbie, sorry, I changed my mind, I'm stopping here, here on Twenty-seventh street, when the phone rang and our bridge loan guy said he had to talk; he'd maybe lined up a syndicate to place the deal, they would need to get a CEO candidate to commit, contingent, he understood, on the funding. The cab continued west. I'd stop there tomorrow. Or, no later, the day after.

The cabbie was gesturing to me. I pulled the phone away from my ear and leaned forward. "Shall I turn here?" he asked.

"Do what you want," I said and sank back into the seat.

About AuthorsFirst

AuthorsFirst was founded by *New York Times* bestselling author Lou Aronica, Tony and Pulitzer Award-winning Broadway veteran Mitchell Maxwell, and Aaron Brown, an international bestselling author who publishes under the name Ethan Cross. AuthorsFirst offers a wide range of instructional sessions (both print and video) at basic and intermediate levels. You can discover these at www.AuthorsFirst.com.